**FROM OUT OF THE SHADOWS
CAME A BEAUTIFUL WOMAN.
SHE REACHED FOR THE
WOLF-STONE
AROUND LENARDO'S NECK.**

"The wolf-stone has saved your life twice now," Aradia said. "Once from the hill bandits, once from those who discovered you are a Reader."

At Lenardo's start of surprise, she smiled and touched his arm to keep him from rising out of bed. "Don't worry. Our first concern now is your health."

As she spoke, a many-branched candelabrum on the table beside the bed moved. Astonished, Lenardo then saw every candle burst spontaneously into flame.

Aradia smiled. "A mere trick. The candles are made to burn. I simply work with their natural inclination."

"Then I suppose," Lenardo said bitterly, "that you savages attack the Empire because of a natural desire to kill?"

Also by
Jean Lorrah

FIRST CHANNEL
(with Jacqueline Lichtenberg)

SAVAGE EMPIRE

JEAN LORRAH

PLAYBOY
PAPERBACKS

SAVAGE EMPIRE

Copyright © 1981 by Jean Lorrah

Cover illustration copyright © 1981 by PEI Books, Inc.

Published simultaneously in the United States and Canada by Playboy
Paperbacks, New York, New York. Printed in the United States of
America. Library of Congress Catalog Card Number: 80-83592. First
edition.

Books are available at quantity discounts for promotional and indus-
trial use. For further information, write to Premium Sales, Playboy
Paperbacks, 747 Third Avenue, New York, New York 10017.

ISBN: 0-872-16794-1

First printing March 1981.

This book is dedicated, with deepest gratitude, to

       Jacqueline Lichtenberg

I would also like to thank the following people, each of whom made some contribution to the inspiration of this work:

       Robert Adams
       Katie Filipowicz
       Anne Pinzow Golar
       Winston Howlett
       Katherine Kurtz

My thanks also go to Sharon Jarvis, my editor at Playboy Books, for her help and encouragement.

If there are readers who would like to comment on this book, my publisher will forward letters to me. If you prefer, you may write to me care of Box 625, Murray, KY 42071. All comments are welcome. I came to professional writing through fan writing and publishing, where there is close and constant communication between writers and readers. Thus I shall always be grateful for the existence of sf fandom, which has provided me with many wonderful experiences, and through which I met all the people mentioned above.

                                  Jean Lorrah
                                  Murray, Kentucky

Contents

Chapter One

Exile

Sword clashed on sword.

Lenardo parried and stepped back, deliberately open as he feinted, came in under his opponent's guard, and pulled his stroke before the blade touched the boy's throat.

"Decius, you were not Reading!" he scolded.

The boy flushed. He would have lost the fight and probably his life. "I didn't want you Reading me, Magister."

Lenardo shook his head. "I am not your teacher today. I am your enemy, non-Reader, open for you to Read and combat."

"Yes, Magister," Decius said contritely—for the dozenth time.

"Let me try him," said a voice from the sidelines.

"That's not fair!" protested Decius, and Lenardo smiled. Where else would a student of swordsmanship consider his opponent to have an unfair advantage because he was blind from birth?

Torio, who was lounging gracefully on the bench where Lenardo and Decius had laid their cloaks, now rose, doffing his own cloak and striding easily forward, Reading his way.

Lenardo had taught Torio swordsmanship—but the student was now more skilled than the teacher. At seventeen, Torio was tall, with a long reach, but his real advantage was his disconcerting eyes. Years ago, he had not been able to concentrate on swordplay and the social amenity of making his eyes appear to focus at the same time. Then he discovered that others were put off stride by a swordsman who was obviously blind.

9

By now, Torio needed no advantage but the skill he had developed with long practice. He had long since stopped showing off; Lenardo Read clearly Torio's eagerness to teach Decius—the sincere desire of a true teacher to share the process of discovery.

Decius was only thirteen, his body just beginning its adolescent growth spurt. Torio adjusted his own skill to the younger boy's as Lenardo watched approvingly.

Decius, however, was watching Torio, becoming fascinated by the milky eyes that drifted, unfocused. A yelp and a clang—Torio disarmed him, then pinned him against the wall. "Don't watch me—*Read* me! By the gods, Decius, you waste your talent! Magister, will you lend me your kerchief?"

"No!" cried Decius.

"You are a Reader," Torio told him. "You have as much talent as I, but you lean on your five senses. Block out the most important of them, and you will have to Read." He tied the fine linen kerchief over Decius' eyes. "There. Now, let us fight as equals."

Lenardo could Read Decius' tight throat and sweaty palms. Now the boy had to Read Torio, their surroundings, and himself, all at once. He fumbled, could not even parry at first, backed against the bench and almost fell. Then, by degrees, he found his way. Within half an hour he had made more progress than Lenardo had got from him in a month.

Torio allowed Decius a touch, saying, "Now you're doing it, Decius. Good work. By the time you've reached your full stature, you'll be a better swordsman than I am."

Blushing at such praise from an acknowledged swordmaster, Decius pulled off the blindfold, blinking in the bright sunlight. Torio smiled and answered his half-formed thought, "Yes, it is as bright for me." //I am still Reading, Decius. I cannot *not* Read, or the darkness enfolds me.//

"Will you work with me again tomorrow, Torio? Oh! Pardon, Magister Lenardo—I didn't mean—"

Lenardo smiled at the boy's confusion. "For this particular skill, Torio is the better teacher. I shall assign you to him."

"Oh—thank you, Magister!" Decius had stopped Reading again—a pity, Lenardo thought, for he missed the warm anticipation from Torio. "Tomorrow! I'll be ready—I promise!"

As Decius hurried off, he also missed the cold apprehension that went through Lenardo at his words. The teacher cut it off, lest Torio Read him. He knew, Read, that tomorrow Torio would not teach Decius. That was all, except for an attending bleak sorrow.

But the blind boy was too enthralled to notice that Lenardo had stopped Reading. "My own student! My very first!"

"Yes, Torio," Lenardo agreed. "You are certainly qualified to teach swordsmanship, even if your methods are . . . unorthodox."

Torio laughed. "But they should not be. Boys come here at eight or nine, completely reliant on their five wits. I came at seven, and within a year I was a proficient Reader —simply because I could not rely on my eyes. New boys would learn much faster if for a portion of each day we blindfolded them—aye, and stopped their ears, too. Then they'd have to learn to Read."

For a moment, Torio's enthusiasm woke in Lenardo the delight he had felt whenever Galen had proposed a new idea—but Galen was gone now. Lenardo's fault for not teaching him to master his enthusiasm. He must not make the same mistake with this boy, who shone above the other boys just as Galen had.

"When you are Master here, Torio, then you may institute your own techniques."

"But you will be Master long before that, Magister. And even now you might try my suggestions."

Will I ever be worthy to be a Master? Lenardo blocked the thought, then covered his discomfiture with a laugh. "Torio, Torio, just appointed tutor today and already trying to run the academy!"

As he had hoped, the boy was distracted. "Tutor! Yes—if I have a student, then I am officially a tutor! Oh, thank you, Magister Lenardo!"

"You deserve the post. I shall consult with Master

Clement about your tutoring one or two beginning Readers. If you don't frighten them to death, you will have the chance to demonstrate whether your method produces good Readers in less time."

"Frighten them? . . . Oh, yes—I understand. I must Read the new boys to comprehend the fear of the dark, for I have never feared it. Dark was all I knew until I was seven years old—and you showed me light."

"It was you who Read me, Torio," said Lenardo, recalling the surge of joy ten years before, when he found in the little blind boy the talent that would release him from his dark and circumscribed world. In those days he had never questioned his calling to teach. Now he was no longer certain—no longer trusted his judgment to guide the young Readers. How well had he guided Galen, that the boy had come to question the law—and been branded a criminal, thrust beyond the pale, where he would have to cease Reading—or die?

Surely he is dead by now, Lenardo thought. *And yet . . . I would know. I loved that boy. I cannot Read for him into the savage lands—but surely I would perceive if he were dead.*

"Magister?"

"What? Oh, I'm sorry, Torio. It's nearly midday. Come —let's see what the refectory has to offer."

As they began to unstrap their swords, however, Torio stiffened. "Magister—Read!" His delicate, skilled hands reversed their actions as the alarm bell clanged, rousing all Readers to open their minds to the message.

//Attack! Adigia is under attack! Battle positions!//

Three years ago, Lenardo would have dashed with Torio to defend the gates. Fifteen years before, he would have run, as Decius should be doing, to hide with the children. Now, however, his place was in the center tower of the keep, deep within the stone walls where the most skilled Readers would direct the battle while remaining safe from the attackers. For Readers were the only defense of civilization against the encroachment of the savages.

Lenardo was well into the passage before it occurred to him that Torio, despite his youth, was an increasingly skilled Reader who should be protected. *I'll put it to Master Clement at the first opportunity.*

The unlit passage twisted and turned, winding stairs deliberately impeding progress. In utter blackness, it was negotiable only by a Reader. A torch would throw hundreds of flickering shadows to fool the eye. For a Reader, though, the passage might as well be open to the sunlight.

Lenardo caught up with Master Clement on the narrow, twisting stairs. The old man was bent with rheumatism that slowed his steps, making the trek to the safety of the tower a painful journey. As always when he Read the Master's pain, Lenardo had to force down the traitorous thought, *If only we had the skills of those savages!*

Even as he took Master Clement's arm to help him into the well-protected chamber, the attacking savages sent their power thundering against the tower itself. Pure mental energy shook the very stone about them.

//What are they *doing*?// Lenardo wondered.

//Wasting their energies, let us hope,// replied Master Clement.

The two men entered the chamber and lay down on the comfortable couches. They would be sending their minds out now to guide the troops in battle; their bodies must be left secure behind.

The routine was already old to Lenardo. He removed his boots and stretched out, carefully composing his long limbs so that no part of his body placed pressure on another, no wrinkle of clothing threatened to cut off circulation. The process took only moments, but Master Clement was already waiting when Lenardo's consciousness left his body.

With no physical sensations to distract, the two men began to Read the battle. The savage warriors had already broken through the town's defenses, and the townspeople were retreating to the stronger-walled academy grounds. The academy, however, was the target. It had been attacked before, but never with such numbers, in such a determined effort!

//Tell Tiberium!// instructed Master Clement, then concentrated his efforts on guiding their troops strategically.

Lenardo reached out impatiently, not wanting to deliver

messages when he was needed **for** defense. But the Master was right—the central government at Tiberium must know that the savages were trying to push the empire's borders back once more—and it looked as if they might succeed!

Concentrating on the academy at Tiberium, Lenardo found himself "there," a faint consciousness floating in the courtyard where young women were practicing the intricacies of an ever-changing dance. The academy at Tiberium was female, as the one at Adigia was male. Briefly touching the minds of those in the courtyard, he found that Portia was not among them. Reading outward, almost at the limit of his strength to hold himself a single entity, he found her in meditation, her thoughts directed inward, not Reading.

Once he had found his object, Lenardo could focus on her, no longer fearing his consciousness would dissipate. How to get her attention? Again traitorous envy suggested, *A savage would tug her sleeve or pull her hair.* But he was no savage; he had no such power, and would not use it if he had. Besides, a savage could not Read.

//Portia!//

No response. She was the strongest and most skilled of Readers; thus her barriers were the most firm against intrusion. However, she would be sensitive to a concerted attempt to intrude, from a strong and practiced mind. So he mentally shouted at her, seeking over and over to Read her with all his strength . . . until at last she yielded to irritation and dropped her barriers for a moment to Read who was pestering her.

//Lenardo!// She Read instantly that he was not physically near—even if he had been before her, she would not have recognized his face, as they had never seen one another. Portia's warm greeting was tinged with apprehension. //Why do you contact me?//

//We are under attack here at Adigia. You must ask the emperor for more troops.//

//They are attempting to push back the border again? Or do they seek to take the academy?//

//Both, I think. Portia, we may be able to hold them off for a few days, but I Read a huge assembly of troops massed in the mountains. They will take us if we do not get help.//

//May the gods protect you, Lenardo. A Reader of your skill should not be left amid the dangers of a border town. Go back now, and tell Master Clement that Portia says an army will be on its way to you by nightfall, or she will take up sword and march to your defense herself.//

//The gods bless you for your help, Portia.// Lenardo withdrew regretfully from Portia's presence. As often as he had contacted her, the Master of Masters among Readers, he had never dared to Read her exterior. Her abilities were renowned throughout the empire. She had to be older than Master Clement, yet confronted with the power and compassion of that vigorous mind, Lenardo could not envision her as an old woman. He could not envision her at all.

Perhaps it was for the best that by law male and female Reader could never meet face to face, unless one or both had been declared unfit for the two highest ranks.

The familiar thoughts flitted through Lenardo's mind in the brief moment it took him to return his conscious presence to the Adigia Academy chamber. Master Clement was Reading the battle, guiding the Readers who led the defenses. Lenardo Read with him briefly, touching Torio's strong mind, the thought coming unbidden, *He could be trained to take my place here, were I sent to Tiberium.*

But then he had no time for personal thoughts. The battle raged at the very gates of the academy. People rushed to put out fires in two wooden outbuildings. Fire was one of the savages' most potent weapons—but they had to see the target to start the blaze. If they could Read, as well as thrust their powers outward, the empire would be doomed.

Only because they could not Read was it possible to defend against them. As another fire appeared on the roof of the bath house, Lenardo directed young Silvius to it. Silvius led a contingent of townsmen, the gruff men and women following the boy's direction without hesitation— nobody questioned a Reader in battle.

Another blow struck the ancient stone keep, shaking it to its foundations. But it only shook—that savage tactic might tumble a wooden barn, but it was a waste of strength against a building of stone, partly carved from the living mountain rock. Why were they doing it? The Readers speculated that the Adepts among the savages used enormous amounts of physical energy in such blows. They must deplete themselves, for if they could continue that kind of effort indefinitely, they could destroy anything. No one knew their exact limitations.

The blow came again. Why? What was the sense of pounding away at the keep? Lenardo tried to Read the Adepts who were striking against the stone building. As he did so, he caught a faint touch of familiar presence. Shock rang through him but was dispelled by the content of the thought he perceived: //. . . flaw directly beneath the keep tower. Direct your power low, right at the fault.//

A Reader! A Reader directing the savages! Relaying that horrifying news to Master Clement, Lenardo sent his mind deep beneath the keep, Reading the stresses in the very stone of the mountain. A fault! Centuries of gravitational shifting had produced slippage of rock layers deep under the ground. It was safe enough, though, unmovable by anything short of an earthquake—or the kind of pounding the savages were now inflicting.

//Master Clement! The savages will bring the academy down about our ears!//

The Master Read with him, and Lenardo felt infinite sadness in the old man at the impending destruction. But neither man took time for sorrow—both began at once to broadcast the alarm. //The keep will fall! Get the children out! Take shelter outside, against the walls!//

Immediately, everyone inside the ancient stone building was on the move—except Lenardo and Master Clement. //Return to your body, my son,// said the old Master.

//And you, Master. Hurry! I will help you out through the passage.//

//No. This is the end of the Adigia Academy. I have lived a full life. It is fitting that it end here, defending the academy to the last. Lenardo—I appoint you Master.//

//No!//

//Yes. You have authority now. Help the Readers to escape. They must not be taken! Especially the youngest ones—the ones our enemy could force to work for them. Find a way to get the boys out if you can, Lenardo. Build a new academy. Go now—I shall stay and direct until the battle ends.//

Until they destroy your body, thought Lenardo, but he blocked the thought and his sorrow. //The gods protect you, Master Clement. I shall revere you always as my teacher.//

//You have far outdone me, Master Lenardo. Remember always the true joy of the teacher—to have one's students reach beyond oneself. And reach they must, if you have taught them well. The gods protect you. My blessing goes with you.//

Reluctantly, Lenardo returned to his body. As always, it felt clumsy and unresponsive, his senses—even his Reading —closed in after the freedom of being pure mind. But Master Clement was right: he must attempt to save as many Readers as possible; none must be allowed to fall into the enemy's hands. Any who did would be tortured to death if they dared Read. Except the children . . . the gods preserve the children!

Drawing a few deep breaths, reorienting himself, Lenardo left the chamber and began Reading his way out through the winding passageway. The familiar presence of Master Clement rang in his mind, directing the children and older Readers out of the building, issuing instructions for escape through the fields behind the back wall in the confusion that would follow the fall of the keep. //Lenardo will lead you. I have appointed him Master, to build a new academy.//

The keep shook again with one of those mental blows— and yet again! What were they—? *They want me! They want to bring the keep down before I can escape! They? . . . or he?*

Another blow threw Lenardo to his knees. Struggling up, he Read deep, deep down into the rock, to the flaw they were battering. This time he searched further, amazed that there was no change since he had Read it before—only minutes ago, but before the latest series of devastating blows.

Sensing a few minutes of safety yet, he paused to Read further. The fault was most obvious just beneath the keep, but he could trace it back into the mountain . . . through the mountain to where it changed from a barely perceptible weakness to a precariously balanced fault that ended only where the sheer cliff face was exposed—where the far side of the mountain had fallen centuries before.

Now *there*—a single blow like the ones aimed at the keep could bring the entire cliff down in an avalanche upon . . . upon the massed troops of the enemy! They were all there in that valley, ready to surge through the pass as soon as the town was taken, to push the border of the empire back farther and farther, until one day they would drive all the way to the sea!

Lenardo pulled his mind from that train of thought. Did the Reader who was guiding the Adepts know that the fault ran through the mountain? Lenardo had lived here twenty years and discovered the fault only today. Another blow shook the keep. Lenardo Read its reverberations along the line of the fault. The greater weakness might be on the other side of the mountain, but the blows were carefully aimed at this side, their strength dissipating through the living rock. At its weakest point, the fault was receiving only faint echoes of pounding force.

At the next blow, the rock deep beneath the keep gave for the first time. At the tiny slip of edge against edge, the stone beneath Lenardo's feet seemed to turn to water, lifting him like a gentle wave, settling again into firm earth. Outside there were screams, and a rickety storage shed tumbled over.

Again Lenardo Read deeply, and he saw that the shift had left a precarious balance; moreover, the crack had extended beneath the mountain, making it possible that this side could tumble down upon them unless. . . .

He cursed his lack of engineering and mathematical knowledge—not proper studies for a Reader, he had been told. Instinctively he knew that there was a stress beneath the mountain such that more powerful blows could go either way. With the fault now connecting both sides, there was a possibility that another shift could bring down not only the keep but the mountain slope above it; or the shift could slant in the opposite direction, dropping the cliff face on their enemy.

And what good would it do me to understand it? he thought bitterly. *I am no Adept, to direct the stress against the enemy.* But would it not be poetic justice if their enemy destroyed its own troops with its own weapon?

It was useless for Lenardo to move at that moment. If the keep came down, so would the whole side of the mountain; there would be no benefit in being outside. So he remained still, concentrating, Reading the forces within the earth as he waited for the next blow, praying that it would reverberate through the mountain to the other side.

It came. The ground shifted sickeningly, but Lenardo's concentration was deep within, hypnotically fascinated by the stress patterns forming, reverberating in shock waves . . . waves causing the ground to lurch . . . concentrating and running along the crack so that the earth shifted far within . . . slow forces, earth moving like incredibly slow swirls of water . . . shifting, flowing outward in both directions from the center . . . but the weakest point was the cliff side! For an instant he stopped Reading, protecting himself.

The rumble reverberated through the mountain. There were screams here—but on the other side Lenardo could not prevent himself from Reading disbelief turning to terror as the sheltering cliff became a rockslide, tumbling down on the massed troops, burying them in the midst of their panic.

And as it happened, as the cliff fell, he Read again that familiar touch, now glaring in panic, Reading fury from three Adepts ranged about him—reaching for him— And they were gone, snuffed like candle flames before the first rocks landed, leaving only the non-Adept army to be buried, screaming, beneath the rockslide.

The battle continued, for the savage troops in Adigia did not know that what had felt like an earthquake had been the destruction of their main army. But the small army of Adigia and the students of the academy, together with the townspeople, drove them back easily once the Adept attacks stopped.

When it was over, Lenardo helped Master Clement out into the sunlight, where the other teachers were already accounting for the students and tending to the injured.

"I never thought to set foot in this courtyard again," said Master Clement. "The gods were with us today, turning the evil of our enemy back upon them."

"The savages were forestalled," Lenardo agreed, "but they will raise another army and return, Master. With a Reader working with them, they have us at their mercy."

"A Reader *with* them? Or one they have forced to Read for them, who deliberately caused their destruction this day?"

"Master, I Read him today. I know who it is . . . and I touched upon his hostility to us. I am convinced that what happened today was the result of divided attention, a single Reader attempting to direct an entire battle. He will not make that mistake again."

The old man halted, turning clear brown eyes upon Lenardo. "You say you know him. Then it is . . . ?"

"Galen," Lenardo acknowledged. "To my eternal shame, my student not only defies the empire but now has joined the ranks of our enemies. Our only hope is that they, who cannot Read, will think he betrayed them today."

"Lenardo . . ." Master Clement put a hand on his arm— a most unusual gesture between Readers. "Galen was your student, true. But you cannot blame yourself."

"My teaching was not strong or clear enough!"

"Lenardo, Galen had the fire and optimism of youth. He truly believed we could bargain with the savages, trade Reading for peace. I could not dissuade him, any more than you could. It is sad that he had to learn his lesson this way—but you have been a teacher long enough to know that the only way some people will learn that an idea will not work is to try it and fail. And at that point the teacher must let the student go."

"You did not touch his mind, Master. There was hatred in it."

"Hatred of the savages," agreed Master Clement. Lenardo wanted to believe him; after all, he had touched Galen's mind only briefly. So he did not protest as the old man continued, "The boy must have suffered bitter disillusionment. What you felt was certainly his despair at being forced to work for the enemy."

But I taught him, thought Lenardo. *I gave him power and failed to instill in him the principles of its use.*

"Magister Lenardo! Oh, please—come and help!"

It was Torio, calling him to where the injured were being tended. The blind boy knelt beside a still form—Decius.

Lenardo Read the younger boy, found him alive, but—

"He joined the fight! He didn't go with the children, Magister, because I praised him this morning. He thought he was ready to do battle. If he dies, it's my fault."

"He's not dying, Torio. Only . . ."

Decius was ashen with loss of blood. The wound was in his leg, above the knee—a vicious slash through flesh and bone. Nerve and muscle were severed. Lenardo Read the wound, which had almost stopped bleeding since someone had tied a strip of cloth around the leg just above it. Someone who had Read what Lenardo did: no empire surgeon could repair that leg. It would have to come off. Decius would be left a cripple.

Torio, Reading with Lenardo, began to sob. "I hoped I was wrong! Oh, why did I encourage him to think himself a swordsman?"

"Torio, you didn't. You merely told him he would make a swordsman one day—and he would have, with you to teach him. Now you must teach him other skills. Teach him to Read as well as you do."

"That won't compensate for the loss of a leg!" Torio said furiously. "Because I can Read, I don't need eyes—but no skill at Reading will make Decius any less a cripple. Our enemies' skills could help him—ours cannot!"

The boy echoed Lenardo's own traitorous thoughts. Yet . . .

"Torio, was not today's battle enough to show you how the savages use their powers? They destroy with them—they don't do good. Their misuse of power brought the attack in which Decius was injured."

"I know," Torio said miserably. "But *why*, Magister? Oh!" He suddenly remembered. "*Master* Lenardo, why must such power be only for evil?"

"It is the nature of power to corrupt," Lenardo replied, the tenet drilled into him since his own power to Read had been discovered when he was eight years old. "Our society is designed so that no one person may hold enough power to corrupt him."

It was a set speech. Torio accepted it, kneeling beside Decius. "Yes," he whispered fiercely, "I know. Still . . . why have we never sought to acquire the skills of our enemy and regulate them as we do our own? We have the society that could do it, Master."

Lenardo sighed. The old argument of youth, rising afresh in each generation. "Torio, when you ask that, you are ready for Master Clement's private tutoring. I will inform him."

"Why won't you teach me, Master Lenardo? You have always been my teacher. There is no reason for us to sit still and let the savages destroy us. Are we savages ourselves, afraid of anything we don't understand?"

Just then, Decius stirred and moaned. Both Lenardo and Torio bent over him, their discussion forgotten as they sought to make the injured boy more comfortable. But the worry preyed on Lenardo's mind. *My teaching did not lead Galen in the right path. Because of my weakness, the entire Aventine Empire may fall.*

As soon as the wounded were attended to, preparations for burial of the dead begun, the homeless given shelter, Masters Clement and Lenardo returned to the chamber beneath the keep to report the result of the battle to Portia. Leaving their bodies behind, they entered a plane of privacy. Only another Reader on the same plane could perceive their thoughts, unless they deliberately directed them to someone.

Portia relayed the message to recall the troops marching toward Adigia, and then listened with sad intensity as Lenardo told her about Galen.

//You are certain it was Galen, and that he was Reading for the enemy? The boy was a fool, but I never thought him so vile a traitor.//

Her words stung Lenardo. //I did not think so either. You know I opposed his exile. Portia, something must be done to stop Galen, or the empire is doomed. Every year, the savages force our borders back further. Now, with a Reader to guide them—//

//Lenardo—Clement—how many others know that a Reader was directing the attack?//

//Why . . . no one,// said Clement.

//Good. Do not tell anyone.//

//But Portia,// protested Lenardo, //something must be done!//

//Indeed, we must put a stop to Galen's aiding the savages—but in doing so, we must not make our own people mistrust us.//

//What do you mean?// asked Master Clement.

//My friends, you have been too long out there along the border, where simple people respect and accept you. Here at the center of government many fear the Readers. We must show that we police our own—or they will fear that any or all of us might turn our talents to abetting the enemy.//

//But this is the first time—// Master Clement began.

//Aye,// she replied, //it has finally happened, the secret fear of non-Readers. Did you think only Readers capable of predicting such an event? Others are as intelligent as we—and many far more crafty. For centuries we Readers have disciplined ourselves. The only restriction the government places on us is that we may not hold office. Do you want to see other restrictions, the academies broken up, non-Readers interfering with the education of Readers?//

//Portia, surely you—// Master Clement began gently.

//No, Clement, I do not exaggerate. You do not know the fight I have had to wage against such measures in the senate—ever since the savages destroyed the irrigation lines seven years ago and nearly caused a famine. Many argue that the Readers should have known what the savages planned.//

//No one can Read so far!// Master Clement protested.

//*We* know that,// Portia agreed, //but the non-Readers who fear us also fear that we do not reveal all our powers. If they find out about Galen, there will be widespread distrust of Readers. Should that happen—should the non-Readers rise up against us, refuse to trust our abilities—the empire is doomed.//

Perhaps the empire is doomed anyway, thought Lenardo. He had meant to shield the traitorous thought, but the rapport with Portia's agile mind was too strong.

//Will you give up without a struggle, Lenardo?// she asked.

//I have been struggling all my life,// he replied, //and yet the savages advance upon us. My family fled the city of Zendi when the savages took it. I remember, though I was only five years old. When I came to Adigia as a child, the academy was safe, secure, well inside the border. But year by year the savages advanced, pushing our borders back. I have fought them stroke for stroke with my sword, and I have fought from afar with my mind. To what avail? Only by good fortune was Adigia not taken today—and next time it will be taken. Master Clement and I have already decided the academy must be moved—but how long before the savages advance again to wherever we rebuild?//

//What would you have me do, Lenardo?// asked Portia.

//Galen is the immediate danger. No one can find him but another Reader—and I am the one responsible, Masters, for I taught him the skills he now uses against us.//

//No, Lenardo!// exclaimed Master Clement. //Your power as a Reader exceeds mine. I have just appointed you Master, and had intended to send you safely to Tiberium, no longer risk your life anywhere near the border. The empire needs you as a Reader, not a soldier.//

//Not a soldier,// Lenardo replied; //a spy. I must stop Galen—bring him home. He is a weapon I crafted;

now our enemy has that weapon, and I feel an obligation to take it from them.//

There was a long pause. Then Portia said, //It may take all your skills, and if you should succeed in persuading Galen—or killing him—then your life will surely be forfeit, Lenardo.//

//Perhaps. Nonetheless, Galen is my responsibility.//

//Portia, you cannot let him—// Master Clement began.

//My old friend,// she said, //I would not send Lenardo if there was anyone else, but only a Reader of his accomplishments has a chance of locating Galen, let alone reaching him. And if Galen has respect for anyone in our empire, surely it will be for his teacher.//

Despite their bodiless state, Lenardo sensed from Master Clement something like the stinging of tears as he said, //Portia, you know there is only one way Lenardo could cross the border and not be slaughtered at once. He would have to be branded a traitor in a public exhibit at the gates—once branded, how could he ever return?//

Out of touch with his own body, Lenardo experienced his fear as pure emotion. He had not thought of that—barred forever from home if he should somehow live through his mission! Barred forever from the rapport with other Readers . . .

//No,// said Portia, //he would not be prevented from returning. Remember the story of Barachus, who went out in the same way among the savages and returned with detailed plans of their stronghold at Galicium? Through his efforts the savages were driven back, and Barachus became a senator, bearing the brand on his arm as a mark of honor to the end of his days.//

//Then . . . we must see that there is no chance that Lenardo will be killed or driven away if he lives to return,// said Master Clement.

//Aye,// replied Portia. //I had meant to keep the plan among the three of us—but you and I are old, Clement. There should be a third who knows, younger than we—a Reader who can tell other Readers if we should not be here when Lenardo returns.//

Lenardo was grateful for the confidence of that "when."

//Lenardo,// said Master Clement, //is there one among our young Readers you would trust with this secret —and your life?//

//Aye,// Lenardo replied at once. //Torio. He shows promise of becoming more skilled a Reader than I . . . and I think knowing what Galen has done will increase his own loyalty to the Empire.//

Thus it was settled, a plan of Readers, by Readers, the emperor himself not to be told of it until Lenardo had succeeded—or died trying. The failure of the enemy to take Adigia gave them some time, for even the savages could not quickly replace the troops buried when the cliff fell. Nor, Lenardo thought, would Galen be trusted soon again.

And perhaps they are right not to trust him. He grasped at that hope. Having lived among the savages for over two years now, Galen might have seen the error of his ways and taken the chance to trick the enemy into destroying its own troops. Perhaps . . . by the gods, perhaps he was undertaking a rescue mission!

In order to have privacy amid the academy full of Readers, Lenardo called Torio into his study. It would be another year before the boy was ready to learn to leave his body, despite his rapid progress. Therefore, once they were seated, Lenardo said, "Torio, I must ask you to stop Reading, and merely listen to me. I am about to trust you with my life, and also the safety and security of all Readers in the Aventine Empire."

Torio paled and broke into a light sweat. His eyes, which had been fixed on Lenardo as if he could see him, drifted unguided as the boy said, "Why me, Master?"

"Because you have the talent that will make you a Master yourself one day. You questioned me today just the way another student questioned, not long ago. Do you remember Galen?"

"Aye. Are you warning me that my questions could lead to the same fate—branded and thrust across the border?"

"No, Torio. I am telling you what you must not reveal

to anyone else: it was Galen who led the attack on the academy today."

"Galen Reading for the savages against the academy? Master, no! Surely any Reader would die first!"

"Torio, we cannot know what methods the savages may have used to force him. It may be that he plotted the destruction of their army today, under the guise of helping them. But either way, he must be taken from the savages."

"How?"

"I am going after him."

Lenardo explained the plan—what little there was of it—to Torio. "You are my final security, should I live to return."

"Let me come with you!"

"Nay, child—a blind boy walking as if he could see? You would be recognized as a Reader immediately, killed by the ignorant peasants. No—I must take care not to reveal my abilities until I can find out who among the savages took Galen in—and to what purpose. You, Torio, have important work to do here. You must mature and fulfill your potential as a Reader and, if I succeed, be my entry back within the pale. Only three people know of my mission: the Masters Portia and Clement, and you, Torio. If no one of you is here to persuade other Readers of my loyalty to the empire, then I must remain forever an Exile among the savages."

In order to be exiled, Lenardo had to pretend to treason—and what more likely than the very treason Galen had committed? It had happened two years before, on a day of failure and triumph. Galen and Lenardo had taken the afternoon to pick mushrooms in the wood not far from Adigia. Lenardo was trying to teach Galen to Read directly whether the mushrooms were poisonous or not, rather than judging by their possibly deceptive appearance. At almost eighteen, the boy did not yet have the sensitivity. He should have had it; Lenardo found himself scolding him several times for not concentrating. He worried about Galen; would his student fail his final test as a Reader?

Master Clement had already voiced that fear. Lenardo redoubled his efforts to teach the boy; that was why he had not let Torio come with them that day.

Despite Lenardo's individual attention, the lesson was not going well. "What does it matter?" Galen demanded in frustration. "I haven't picked any poisonous ones. Non-Readers don't poison themselves either."

"Galen, you are old enough and bright enough to know that mushrooms are not the point. You will need this same sensitivity when you go for your medical training. You must be able to Read what poisons may be in the body of a sick person, or you might give him the wrong medicine."

"I have more than two years," Galen said defensively. "I'll learn it!"

"You should have learned it already."

"You think everybody should be like your precious Torio!" Galen snapped. "Don't bother to tell me *he* could Read these stupid mushrooms, and he's not sixteen yet."

"I wasn't going to tell you that. Galen, you need not compete with Torio. There is no competition among Readers. But you want to stay at the academy, don't you?"

"Of course I do. I plan to be a Master Reader."

Lenardo doubted the boy had that much talent. Nonetheless, it was a proper goal. "Then you must learn to concentrate. Here—try again. Just behind those trees—"

"I can Read them!" Galen said impatiently, and Lenardo withheld the chiding comment he should have given for the boy's rudeness. Recently Galen's attitude had deteriorated severely, but all the teachers had found that scolding him and punishing him only seemed to make it worse. What had happened to the boy who had so loved to learn?

"Stay where you are, and tell me if those mushrooms are edible," Lenardo directed as if he hadn't noticed Galen's tone.

Galen frowned in concentration. He was a beautiful boy who had never gone through a period of adolescent awkwardness, perhaps because he had not shot up in height as most boys did. He was still more than a head shorter than Lenardo, slender, younger looking than his years. He had outgrown sickliness in childhood but still looked delicate, ethereal. His hair was reddish blond, his skin pale and faintly freckled, with no trace of beard yet. Perhaps his appearance had caused all the teachers to baby him.

Soon he will be eighteen, and he will be put to the test like any other Reader. I must see that he does not fail.

Deliberately not Reading, so he would not accidentally transmit information to Galen, Lenardo watched the boy's concentration. "There's a big patch of them," Galen said finally, "all edible."

"Very well," said Lenardo, concealing his disappointment, "let's go have a closer look. It's a good thing there are plenty to top off our basket—there's a storm coming."

What Galen had missed was one small patch of death cup mushrooms to the side of the unusually large clump of common edible ones. Perhaps he had not concentrated on them at all, pulling his old trick of deducing what he could not Read. His high intelligence compensated for weak Reading skill in the classroom; it was in the field that Galen's inadequacies showed.

Still not Reading, Lenardo bent beside Galen, gathering the fresh mushrooms, leaving the older stalks. Tonight there would be a casserole of eggs and mushrooms on the refectory table.

According to the lesson, Galen was supposed to be Reading each mushroom as he picked it. Lenardo carefully picked in a pattern that edged Galen toward the poisonous ones. The boy finished plucking all those he could reach, looked around, and moved toward the group of death cups. Lenardo's heart sank. He shouldn't have to go near them to Read they were poisonous!

To Lenardo's horror, Galen reached out and broke off two of the deadly mushrooms.

"Galen!" he exclaimed before the boy could toss them into the basket. "If you're not going to Read, *look!*"

"But I—" The boy stared at the mushrooms in his hand, turned pale, and then an angry red. "That's not fair! You pushed me this way!"

"Yes, I did," said Lenardo. "I thought you would discover the death cups for yourself, and then I could have praised you. Look—the moment you bothered to use your eyes you saw the fatal cup around the stem."

The boy threw the poisonous mushrooms aside and scrubbed his hand roughly against his robe, fighting down tears. Trying to guide him to make something positive of the experience, Lenardo asked, "What can you learn from this mistake?"

"That I might have poisoned myself and everyone at the academy!" Galen said grimly.

"No," said Lenardo, "you already knew that a Reader's mistake can cost his life or those of others. It is the corollary to that lesson that you refuse to learn, Galen—and that, more than any deficiency in your Reading skill, is what will cause you to fail your final test. Do you know what I'm talking about?"

"Know your limitations," Galen quoted.

"Not only know them, but admit them," Lenardo added. "You have many years before you will come to the peak of your Reading skills. No Reader under thirty is yet in full command of his powers."

"I know that," Galen said dully.

"No," Lenardo replied, "you have heard it time and again, but you refuse to *know* it. And that makes you dangerous. Galen, you knew you were not Reading the mushrooms properly. Any ten-year-old would have had the sense to *look* at them!"

"I *did* look!" Galen protested. "I looked when you told me to Read them from behind the trees. They all looked edible!" His vehemence died. "I guess I didn't check every single one," he admitted. "Cook would have caught—" He hung his head. "No, don't say it. That's not the point. I won't let it happen again."

That was the Galen Lenardo loved, able to admit his mistakes and go on.

"Good. Now I want you to practice checking your Reading through your other senses. I do it. Even Master Clement does it. It's only common sense."

"You scold me for doing it in class."

"Galen, don't pretend stupidity. How can you know your limitations if you cheat when we are testing them?"

"Yes, Magister," the boy said resignedly. Lenardo longed to Read what was going on in his mind, but Galen had not invited such scrutiny, and so the Law of Privacy prevailed. But if the boy's sunny enthusiasm continued to disintegrate into these mood swings, how was he to learn the final lessons that would allow him to reach the top ranks of Readers?

Among the older boys, only Galen and Torio showed the deep sensitivity that would keep them in the brotherhood of the academy. The others would be trained to the fullest extent of their abilities, then assigned to places where even a Reader of limited capacity would be welcome. Most would serve with the army for two or three years, directing the troops in the constant battle against the savages. Then they would be married off to similarly limited female Readers, to lose much of whatever powers they had in breeding a new generation of Readers. Lenardo's parents had been assigned in that fashion to the city of Zendi. He remembered little of them now, except their determination that their children would not fail their final tests and suffer a similar fate.

As Lenardo and Galen came out of the woods into the fields around Adigia, thunder rumbled and the first fat raindrops fell. Lightning flashed, and they quickened their pace. The rain remained light, but the lightning and thunder increased, coming together as the storm approached. Harvesters in the fields ran to hold their frightened horses lest the loaded wagons overturn.

"Ho! Magister Lenardo! Can I give ye a lift?"

"Thank you kindly," Lenardo began as one of the hay wagons slowed beside them, the driver fighting the frightened team. Setting his heels, the man rose to his feet, hauling on the reins as Lenardo, panic striking through him with the flash of foreknowledge, cried, "No! Get down!"

But it was too late. Lightning bolted the man to the wagon for one paralyzed instant as the crash of thunder shook the earth. Then the screaming horses dashed forward, and the driver tumbled to the ground, limp as a poleless scarecrow.

Both Lenardo and Galen were on him at once, working in unison, Reading for broken bones or internal injuries before they spread Lenardo's cloak and laid the man on it. It was the work of moments. //His heart's stopped,// said Galen. //He's not breathing!//

//Pump his lungs,// Lenardo instructed, for Galen already knew basic emergency procedures. The boy bent to his task while Lenardo Read for the right spot to place his hands, where the force he might apply would be transmitted to the man's heart. Then he was working automatically, Reading, hardly thinking.

Is he dead? There was not enough damage from the lightning to account for the lack of response in the limp body. As the rain began to pour down on them, the man's body temperature started to drop. Were they trying to revive a corpse? There were fine nerves, infinitely small structures in the human body that Lenardo had not the sensitivity to Read—no Reader had. He could Read no unconscious mind either—just a physical shell.

//It's no use,// he told Galen.

//No!// the boy protested, continuing his ministrations. Lenardo remembered that this was the first time Galen was putting what he had learned to use in a real emergency. How hideous to have his first patient die!

//Galen, he was dead before we touched him.// He sat back on his heels, rubbing his hands.

"No!" Galen cried out loud. He was soaked through now, his hair plastered to his skull as the rain beat on them. Still he moved quickly to the other side of the man's body and took up trying to pump his heart.

"Galen, it's no— Wait!" A flicker—a mind. "You're right, Galen! Go on!" Lenardo took up the task of forcing air into the man's lungs.

Galen said, his voice shaken by his stiff-armed bouncing on the man's chest, "If—I were—one of those—savage Adepts—I'd *force*—his heart—to work."

//Hush!// Lenardo warned him. //People are watching us.// For, indeed, a crowd had gathered to watch the revival effort.

Suddenly he Read a heartbeat. A pause, then another, agonized spasms, and then an unsteady rhythm. At the same time, the man gasped, groaned, and began to breathe stertorously.

The two Readers sat back, watching, as a murmur of wonder came from the gathered workers. Then a young man came to kneel beside them.

"Father?"

"He can't hear you," said Lenardo, "but he's alive."

"Thank the gods you were here!" the man said.

Lenardo projected warmly to Galen, //Thank the gods you wouldn't give up!//

As soon as the man's condition seemed stable, they carried him to his house, where his wife scurried about, putting him to bed, then insisting that the two drenched Readers warm themselves before the fire. Lenardo intended to stay until the man regained consciousness, for he feared that after the length of time he had been . . . dead . . . there might be irreparable damage. For that reason, he tried to send Galen on to the academy, but just as the boy was about to leave, their patient suddenly woke with a hoarse cry.

The man sat up, staring, uttering garbled noises. He lifted his arms, but his right hand flopped limply, out of control. He stared at it in horror and made more panicked sounds. His wife rushed to his side, trying to push him back on the pillow as she said, "It's all right, Linus. You're alive. You're at home."

His eyes became even more stricken as he stared at her, and Lenardo Read that her words were being twisted by Linus' wounded mind into the same incoherent nonsense that he was uttering. The couple's son, who had stayed to help his mother, cried out, "No! The lightning addled his brain!"

"He can be helped!" Lenardo quickly assured them. "At the academy, Readers can reach his mind." The symptoms were similar to those of a stroke. Readers could touch the unspoken desires of such a victim and help lead him back to communication.

Lenardo sat on the edge of the bed, looking into Linus' face, not speaking lest he frighten the man further. Linus stared at him in confusion. Then he spoke—the words were nonsense, but beneath them Lenardo Read, //Magister Lenardo?//

Lenardo smiled and nodded, taking the man's left hand and squeezing it as additional assurance that he understood.

//Help me?// This time Linus made no effort to speak aloud.

Again Lenardo nodded, then reached out to close the man's eyes, urging him to rest. Relieved that there was someone who understood, Linus relaxed and drifted toward sleep.

"He recognizes people," Lenardo assured the man's wife and son. "I don't think his intelligence is impaired. Let him sleep through the night here, and in the morning we'll take him to the academy. One of the Readers will come back and spend the night, in case he needs anything."

"You can make him well?" Linus' wife asked.

"I've seen others with the same problem cured," Lenardo replied. No sense telling her now that a few never improved and that almost every victim retained some impairment.

"Thank you for saving his life," she said fervently.

"You can thank Galen," Lenardo began.

"I should have let him die!" the boy burst out. "You knew what would happen! Why didn't you make me stop?"

The boy had not yet been to Gaeta, where Readers studied in the great hospital. He had not seen the seeming miracles Readers could perform in curing afflictions of the mind, or the skill they had developed in curing the body when they could Read the cause of the illness.

"Galen, you did the right thing," Lenardo said aloud, for Linus' family to hear. "Linus will recover." //Will you be quiet and stop frightening these people?// he added, but Galen was stubbornly closed to Reading.

"It was too long!" the boy insisted. "You knew! We couldn't save him with our hands. Only an Adept could have revived him in time!"

That again. "Galen, stop it! Do you want these good people to think you're a fool? You're not thinking."

"I've thought it out before, and no one will listen! Healing is the one thing we can trade with the savages—a place to start. Why won't the emperor even *try?*"

"Shut up, boy," growled Linus' son. "You don't talk treason in my father's house!"

"Your father almost died! Now he'll suffer for the rest of his life—but if there'd been a savage Adept with us—"

Lenardo grabbed Galen in anger and fear, shaking him soundly. "The savages kill. They don't cure; they *kill!* Stop this before you get yourself exiled so they can kill *you!*"

But it was too late. Linus' son reported Galen's words to the commander of the local army. Lenardo often thought it was the horror of his father's condition that caused the younger man to take a kind of revenge on Galen. Had Linus either died or recovered with only minor problems, his son would probably have ignored Galen's outburst. But visiting his father day after day, finding him still unable to understand or communicate, he had to take out his frustration somehow.

Galen was no help to his own cause. He took his trial as a forum to propose that the empire sue for peace by offering the savages the services of Readers. Nothing Lenardo or Master Clement could say about the folly of youth did the least good. Galen was condemned to exile. His words upon being sentenced were a final defiance: "Then perhaps I shall have to bring about peace by myself!"

Lenardo had feared then that the sentence would be changed to death. But no, Readers had been exiled before, and none had ever succeeded in ingratiating themselves with the Adepts. The empire knew that, for a Reader, exile did mean death. He wondered if any non-Reader could understand. Even if a Reader did not give himself away, being cut off from the rapport with other Readers would make death seem preferable to such a life.

Galen was to be sent into exile the next morning. Le-

nardo spent the night in a fruitless attempt to teach the boy
the technique of leaving his body, so he could avoid the
pain of branding. It was a lesson Galen would have begun
on his eighteenth birthday, less than a month away—but it
was a rare Reader who learned it on his first attempt.
Lenardo knew there was little hope that Galen could
achieve it in his state of emotional turmoil, but he had to
try.

What he learned was that Galen thought himself incapable of that final test—that he expected to fail and be
removed from the academy. And that he thought it was
not fair.

Lenardo touched that night on fragments of Galen's
feelings kept hidden up to now. Although the teacher had
no intent to invade his privacy, the student was so upset
that his private thoughts kept surfacing . . . or perhaps
something within him wanted Lenardo to know them.

Why were Readers kept out of government? Surely with
their strictly enforced Code they were more trustworthy
than the non-Readers who entered politics. Why were the
tests for Readers so stringent? The academies never had
enough staff because they insisted on that final ability to
leave the body before one was safe from being married off,
one's sensitivity destroyed through sexuality. He'd even
heard that reluctant couples were drugged—

"Galen, why didn't you tell me these things were on
your mind?" Lenardo asked in dismay. "You've been listening to ignorant, vicious gossip. Those stories are simply
not true. I would *know!*"

"How would you know? They didn't marry *you* off—but
then you always perform the tricks they ask, don't you,
Magister Lenardo? Just like a trained dog, never questioning, always getting patted on the head by the Masters."

Lenardo let the insult pass. "Galen, you know the answers to your questions. The powers Readers have are not
appropriate to governing. And as for why not all Readers
can remain secluded in the academies, where would the
next generation of Readers come from? Non-Readers
sometimes have Reader children—but Readers always do.
And since the act of procreation severely diminishes a

Reader's ability, does it not make sense that the very best Readers should be spared?"

"I have no quarrel with that," said Galen, "but *more* should be spared. You know a Reader of my ability could be a great help here at the academy, tutoring, healing—"

"That is true," Lenardo agreed. "However, those Readers who are not quite the best are the very ones who must produce the next generation, if the best Readers cannot. And, Galen," he added, "you have now seen to it that you will never know if you would have made it into the top ranks. Is that what you intended?"

Instead of opening to cleansing grief, as Lenardo hoped he would, Galen just said, "I don't know what I intended— except to make people see the truth. You have all those standard answers, which let you ignore the questions."

"I don't understand you, Galen."

Galen's eyes fixed on Lenardo's. "I know, Magister Lenardo," he said sadly. "I know."

Now, two years later, Lenardo still felt the same frustrated guilt. He found it strangely easy to say Galen's words publicly, even though he did not believe them. At his own brief trial, he insisted that the last savage attack on Adigia, using the force of an earthquake, had convinced him that the empire had no hope of surviving against such power. He then presented Galen's argument—that the empire should seek peace with the savages by offering Readers' abilities—as if it were his own.

For a moment, as he awaited sentencing, Lenardo wondered how much the non-Reader tribunal knew. Had they got wind of the fact that the last Reader they had exiled was now working for the enemy? Would the sentence be not exile but death? In horror, he discovered that some small part of him hoped it would be.

No. I must correct my mistake. How often had he made his students do their work over, insisting, "Mistakes are meant to be learned from." So now he must try again to persuade Galen. He stood firm as the sentence of exile was pronounced.

.* * *

To be sure the the empire's exiles could not return under assumed identity, each one was branded on the right arm with the head of a dragon, symbol of the mindless power of the savages. As Lenardo, dressed in sturdy traveling garments, was led to the gates of Adigia, he couldn't help shuddering at the sight of the brazier, the iron already heating in the glowing coals.

He remembered when Galen was branded. Out of some strange mixture of expiation for himself and reassurance for the boy, he had meant to Read the pain with him. No Reader could shut out that kind of pain entirely—every Reader in Adigia suffered when someone in town felt agony, except the very young boys who could not yet Read beyond the confines of the academy. But Lenardo had intended to make no effort to close Galen out.

Deliberately he turned his mind from the thought as he approached the north gate of Adigia on his own day of exile. Torio and Master Clement walked on either side of him, dressed all in black—symbol of his death to them. In the gathered crowd were many familiar faces, a few students, townspeople, soldiers. He saw Linus with his wife and son. If—when—he found Galen, he would give him the good news that in two years the man whose life they had saved had recovered enough to work, to play, to enjoy life. He still spoke haltingly and walked with a slight limp, but he was alive and grateful to be so.

Lenardo Read great confusion from the crowd—a Master Reader exiled? Many of them wondered why the government would not heed the words of so wise a man. *If they only understood that Reading does not automatically confer wisdom!* he thought bitterly.

Others were scornful, though. A number of times he half-heard, half-Read someone say, "The savages will show him. *They* know what to do with an exiled Reader!"

The soldiers waiting to perform the Acts of Exile were men he had known for years, non-Readers he had fought beside many a time before his skills had reached the level at which he could retire to the keep to direct the troops. Now one of the men gazed at him with contempt, but the other, a grizzled old warrior with a scar down his cheek, had tears in his eyes. "Ye were ever a good man, Master," he said gruffly. "I dinna understand. Ye guided us against the enemy not two weeks ago, and now they say ye be a traitor."

"The emperor thinks my beliefs dangerous," Lenardo replied neutrally.

"Aye, and it not be dangerous to leave Adigia wi'out ye? Ah, Master, may the gods bless and protect ye. Here." He pulled at a chain about his neck, drawing an amulet from under his tunic. "I took this off one o' them savages in my first battle. 'Tis said to be a powerful protection, Master, from one o' *their* gods. And indeed, with all the battles I've been through, here I am, alive and healthy."

"I cannot take your protection, Quintus," Lenardo protested.

"Nay, lad—I am old. If I die in battle, that will please me better than living to weaken with age. You are young and going into danger."

"Why do you want to protect a traitor?" snapped the other soldier.

"I dinna believe he be a traitor," replied the old man, putting the chain around Lenardo's neck.

Lenardo looked at the amulet for a moment—a wolf's head carved from alabaster, the eyes a natural vein of violet just deep enough beneath the surface to show where the eyes were carved out. The stone was warm from the old soldier's body. Lenardo realized that his hands were very cold.

As the crowd gathered to watch, Lenardo's arm was strapped into the brace that would hold it for branding. Remembered shame rang through him: when Galen was branded, Lenardo had not been able to stand it. When the iron touched the boy's skin, the pain was so unendurable that he had had to stop Reading, enduring only what he could not block out. Trapped in his own body, Galen had had no escape from agony.

But I have.

Lenardo watched in hypnotic fascination as the brand

was prepared. As it approached, Torio and Master Clement supported his body. He relaxed against them, leaving his body, floating above, Reading the scene until the iron was taken away and Master Clement began to cover the wound with an ointment to ease the pain.

Sliding back into his body, feeling Torio's arms supporting him, Lenardo moaned as incredible pain shot up into his shoulder and down into his hand from the burn. It was as if the red-hot iron were burning into him right now!

Both the other Readers gasped with Lenardo's pain. The ointment did nothing to stop it. He was nauseated by the smell of burning flesh—his own flesh. A moan escaped him as he stared at the brand, the dragon's head, not a quarter the size of the back of his hand, but burned deep into his forearm forever.

The ointment glistening on the red wound did not disguise the burn's depth. He had not looked at Galen's brand, never realized that it bit deep into the muscle under the skin. He would wear the mark of the traitor for the rest of his life.

Finally the pain let up enough that he could perceive there was a world around him, people staring, Torio and Master Clement waiting to escort him to the gate. Quintus unstrapped his arm, saying, "I ne'er did a sadder day's work. The gods protect ye, Master."

Silently, Lenardo walked to the gate between his teacher and his student. Master Clement said softly, "My hopes go with you, Lenardo. I know you will do all you can to stop Galen. Shall I Read for you?"

"Nay, Master, that would be too dangerous—and within a day or two, long before I could hope to discover anything, I shall be out of range. But think of me."

"You know we do!" Torio groped blindly, found Lenardo's shoulders, hugged him. Alone of all Readers, Torio had no aversion to touching because he had "seen" with his hands the first seven years of his life. The contact was not offensive. Lenardo held the boy warmly for a moment as Torio whispered fiercely, "Come back to us! The empire needs you, Master Lenardo. The academy needs you."

"Take my place, Torio. I will return if I can—but you must prepare yourself as if there were no hope at all. Promise me."

"Yes, Master," whispered Torio, but as he pulled away he added, "but you will come back—you *must*!"

Chapter Two

The White Wolf

Lenardo walked a familiar road out of Adigia, for in his boyhood the border had been far distant, and this land had been part of the Aventine Empire. Now it was a no-man's-land between the walls of the empire and the lands the savages had taken. They built no walls to hold their borders; rather they pressed and pressed against the walls of the empire, driving ever farther toward the sea. Lenardo's family had fled southward along this very road, before the retreating army, when the savages had taken the city of Zendi.

For some distance the road was wide and smooth, and Lenardo Read no one nearby. His arm ached and throbbed, making him wonder what he would do if it became necessary to use his sword.

Surely, though, he could avoid that possibility until his arm healed. What was known of the savages indicated that while they fought fiercely in battle, they were reasonably peaceful with one another. They were all mind-blind; the only way they would discover he was a Reader would be if he stupidly answered an unspoken question or revealed something he could not have known otherwise. They killed Readers out of superstitious dread. Otherwise it was a catch-as-catch-can world in which an Aventine exile had as much chance as anyone of carving out a place for himself. When that exile was a Reader, though, isolated among non-Readers, life would mean little.

Exiles were frequently seen among the savage troops. Lenardo had himself twice fought sword-to-sword with men who bore the brand but were otherwise indistinguishable from the mass of savages.

A scruffy lot the savages were, hair and beards long and tangled, armor primitive, barbaric trousers flapping about their legs. But they could fight! And they could die nobly, on the battlefield or under interrogation when captured. Lenardo had sometimes been called in to Read prisoners, but the common soldiers knew nothing of value to the empire.

The officers, of course, could not be captured—or if one was, he could not be kept. It seemed all officers had some degree of Adept powers. Before such people chains snapped, locks opened, and guards fainted dead away.

Through Reading and interrogating prisoners, Lenardo had learned a little of their language—or languages. Even in his small experience he had encountered variants far more disparate than the dialects of the empire. He hoped his knowledge would be adequate, but it should surprise no one if an exile with a still-fresh brand spoke the savage language haltingly.

The well-kept Aventine road narrowed, weeds and tree seedlings encroaching from either side, leaving barely room for a wagon to pass. Occasionally, where the roadbed had shifted, Lenardo had to skirt around holes full of stagnant water.

He had been exiled with only the clothes on his back and whatever he could carry. Master Clement had given him a small pouch of gold coins—good currency anywhere. Otherwise, besides his sword, he carried only a small pack of necessities.

By afternoon he began to see people here and there—peasants, barefoot and ragged, working in the fields. The crops looked good; he wondered why the people tending them should be unkempt and undernourished.

The road passed by a cluster of mud and wattle huts—surely no fit dwellings for human beings! The stench of garbage and excrement reached him, yet he saw stick-thin children playing before the huts, heard a baby crying. Reading, he found she was hungry, the pains of starvation cramping her swollen belly.

What manner of people were these? The savage soldiers

sent against the empire were strong, sturdy, well equipped, well fed. Was that it—was all effort poured into the army, to the detriment of everyone else?

As he moved on into more populated areas, Lenardo Read the occasional thought to confirm his conclusion. There was sorrow in the land—everyone had lost husband, brother, son, or friend in the avalanche outside Adigia. In the simple peasants the loss was one of many sorrows, the latest tragedy in a string of miseries.

He approached Zendi, the border town of his childhood, near sundown. Lenardo remembered it as a large and beautiful city, bustling with life, a trade city of exotic sights, sounds, and smells. He had been happy there, playing with other children in the wide, clean streets. That was many years before he had seen the capital city of Tiberium, and to a small boy Zendi's forum, surrounded by temples, government buildings, and the huge, elaborate bath house, had seemed a magical place.

Although he knew the savages would not have left Zendi in the state he remembered—indeed, parts of the city were going up in flames when he and his parents fled—Lenardo hoped that it would retain some degree of civilization. He wanted to find a room for the night, where he might lock the door and leave his body—and his pain—behind for a few hours. His arm could heal while he Read through the city for clues to Galen's whereabouts. He didn't really expect to discover anything so soon, but he knew of no way to search except to move from one heavily populated area to another, Reading. The breach of the Law of Privacy was necessary now, just as it was in medical cases; Lenardo would not linger over thoughts that did not concern him.

Zendi, he found, had changed greatly since his childhood. The first thing to hit him, a good distance from Southgate, was the smell. It stank like the cluster of peasant huts, intensified. As he approached, he almost gagged —but slowly the miasma seemed to deaden the inside of his nose.

The source of the stench was the open sewer running down the middle of each crowded street. Lenardo hugged the walls, appalled by the filth and squalor. What had happened to the efficient underground sewers of every Aventine city?

The answer was easy to guess. Haphazard structures rising several rickety stories replaced the well-built wooden houses burned when the savages took the city. There were at least five times as many people crowded within Zendi's walls as the town had been built for. Such an influx had undoubtedly overloaded the system—and when it broke down, no one knew how to fix it.

And what of their vaunted magical powers? Lenardo wondered. *Have they put all their Adepts to making war, leaving them no time to help the common people?* There were soldiers everywhere in the city, the only people who looked healthy, well fed, well clothed.

Beggars came up to Lenardo, tugging at his cloak, grimy hands outstretched. "Coin, Meister?" they asked plaintively, but Lenardo brushed them aside, shielding his injured arm against his body. Each time he was jostled, new shocks of pain surged through it, keeping him from concentrating on Reading the city. He dared not answer any comments thrown at him, lest he reply to a thought rather than a word. Let them think he knew nothing of their language at all.

He decided that he could not stop in the town. He would walk straight through, Reading as he went, and take the north road out into the fresh country air again before seeking rest. Darkness held no terrors for a Reader, but in the open he dared not leave his body. He noticed a diminishing of his Reading powers already; the weaker his body grew, the less he would be able to Read and the greater the chance of missing some clue to Galen's fate. He had hoped tonight to let his body do the healing it could accomplish only at perfect rest.

But exiles who were not Readers survived branding. His arm would heal, even if more slowly than he had hoped. He felt eyes on him, not the curious glances from every side, but a steady stare. An officer was looking him up and down, studying him carefully.

Lenardo knew what he saw: a tall, well-muscled man approaching thirty years of age, wearing a sword. No man would wear a sword unless he could use it. Thus Lenardo was not surprised when the officer approached him and spoke in slow but understandable Aventine.

"Fresh across the border, I see," he said with a pointed glance at the blistered brand. "Welcome, stranger."

Surprised, Reading that the young officer truly regarded him as a fortunate discovery, Lenardo replied, "Thank you."

"We can use strong men like you in Braccho's army," said the officer. "It's a good life, all you can eat, warm clothing, good pay, and battle rights. Braccho's not one to take away what his soldiers find, women or treasure."

"It . . . sounds a tempting offer," Lenardo lied. "However, as you noted, I have come from that ungrateful empire this very day. Before I commit myself again, I would like to see what this side of the border has to offer. Your leader—Braccho?—would not want a pledge given in ignorance."

The young officer grinned cheerfully. "No, but I'll warrant in a day or two you'll agree there's no better life to be found. Come to the East Barracks and ask for Arkus. We'll show you how to get back at your tormentors for—that." As he spoke, Lenardo's cloak pulled away as if of its own accord, revealing the brand clearly. But as the cloak fell against it again, he winced at the contact and the officer said, "Aye, we know how to take the sting from such a wound—revenge is sweet balm."

"I shall remember that, Arkus," said Lenardo. "Perhaps you are right. If I decide to join your army, I shall certainly seek you out."

"Soon, I warrant," replied the officer, and he strode away.

When Arkus had spoken of revenge, Lenardo had picked up the man's own desire for revenge—not a clear thought but a kind of simmering anger surrounded by vague images. He felt betrayed, not personally, but as a soldier and a citizen. A split-second memory gave Lenardo some information, but it was negative: it was not Galen's betrayal

being avenged when six huge shields were hung up—in the
forum? No, they had been there, a permanent fixture. The
top one was the largest, black on gold. Below it five smaller
emblems in blue, white, gold, green, and brown. The image
flashed so quickly through Arkus' mind, and was gone
again, that Lenardo got no clear sight of the shields.

There was, along with the image, a sense of frustrated
anger and the smell of scorched leather. That was all, as
Arkus had not remembered the entire scene but merely had
a flash of recall associated with the idea of revenge.

Aside from the fact that Arkus' anger was not directed
at Galen, Lenardo had not learned anything of immediate
use. The name Braccho, apparently the general of the local
army rather than a ruler, he stored away as a possibly
useful fact. Another name, too, had been in Arkus' mind—
a name he would hardly let himself think because it
brought such mixed emotions.

Lenardo could not tell, because Arkus could not, if the
feelings were fear, anger, revenge, or admiration. The
name that conjured them was . . . Aradia.

When he reached the forum, Lenardo saw in actuality
the source of Arkus' memory. The shields were hung up
there, the top one bearing the dragon's head in black on a
field of gold. The five smaller shields below it were grouped
in two rows. One in the first row and two in the second had
been burned; only the frames remained, tattered fragments
of leather clinging to them. The other two were painted,
one with a green spear and the other with a brown horse's
head.

As Lenardo skirted the edge of the forum, a woman
approached him, hardly more than a child, wearing only a
tabard cut off at the hips. Her body was still adolescent,
but she flaunted it boldly. "I can give you pleasure, Meister.
You got money? One copper, I—"

"No, thank you." He tried to push past, quelling his
disgust at a society that reduced young girls to this.

The girl clung, dogging his steps, slipping ahead of him
to run backward as she offered, "Anything you want to
do, Meister—or I will show you new tricks. You want
to—?"

She began to catalogue her techniques, in graphic detail. Lenardo blushed furiously, to the amusement of the passing crowd. They, he noticed, took the girl for granted; his reaction was what made them laugh.

Finally, to get rid of her, he stopped and lifted his cloak to display his blistered arm. "Child, I am in pain," he said. "Can't you see I have no use for your talents tonight?"

At home, he would have worn the robes of a Reader, and no one of this girl's profession would have approached him—certainly not in such fashion! In the Aventine Empire soliciting rudely in the street was unheard of.

"Please, Meister—I'll soothe you, help you sleep. Maybe a bed for the whole night?" Her eyes lit, and he Read that she was hoping for a comfortable place to sleep without having to do anything but—

Oh, ho. There was her plan. She had the Adept power to put people into deep sleep. She planned to rob him. He smiled to himself and told her, "Away with you, now. When I want a woman, I'll find a woman, not a half-grown girl."

But he wouldn't want a woman. He was a Master Reader—he had learned to focus the yearnings of his body into positive channels when he was Torio's age.

Tonight the only yearning of his body was for rest and ease from pain. He ought to eat, he knew—had, this morning, planned to find a hot supper in Zendi. Now, though, pain had killed his appetite, and besides, there was no inn in the filthy warren Zendi had become where he would trust the food.

He was thirsty, feverish, fighting lightheadedness. He had to get out of town, find a place to rest.

A fruit-seller passed him, and for the first time something tempted him: juicy golden citrus fruit. He chose two oranges. All he had to pay with, however, was a gold coin.

Even though he was not Reading as he concentrated on speaking with the vendor, he could feel empathically that his money pouch was being eyed, weighed. He dropped the silver and copper coins the boy gave him in change back into the pouch and determined not to make that mistake again. He must hide his small supply of gold inside his pack and carry only coppers and perhaps a silver piece where they would be seen if he made a purchase.

Pretending he hadn't noticed anything, he walked away, Reading the two men flitting through the crowd, following him at a safe distance. Together? Yes. Very well. He Read crowds in several streets radiating from the forum—mustn't get caught in a deserted area. Reading the men trailing him, he wove through the crowd to get out of their sight, ducked into a side street until they had passed, and came out behind them. Then he eluded their search in the crowd, and escaped through Northgate just as the strangers' bell rang. Soon the gate was closed behind him for the night, the thieves remaining in Zendi.

For some time, Lenardo walked among people returning home from a day's business in Zendi. The crowd gradually thinned, until he walked alone again. He located a sheltered spot well off the road, ate a piece of fruit, and lay down to sleep.

With a Reader's discipline, Lenardo was able to put himself into a light sleep from which he would awaken at any disturbance. It was a troubled sleep, as he usually slept on his right side; each time he would truly fall asleep he would try to turn over, sending waves of pain through his sore arm. By morning it was badly swollen, his right hand stiff and clumsy.

Still very tired, he set off along the road again, now in territory completely strange to him. It was more of the same—fields, peasant huts, squalor and misery. He felt a kinship with the landscape.

He stopped to bathe his arm and spread ointment on it, but the pain just from doing that was almost too much to bear. He drank feverishly at the brook and staggered back to the road for a few hours. By early afternoon, he knew he could go no further.

There was medicine for fever in his pack, an opiate that dulled the physical senses and sent the mind roaming in precarious realms. He dared not use it unless he were safe, where nothing could disturb his body. On the road, there was no such place.

There were hills off to his right, however. He had a full
skin of water, food, and medicine. If there was a cave in
those hills where he might hide for a night and a day . . .

When he left the road, he found it even harder to walk.
His head seemed to lift from his body, then return with a
stabbing pain. Twice he fell, dragged himself up again, and
continued his nightmare journey. At one point he was
seized with teeth-chattering chills, but most of the time he
was in a clammy sweat.

His vision became distorted, and as he tried to Read
both the way he walked and the surrounding countryside,
the two perceptions blurred into confusion. He had to concentrated on his own steps, narrowing in to force one foot to
follow the other . . .

How long he traveled thus, he didn't know. He had
reached the lower slopes of the hills and was clambering
over a rocky outcropping when he suddenly Read people—
savages—all around him.

Alert, he could have avoided them. As it was, they were
upon him, hill bandits on helpless prey. He only half
understood what they were saying.

"An exile."

"No one will be looking for this one."

"They always have good clothes, sometimes money."

Then harsh hands grabbed him, and laughter rang out as
he howled in pain, trying to shake them off, reaching for
his sword with numbed fingers that scrabbled at the hilt.
More laughter as he was disarmed, his cloak ripped away,
his arms twisted behind his back, forcing another scream
from him.

He was staring into the face of a man perhaps his own
age, but the face was bearded, the mouth open to show
teeth missing, and those present black with rot.

"What have you got, exile? What can you give us for
your life?"

"Nothing," Lenardo gasped, knowing they wanted him
to grovel and plead before they killed him anyway.

The bandit hit him in the stomach. Gratefully, Lenardo
blacked out. He came to with the pain of someone twisting
his branded arm again. "Beat him," the bandit instructed,

and while two held him, others punched and kicked at him, ever careful to keep him conscious. Against the pain in his arm, the blows hardly registered. Hanging limp between the bandits, he waited for death to release him from pain.

Suddenly he was dumped to the ground, stripped of scabbard, boots, money pouch. Then one of the bandits felt under his shirt and pulled forth the amulet old Quintus had given him.

There was a gasp. The bandits dropped Lenardo and the amulet as if both had become red-hot.

"The wolf-stone!"

"Aradia!"

They scattered like startled birds, disappearing into the hills. Lenardo tried to sit up. They had taken everything, leaving him weaponless, without even boots to protect his feet from the rocks or a cloak to wrap up in against the night. He needed water, but they had taken the water-skin too.

He tried to Read around him, not moving. There must be a spring somewhere in these hills. He was deathly thirsty, and he had to clean the wound on his arm, where the bandits had burst the blisters with their filthy hands.

Far, far up in the hills, he Read water. He couldn't stand; he could barely get to his knees to crawl. After a while, it ceased to matter. He slumped into unconsciousness.

Feverish sleep possessed him, thirst and pain awakening him several times to see stars overhead. One time he was freezing but couldn't find cloak or blanket. Then he was burning, his lips splitting with thirst, the sun blazing down on him. The pain in his arm was gone.

Somehow he found the strength to turn his head, meaning to look at his arm, but caught instead by a vision. *Hallucination,* he told himself firmly, but still before his bleary eyes, swimming in and out of focus but stubbornly remaining, sat the white wolf.

It was not the abstract alabaster symbol, but a living animal, dusty about the feet, watching him curiously from a safe distance. Safe? Who was the one in danger here?

Perhaps the animal would tear him apart, and his troubles would be over.

The wolf rose and made a sort of whining noise, like a dog. It ran a few paces away, turned to look at Lenardo, came back to its original position, and whined again. Twice more it repeated the performance. Bemused, Lenardo wondered, *You want me to follow you, boy? I'm not going anywhere. Probably not ever again.* The effort of focusing his attention on the animal sent him back into unconsciousness, and when he next woke, the wolf was gone. *If it was ever there.*

He focused his eyes on his right arm, lying like a separate thing, swollen, red streaks running from the yellow, scabrous brand up toward his shoulder. He had seen such marks before. It meant his arm must come off if he were to live.

But I'm not going to live, he thought. Alone, far from help, he would die of thirst before the day was out. Carefully assessing his situation, he came to the same conclusion twice more and decided he was thinking clearly enough. It was truly hopeless. There was no need for him to suffer the lingering hours. He could not move to compose his body, but it didn't matter. He would not be returning to it.

In utter peace, he Read outward until he floated above the wreck of his physical form. Now there was no pain or fever; he was free. When his body died, he would be fully released—but while it still lived he must see Master Clement or Portia. They must know he had failed, must do something about Galen . . .

Before he began to concentrate on Adigia, however, other minds attracted his attention. Four men were coming from the hills. More bandits? He Read them and found there were five, one of them shielded against Reading. An Adept!

The savage Adepts could not Read, but neither could they be Read; a part of their training apparently included barriers against such intrusion, even though it could not come from their own people.

Focusing himself to see and hear, Lenardo saw five men in clean, serviceable clothing, moving purposefully down the hillside. One of them stopped, pointing to Lenardo's body. "Look! There he is!"

They all began to run toward the crumpled form. "Is he dead?" asked the oldest of the group, a stoop-shouldered man with a gray beard.

"Do you know him, Wolf-stone?" asked another as the apparent leader of the group knelt beside Lenardo's body.

"No," he said, and Lenardo Read that this was the one barricaded against him. He was a young man, a Nubian—a Nubian Adept? But if not Adept, why shielded? And they called him Wolf-stone? He was lifting the alabaster wolf's head with the violet eyes, comparing it with one he wore about his own neck. Lenardo wondered vaguely if the white wolf had gone to get him. "He wears the wolf-stone," the black man said. "It is the sign—yet . . ." He examined Lenardo's wounded arm. "An exile fresh from the empire —how can he wear Aradia's sign? Never mind; we must take him to her if he can survive the journey."

"Is he alive?" asked the graybeard.

"Oh, yes. Don't you see him breathing? He will suffer less if we can avoid waking him. Helmuth, wet his lips, but be careful he does not breathe water in. The rest of you prepare the litter."

Reluctantly, Lenardo realized that he was not to be relieved of his mission. He must return to his body and live—for wherever these men took him, he might learn more of Galen. He would lose his right arm, his sword arm, but, he thought with bitter humor, the brand of dishonor would go with it. If he should ever return to the empire . . .

If there was to be an empire to return to, he must regain his body. He had not thought to have to do so. It was a slow, painful, nearly impossible process when the body was as debilitated as his was. Finally, he opened gummy eyes to see the gray-bearded face swimming above him, as gentle hands wetted his parched lips from a water-skin.

Thirst was his first concern. Helplessly, he tried to speak, had no voice, but the old man lifted his head so he could drink, saying, "Lie still, son. You're all right now."

The black man immediately turned back to him. "Don't give him too much at once, Helmuth."

Then he spoke to Lenardo. "Do you understand me?" He now spoke in Aventine.

With the water to release his throat, Lenardo managed, "Aye." It was too much effort to say that he understood the other language too.

"You're safe now. We'll take you to Aradia. I'm going to make you sleep, so the journey will not pain you."

Lenardo wanted to protest, but he was too weak. The black man began to chant something in a language Lenardo didn't know, and he fell into dreamless sleep.

The dreams came later, as he was carried smoothly along in the litter. Or was that a dream too? Four men walking could not carry a litter so that it did not lurch or bump.

The confusing smooth motion was interspersed with strange images—worry about his pregnant wife . . . her time was due . . . when he got home, he might have a son. He tried to cry out to hurry—yes—the babe was born. A fine, healthy boy. Maj is fine . . . happy. . . .

A horse . . . lame . . . nothing seemed to help. Poultices. Must ask Aradia. . . .

Lovely girl. Halja . . . laughing blue eyes, light brown hair. Could he manage the marriage fee before her father gave her to another?

And woven through all the dreams the image of a woman . . . a woman who blended somehow into the wolf-stone, the two images shifting . . . shifting . . . white wolf . . . alabaster woman . . . violet eyes . . .

He woke in a room, at night, lying in a bed. The black man, sitting beside the bed, rose and gave him water. "Are you in pain?" he asked, still in Aventine.

"No," Lenardo replied, a pang of sudden fear as he remembered, looking for his right arm. It was still there, lying atop the covers like a dead thing, bloated, the streaks of red no worse than before but still there—

"Are you rested enough to speak?" asked a low-pitched female voice. Out of the shadows at the foot of the bed moved a woman with palest blond hair, her eyes dark pools in the dim candlelight. She reached for the wolf-stone about Lenardo's neck. "How do you come to wear this? I know you not."

"When I was sent into exile, a friend gave it to me. He thought it might protect me."

Her delicate eyebrows rose. "It has, indeed. The hill bandits have enough respect for it that they dared not kill you. It saved you a second time in that you are a Reader, and anyone else might have had you killed."

At Lenardo's start of surprise, she smiled, her pale face momentarily beautiful. "In your delirium, you talked of everything on the minds of the men carrying you—Helmuth's lame horse, Jorj's marriage plans, Gron's son . . . and Gron did not even know he had been born yet." Pure shame rang through Lenardo. Delirium or no, his training should have kept him from invading the men's minds, let alone babbling out their secrets. But the woman continued reassuringly, "Fortunately, no one but Wulfston spoke your language, so you did not frighten the poor men out of their wits."

"Wolf-stone?"

"I am Wulfston," said the black man.

Confused, Lenardo touched the alabaster wolf's head. "You are called—Wolf-stone?"

"Yes, that is what my name means. When you are well, I will explain how I got the name."

"I am Aradia," said the woman. "May we know your name?"

"Lenardo."

"Well, Lenardo, our first order is to put you back in good health. Let me examine you." As she spoke, a many-branched candelabrum on the table beside the bed . . . moved. Lenardo saw it only out of the corner of his eye and glanced toward it. It was perfectly still now—no, he must have imagined—

As he watched, every candle burst spontaneously into flame. At his astonishment, the woman said, "That is an easy trick—the candles are made to burn. I simply work with their natural inclination."

"How can candles have a natural inclination?" asked Lenardo.

"All of nature has desires," said the woman. "Water desires to run downhill. Crops desire to grow. What you call magic is nothing but encouraging things to follow their natural desires."

"Then you savages attack the empire because of a natural desire to kill?"

"No," she replied gently, "because of the natural desire to grow. Now, if you will let me examine your wounds—"

Wulfston stripped away the blankets, revealing Lenardo naked on the bed. "There were no signs on his back, my lady. They seem to have beaten his face and stomach, and he bruised his knees trying to crawl to shelter."

"To water," said Lenardo, recalling that deathly thirst.

Gentle pale fingers probed his cuts and bruises, pressed on a rib until he winced. "I wonder if—" She laughed, a light, lovely sound. "But you can tell me, can't you? Is this rib broken?"

He Read it. "Cracked, not all the way through."

"Can you Read other people that easily?"

"Physical things? Yes. No one can block that."

"What help you will be at healing!" she exclaimed.

He had never heard of savages healing or using their powers for anything but destruction. Could Galen be right? But this was an opportunity to gain her trust, without doing anything that might harm the empire. "I will be glad to repay your kindness by helping you at healing." Perhaps he could gain enough freedom of movement thereby to search for Galen.

Aradia was doing something with her hands over the broken rib, frowning in concentration. He felt heat within the bone, Read—and found that it had knit! It was not completely healed, but the strength was there, the pain gone!

"None of the rest of these scrapes and bruises are serious," she said. "Now let me heal your arm."

She lifted the arm as Wulfston pulled the blankets back

over Lenardo. He had braced for pain when she touched it, but he felt nothing. It was as if it were someone else's arm.

"There is nothing you can do," he said. "It's already dead."

"Oh, no—you don't feel the pain because Wulfston blocked the nerves at your shoulder, so you would not suffer on the journey here. Can you Read for me how deep the infection goes?"

"The entire arm—and the poisons are in the blood. Surely if you practice healing you know the meaning of those red streaks. If you want to save my life, you will have to cut off my arm."

Both Aradia and Wulfston were shielded againt Reading of their thoughts, but Lenardo's empathy picked up their horror and disgust at his words. "You call *us* savages?" demanded Aradia. "You, who come from a land where they do *that* to a man?" She pointed to the brand.

"What of the tortures you inflict on your prisoners?" he countered.

"Tortures? We have no need of torture. I do not know what you have been told of us, Lenardo, but the only people you will find in my land bearing marks of torture come from other lands . . . and some bear the same mark you do!"

The shock of his experience was beginning to dull his senses. "What of your bandits?" he asked weakly.

"I suppose no one ever breaks the law in the Aventine Empire? How did you come to be here? But come now, you are tired. You must rest and heal."

Aradia's hands moved gently over the bloated flesh, and Lenardo felt something—not pain, but the warmth he had felt in his broken rib, intensified. "It is the desire of the body to be whole," she said. "It is the desire of the body to be well, to cast out all poisons, to heal, the flesh clean and free of taint." Her voice continued, but he could no longer understand her words.

The warmth in his arm became a fire—a cleansing, purifying flame. It was the strangest sensation he had ever known—a terrible, intense heat, without pain. His arm should have been charred into ashes; instead, he Read the blood pumping through it, carrying away the poisons rendered harmless by the fire.

The blazing heat continued as Aradia lifted her hands away. She smiled at him. "When you wake up, tell me if you still want me to cut off your arm. Sleep now."

She pressed gentle, warm fingers over his eyes, and he sank helplessly into blackness.

Lenardo woke to sunlight streaming in the window. He was curled up comfortably on his right side, waking naturally just after sunrise . . . but he was not in his room at the academy.

For a moment he was completely confused by the unfamiliar surroundings, and then his mind cleared. His arm!

Sitting bolt upright, heart pounding, he held his right arm out in front of him. It moved normally, naturally, felt as it had always felt. He Read completely healthy flesh and bone.

To the eye, the skin had a sickly pallor, but he saw and felt that his calluses were gone, his hand as smooth as a baby's. After all the swelling and blisters, the skin must have sloughed off. This was new skin, pale because untouched by the sun.

How long—?

He drew right and left hands together. The outdoor tan on his left arm had hardly paled at all. He could not have been unconscious for very long.

He sat for a moment, staring at his arm. The brand that had caused all the trouble now appeared an old mark, seared deeply and permanently into his flesh, but with no remaining soreness.

Bewildered, he rubbed his face and found he was badly in need of a shave—but again, it was several days' stubble, not a growth of many weeks. He decided the best thing to do was to get up and find someone to answer his questions.

He was still naked except for the wolf's-head pendant, but his body felt clean. His clothes—what the bandits had left to him—were nowhere to be found, so he draped a blanket over himself like a toga and started out the door.

It was locked.

Feeling like an utter fool, he stood there, Reading through it. There was no one in the hallway outside. They didn't think it necessary to guard him.

No sense shouting and pounding on the door. He went to the window and saw the courtyard of a castle. He was two levels above the ground, looking down at the blacksmith setting up for the day's work in the corner below him. He was a slender man, not the well-muscled type one usually associated with smiths. As Lenardo watched, he turned to his forge, waved his hand, and the fire blazed up! Lenardo realized there was no bellows.

Why would an Adept be smithing? He recalled the young prostitute in Zendi, who had planned to put him to sleep as Aradia had done. Were Adepts so common in this society that there was no need to seek them out, as the empire sought Readers? Were they not a precious resource, to be carefully trained and guided?

Just then he Read Aradia at the door to his room. No lock clicked, but the door swung open, and she entered, carrying a tray of food with both hands. Behind her, the door closed itself.

"Nice trick," observed Lenardo.

"What? Oh—the door? If I'd had a hand free, I'd have given it a shove. No use wasting energy. I came to wake you. Your body has been doing an immense amount of work. You should be hungry."

He realized he was ravenous.

She uncovered soup, bread, a dish of soft farmer's cheese mixed with fruit. "Eat the soup while it's hot," she directed when he reached for the cheese and fruit.

"It's made with meat," he replied. "Eating meat dulls the ability to Read."

"Does it really?" she asked. "Strange—it improves an Adept's powers. But meat provides energy and is quickly absorbed into the blood. Will it do permanent damage if you eat some the next few days, until you get your strength back?"

"No, I suppose not." The aroma of the rich soup was enticing, although he usually found the smell of meat faintly repellent. His body was probably telling him he needed this nourishment.

As he ate, he asked, "How long did I sleep?"

"Three days. It takes time to heal such a desperate wound. If Wulfston had found you a day later, you would have been right—I could not have saved your arm."

"I'd have died of thirst before then. But . . . now that you've saved my life, what do you plan to do with me?"

She smiled, completely unReadable. In the daylight, he saw that her eyes actually were violet. He fingered the wolf's-head pendant and recalled some distant vision in which Aradia and the white wolf kept blending into one another.

Her pale skin, pale hair, and violet eyes gave her the coloring of the amulet, but she was hardly wolflike. At the moment, in a tan dress with a spotless white apron, she looked like some charmingly pretty country girl when she smiled—far from the powerful sorceress he knew her to be.

At that thought, he was suddenly uncomfortable in her presence, particularly wearing nothing but a blanket. Male and female—

But she's not a Reader, he reminded himself. And obviously, if Wulfston was her apprentice, there was no segregation of male and female among Adepts. Nonetheless, he felt ill at ease.

She must have noticed, in the way non-Readers had of perceiving emotions, for she said, "The first thing we must do is get you some decent clothing. Then I'll show you around the castle. You'll be very tired the next few days, until your body builds back all that the healing took out of it."

"But *you* did the healing."

"Oh, no. I just directed your own resources to do it. It is the nature of the body to be healthy."

"I certainly *feel* healthy," he agreed. "I'd like a bath and a shave, though, to feel myself again."

"In time," she replied. "We're keeping your body clean until you have enough strength for a bath. You really do not understand how weak you are. When you feel up to it, you may leave this room with Wulfston or me—but until you learn your limits, you are not to go off alone. Do you understand?"

"Are you going to keep me locked in here?"

"It is for your protection, Lenardo. You have much to learn of our ways before you will be safe outside the walls of this castle—or even some places within them."

"What you are saying, then, in spite of the face you put on it, is that I am your prisoner?"

"Oh, no!" She cocked her head to one side, mischievous country girl blending totally with dangerous wolf toying with its prey. Her smile was suddenly a pulling back of lips to reveal sharp teeth as she said in the most casual, reasonable tone, "You are not my prisoner, Lenardo. You are my property."

Chapter Three

Aradia

When Aradia had gone, Lenardo paced the room, anger burning up his small reserve of energy until he quickly reached exhaustion. Collapsing onto the bed once more, he fell into heavy sleep.

He woke again when someone entered the room—Wulfston. The black man brought him tunic, robe, and soft woolen slippers, which Lenardo donned gratefully. "The tailor is taking your measurements from the garments you arrived in," Wulfston explained. "By the time you are strong enough to leave this room, you will have suitable clothes."

"Thank you," said Lenardo, quelling his anger. Wulfston, after all, was merely Aradia's servant—perhaps her property. That might be the meaning of the wolf's-head pendant. "I feel strong enough to leave right now."

"I know," the black man replied. "You are not ill; all the poisons are gone from your body. But the cleansing power to drive them out came from every cell of your being; it will take days of eating and sleeping to replenish those reserves. You do not realize how weak you are. Are you hungry?"

Lenardo was startled to find that he was, although only three hours had passed since his last meal. "You're right about my needing more food than usual."

Wulfston smiled, then closed his eyes for a moment, frowning slightly. "There. Your food will be brought up."

"What did you do?"

"I rang the bell in the kitchen. Now your food will arrive piping hot."

"But . . . I thought an Adept had to see an object to affect it."

"Oh, but I *have* seen that bell, many times," Wulfston replied. "As long as I know exactly where it is, I can control it."

Of course. That was how Aradia had healed Lenardo's broken rib, and how Galen could provide directions to the attacking savages.

"You are Aradia's apprentice," said Lenardo. "She is your teacher?"

"Indeed, as her father was, until . . ." The man's eyes grew sad, and even without being able to Read the Adept, Lenardo again caught an emotion, this time a frustrated grief when Wulfston spoke of Aradia's father.

"You cannot be much younger than Aradia."

"Five years. However, I remain as her apprentice because she is the most powerful Adept I have ever seen, except her father. I still have much to learn from her."

Lenardo fingered the pendant about his neck, looking at the one Wulfston wore. "Could you leave her if you wanted to?" he asked. "Are you not her property?"

"Certainly not!" Wulfston replied indignantly. "I am Aradia's sworn man, of my own will, loyal unto death!"

"But the pendant—I thought—"

"I do not know why Aradia allows you to wear it," Wulfston said. "Very few have earned the right to swear fealty to Aradia—and you most certainly have not."

"Wulfston, exactly what claim *does* Aradia make on me? Does she think she can make a slave of me?"

"You are like a member of a captured army—you cannot be trusted, and you must be controlled. The ruler who has captured you claims you until you prove your worth and loyalty. Aradia may do with you whatever she pleases —including taking your life."

"Doesn't she hold that right over all her people?" asked Lenardo.

"She holds that *power*. So do I. But neither of us has the *right* to take the life of a freeman without cause. Aradia is no tyrant like your emperor."

Lenardo let that pass to ask, "Then I may earn my freedom?"

"Earn Aradia's trust, and give her your loyalty."

As Lenardo pondered the problems inherent in such acts, they were interrupted by the appearance of a woman with a tray of food. She opened the door with one hand and at Wulfston's instruction set the tray on a small table. Lenardo watched, Reading her as she left. She was no Adept, and the uppermost thought in her mind was that the cook had scolded her for scalding a pan of milk that morning. Yet she opened the door as easily as Aradia or Wulfston. Perhaps Wulfston had removed the locking device and would reset it when he left. *Could I distract his attention and make him forget?*

There were two trenchers on the tray, but only one goblet and a pitcher of wine. A joint of meat steamed on a platter, surrounded by leeks and potatoes, all cooked. A bowl held grapes and apples, and that was all.

"I'll join you, if you don't mind," said Wulfston, setting two stools at the table. "I haven't eaten yet today."

Lenardo looked at the meat and overcooked vegetables and wondered if he was really hungry. Fresh, crisp bread and cheese, with a salad—that would have been his choice.

The great chunk of hot meat, dripping juices, was much harder to face than the soup Aradia had brought. Still, there was no choice—his stomach clamored for more than a bit of fruit.

As he seated himself, Wulfston was slicing slabs of meat and placing them on both trenchers. Then he filled the goblet with wine, tasted it, and handed it to Lenardo. At the Reader's hesitation, he said, "It's a very light wine. It doesn't interfere with an Adept's powers, so I wouldn't expect it to affect yours."

Lenardo was satisfied to let Wulfston misinterpret his hesitation, which was actually due to being expected to drink from the same goblet as another person. "No," he replied, "Reading is not affected by a cup or two of wine."

He poked at the meat in front of him, swallowing a few morsels as Wulfston ate heartily and cut some more. "Do you have hot food like this every day?" Lenardo asked.

"Mostly plain fare," said Wulfston. "Only at great feasts are there elegant dishes made with exotic spices. Are you used to more complex dishes?"

"No—simpler," said Lenardo. "Readers don't eat meat, and I'm used to raw vegetables."

"Raw?" Wulfston wrinkled his nose. "Well, that's easy enough—but how do you live without meat?" His eyes swept over Lenardo's body. "You're built like a warrior. Where do you get your strength?"

"Eggs, cheese, occasionally fish. It's meat that clogs the digestion and interferes with Reading."

"And meat that gives Adepts their strength," Wulfston mused. Then he shook his head. "No, it can't be just diet."

"What can't be diet?" Lenardo asked.

"The differences in our abilities."

Before Lenardo could ask where Wulfston got such a peculiar idea, there was a sudden crash behind them. The heavy candelabrum had fallen from the stand beside the bed. "How could—?" Lenardo began, but Wulfston was already on his feet.

"Nerius!" he exclaimed as a shield hanging above the fireplace went sailing across the room to splinter against the opposite wall. "I must help Aradia."

Lenardo ducked the flying shield. "What's happening?" he asked—too late. Wulfston was already out the door.

Outside he heard a crash and Read a heavy oak table split down the middle. Following Wulfston mentally, he Read him run through the hall, meeting Aradia at the entrance to the tower stairs. "It's getting worse," she said in a worried voice and raced up the winding, treacherous steps.

Wulfston didn't answer but followed Aradia up to a room above Lenardo's, where a frail old man lay in bed, a woman trying to restrain him as his body convulsed, each spasm corresponding to another crash somewhere in the castle.

Lenardo could not Read the man, beyond his physical condition. Another Adept, but one whose powers had gone wild, striking arbitrarily, draining energy from his already depleted body.

Aradia flew to the old man's side. "Father! No, Father, please!"

"He can't hear you," said Wulfston. "You'll have to restrain him again."

"How long?" she murmured, then spread her hands over her father's heaving body and began to concentrate. Slowly the spasms subsided until the old man lay limp, unconscious.

Aradia lifted tear-filled eyes to Wulfston's. "Why can't I heal him? All I can do is stop the attacks—but each time they return more quickly and more severely."

"You're doing everything you can," said Wulfston.

"It isn't enough!" Aradia said angrily. "Why does his body refuse to heal?! It's against nature for it to destroy itself this way."

"Aradia . . ." Wulfston moved to her side, putting his arms around her, letting her lean on him. Shocked, Lenardo withdrew from Reading any further such a private scene. The sick old man had nothing to do with his chances of escape, and so he had no right to intrude further on the privacy of non-Readers.

As he picked up the fallen candelabrum and replaced the candles, Lenardo suddenly realized that the old man's attack might indeed have given him a chance to escape. The way Wulfston had rushed out—

He went to the door and tried to open it. Locked. He curbed a frustrated urge to kick the door and a secondary longing to fling himself down on the bed like a child in a tantrum. Instead, he forced himself to finish his meal, then lay down to rest again. It was, after all, sensible to save his strength, eat and sleep as Wulfston suggested until he built back his reserves. It had taken unusual effort to Read the scene in the upper room—so close, and only a superficial visualization. His powers were badly impaired, and would probably not return to normal until he recovered his physical strength and then performed a fast to rid his system of the effects of the meat diet.

Each day he was detained here was another day he could not search for Galen, and another day for the Adepts the boy was working for to rebuild their forces. He had to get away at the first opportunity—all the more reason to build his strength back as quickly as he could. And his arm was completely healed. He was better off than he might be; surely he would soon find a way to get away from these savages. Meanwhile, if he kept alert, he might Read something to tell him which direction to take in his search for Galen. One thing that would help restore him was sleep.

Lenardo woke to a minor commotion. Two men carried a wooden tub into the room and set it by the fire, along with a vessel of steaming water. Aradia followed them in, carrying an armload of clothing and a small leather case. "Time for a bath and a shave," she told Lenardo. "Then you can try on your new clothes."

The servants left, and Lenardo got up, pulling on his robe as Aradia poured hot water into the tub. What a cumbersome way to take a bath; no wonder the savages went dirty most of the time. One thing Lenardo hadn't thought about missing was the convenience of a bath house.

Aradia turned from her task and laughed. "Is it empire custom to put clothes *on* to bathe?"

"Of course not. As soon as you leave, I shall bathe."

"Don't be stubborn. I'm going to bathe you." She was dressed more as if to bathe a dog or an obstreperous child, in a blue dress faded from many washings, a white apron, and a white kerchief tying back her hair.

"I am perfectly capable of bathing myself," said Lenardo. "I've done it since I was four years old."

"Then the middle of your back hasn't been scrubbed in all those years! Come on. Get in the tub. What's the matter with you?"

"It . . . it is not customary where I come from for a man and woman to be naked before one another . . . unless . . ."

While Lenardo fumbled for polite words, Aradia burst into laughter. "*I* have no intention of taking my clothes off," she said. "Whatever were you thinking of? I am an Adept, virgin-sworn. You are my patient, still weak after serious illness. I'll not have you fainting in your bath."

Lenardo felt compelled to explain. "I too am 'virgin-sworn,' as you put it. You are not a Reader. If you were, you and I would never meet face to face, let alone . . ."

"Why not?" she asked blankly.

"To tempt the flesh with what it may not have is to incite lustful thoughts that interfere with concentration." Lenardo recalled being caught kissing the innkeeper's daughter at the age of twelve. Despite a whipping that had left him unable to sit for a week, and hours of meditation exercises meant to banish the incident from his thoughts, for months, every time he let his guard drop he would feel the softness of her lips on his, the strange, warm sensations in his loins.

With a Reader's discipline, Lenardo banished the memory instantly. Aradia was saying, "You mean until you were exiled you lived entirely segregated from women?"

"Oh, no! Just from female Readers. I was at the academy at Adigia. There were only boys there, in training to be Readers, but we went among the townspeople often. We had had to leave our own mothers, so many of the women in town were very kind to the younger boys."

"What about the girls in town, as you grew older?"

Could she Read—? No, had she noticed some look in his eye a few moments ago? "We had to learn to resist, of course. The blood of youth runs hot; one of the hardest lessons we must learn is to abate that heat."

She smiled again the dangerous smile that half transformed her to a wolf. "I wonder just how well you have learned that lesson? But come—take your bath while the water is still warmer than your blood. I am no Reader, nor bound by your strange customs. You have a fine body, Lenardo. If the sight of it should heat my blood, all the better—I can make positive use of such energy!"

It was maddening not to be able to Read her when she teased him so. Embarrassed, he retreated into stubbornness, stiffly clutching his robe about him and looking at her defiantly.

"Do you expect me to waste my energy disrobing you?" she asked at last.

"You will have to if you think to get me into that tub with you still in the room."

Exasperated, she said, "Very well—prove to yourself how weak you are. I'll be right outside." She took a step, then turned back. "Lenardo, what sense does it make for a Reader, of all people, to be embarrassed about the exposure of naked flesh? Certainly you can all Read through one another's clothing if you want to."

"Precisely," he replied. "That is the reason the Law of Privacy must be so deeply ingrained in us."

She tilted her head to one side as she always did when she was thoughtful. "I'll have to consider the logic of that," she said and left.

When the door had closed behind Aradia, Lenardo stripped off his robe and stepped into the tub. He had to fold his long legs so his knees almost touched his chin when he sat down, but the warm water felt good. He leaned back, getting as much of himself as he could under water, luxuriating in the minor pleasure that he would know infrequently on this side of the border.

There was soap, a sweet-smelling bar of pale gold. The empire had never found the secret of making it; the luxury item was purchased from seamen who also traded with the savages. Only a very few times had Lenardo bathed with soap; on holidays and other rare occasions the housekeeper at the academy would break out their meager supply, and the bath house would be awash in bubbles.

Lenardo laved suds through his hair and beard, sat up to soap his arms and chest, and started to stand to get at the rest of himself. The sudden movement after the heat of the bath made him dizzy. He staggered and, trying to catch himself without knocking the tub of water over, stepped out of the tub, his legs at an awkward angle for support. He reached toward the closest item of furniture, a light chair onto which he had thrown his robe.

Soap-slick hands clutched at the chair at the same moment his wet foot hit the smooth floor. Neither achieved support, and he went down in a heap, overturning the chair with a ringing clatter.

By the time he'd got his feet under him and was trying to rise, Aradia was beside him, her worry turning to anger the moment she realized that he was unhurt. "I told you you'd faint!"

"I didn't faint. I slipped."

"Oh—get back in the tub. I suppose we're lucky you didn't flood the whole room!"

Lenardo cringed inwardly when Aradia picked up soap and sponge and began to scrub him, but embarrassment held him silent long enough to realize that her touch was impersonal. She made him move so she could reach every part of him, and he submitted in silence, sensing that she had no interest in him except as a patient—or perhaps her property to be maintained.

Nonetheless, when he was dry and wrapped in his robe once more, Lenardo felt more at ease. "I can shave myself," he said as Aradia opened the razor case.

"Indeed? Hold out your hands."

To his dismay, they trembled; all his force of will could not steady them.

"Tomorrow you may shave yourself," said Aradia, "but today I'll do it—unless you would like to grow a beard?"

He realized she was serious. A good number of the savages wore beards, not all of them shaggy and unkempt. All he had seen among Aradia's men were neatly trimmed. Still, he associated beards with savagery. "I wouldn't know myself," he joked feebly.

"Do you want to?" Aradia asked, quite seriously.

"What do you mean?"

"Lenardo—you committed some crime within the empire, or you would not have been exiled. Will you tell me what it was?"

"I . . . would rather not." If the Adepts ever found out what he had said . . .

"Good." She smiled. "I'd rather have an honest refusal than a lie—and I don't think you yet trust me enough to tell the truth."

"Why should I?"

"Because you must trust someone. Your old life is over —that brand means you cannot return to it. You will not survive if you cling to the past. I can offer you a new life—indeed, I can offer you life itself, despite the fact that you are a Reader, and we have always before systematically destroyed people with such powers."

"But you will expect me to use my abilities to help you gain power."

"I hope you will come to want to help me do what is right for my people. Right now I do not trust you any more than you trust me. However, do you agree that it is in both our interests that you should regain your health, not just physically, but emotionally as well?"

"I am not—"

"Lenardo," she chided, "you are clinging to the past. I'm sorry I made fun of you about the customs you grew up with, but for your own good, you should rid yourself of everything that reminds you of the empire. Become one of us. It is perhaps fortunate that you were robbed of everything you brought from the empire. Now you must start fresh, with nothing to tie you to your old life." She touched the wolf's-head pendant. "And is this not an omen, that you were sent to me?"

Had he truly been an exile, Lenardo realized, Aradia's words would have been the best advice anyone could give him. In fact, if he were to carry off the deception, he ought to think of himself as permanently exiled. "That is why you think I should grow a beard? To appear like one of your men?"

"Yes. Leave your old self behind. Become one of us."

"Very well. At least I'll try the beard." He picked up the small looking glass she had placed on the table. "It looks rather scruffy right now, though."

"Let me trim it for you," said Aradia. "It will look better in a few weeks, but I can make you presentable today. I trim my father's beard for him, since . . . he went blind."

Lenardo thought quickly. Best not to let her know he had Read the scene in the upper room. "Your father is lord of this castle?"

"In honored title. He is very ill and cannot leave his bed. He has been slowly weakening for years, and I have taken over all his duties." She spoke flatly, through pain so old it had worn itself to a dull throb in her throat.

"I'm sorry," Lenardo said in true sympathy.

The violet eyes studied him for a moment, but Aradia said nothing. Then, in businesslike fashion, she went to work on his beard. "There now—put your clothes on, and we'll go downstairs and find something to eat."

"You mean you'll finally let me out of this room?"

"As long as I'm with you. Here—see if these fit properly."

The clothes fitted but were not at all what Lenardo was used to. The best he could say was that at least there were no trousers—the beard was enough of the mark of a savage for one day. The hose and undergarments were such as at home he would have worn under a knee-length tunic and floor-length robe.

The pile of clothing Aradia had tossed on the bed shimmered with rich colors, dark green and gold so deep it verged on brown. The hose were green, the undertunic dark gold silk—he had never worn silk in his life!

Over that went a silk shirt with full sleeves, gathered at the wrists, also in dark gold. Finally he drew on a sort of short cyclas or tabard of richly embroidered dark green velvet. It was seamed from waist to hips and cut off short there, exposing the full length of his legs. Wulfston wore something of the sort, but Lenardo did not recall its being so short or so closely fitted. Lenardo felt displayed, like some slave girl in the marketplace, discreetly draped in such a way as to reveal every attribute.

He looked at Aradia in her simple cotton dress. "This is . . . surely not everyday attire."

"Indeed it is," she replied, then answered his unspoken question. "You have seen me dressed to tend the ill. They often bleed or vomit on one—or splash water." Lenardo managed a rueful smile, and Aradia continued, "If you are ready to care for yourself now, I shall dress more appropriately to my station. But tell me—don't you think my tailor has done a good job?"

Half from curiosity, and half to see how badly his powers were still impaired, Lenardo Read his appearance as if he were across the room, looking at himself. It was a simple trick, theoretically no more than any visual Reading from a point where the Reader actually was not. However, having oneself as the subject was disconcerting, and at first highly disorienting to young Readers. Torio was the only one he knew to master it as quickly as any other shifted point of view, without suffering dizziness or nausea.

Lenardo had learned it many years ago, of course, but rarely used it. The last time was when he had first put on the black Magister's robe, years ago. There had been no time before he left Adigia to invest him with the scarlet robe of a Master. *Will I ever wear it?* he wondered as he stared mentally at the stranger Aradia had created.

He did not know this man; certainly he was no citizen of the Aventine Empire. Somehow, he appeared younger than before—the vivid colors and lack of professional dignity in his costume, Lenardo decided. The green and dark gold played up the shifting colors of his hazel eyes—he'd always thought they were brown!—and the beard gave him a faintly sinister look. Hair and beard were the same dark brown as always, but at home he would have trimmed his hair when it reached this length.

The close-fitting clothing was what made the major difference. Lenardo was tall, his body in good condition from constant exercise. The intent was health, not appearance, but the costume he now wore emphasized the broadness of his shoulders, the narrowness of his waist, and the muscular curves of his legs. He was right: Aradia had put him on display.

When he looked through his own eyes again, he found Aradia staring at him. "What did you do?" she asked.

Lenardo shifted his weight hurriedly and awkwardly as a moment's dizziness siezed him. Again? And this time from Reading? Immediately his mind swarmed with guilt at his delirious outpouring of other people's thoughts on the nightmare journey to Aradia's castle, Intentional or not, the misuse of his power was taking its toll.

At his stagger, Aradia flung an arm about him. "What is it? Do you feel faint? Do you want to lie down? I'm sorry—when your eyes went out of focus I just thought you were Reading something."

He was very much aware of the warmth of her arm against his back as he answered, "I was. I was looking at myself—it's a child's trick. I became disoriented, that's all."

She looked up at him, her smile showing the tips of her white teeth. "Yes," she murmured, "you do look different ... handsome...." Her hand slid up to his shoulder as she turned to face him, lifting her other hand to cup his cheek. "You could become very important to me, Lenardo." She half-closed her eyes, tilting her head back.

Lenardo felt his heart pounding, and the strange pain/pleasure stirring in his loins that he had known at the moment of his first kiss. Did she—? Could she expect him to kiss her? Something in him wanted to, but a more rational part of his mind told him she was testing his declaration of celibacy. As an Adept, no matter what he did, Aradia could maintain control. Then he remembered her statement that she could make use of any energy caused by her response to him. *She's using me!*

The thought cooled the heat that her closeness woke in his blood, and he gently removed her hands from him. "Perhaps I will be important," he agreed, "but not if I remain forever in this room. You promised to let me out today." The first step in the freedom he had to have to continue his search for Galen.

Aradia seemed not to notice the rebuff. "Very well. But don't be ashamed to lean on me if you feel faint—and remember, only Wulfston and I know you're a Reader."

At last Lenardo saw Aradia's castle first hand. This wing was three stories high, with a tower over the widest part, containing Aradia's father's room. Lenardo Read that the narrow winding stairs led down as well as up, but Aradia took him down by way of a wide staircase into the great hall. It was empty now, except for a heavy table across one end. Behind the table were several chairs, the middle one large and ornately carved.

On the wall behind the table hung three decorated shields, the kind he had seen in the forum at Zendi. The central one bore the white wolf's head, while the one to the left was painted with the figure of a lion in vivid blue, and the one to the right boasted a golden boar.

"You may come into the great hall anytime," Aradia told Lenardo, "or any of the pantries or the kitchen. All of these rooms lead to the courtyard, where you are welcome to walk in the fresh air. Come—we'll take some food and sit in the sunshine."

The kitchen was permeated with the smell of roasting meat. Lenardo saw what appeared to be the carcass of a boar spitted over the fire, and he turned his eyes away. As he fought queasiness, he paid little attention to what Aradia was doing until she called to him.

He followed her outside, welcoming the fresh air. The clang of the blacksmith's hammer came across the open space, while a young boy raked straw from the stables that formed the ground floor of the opposite wing. *Horses. If I could steal a horse, I could move much faster than on foot.*

The courtyard was a work area; there was no garden. Aradia led Lenardo to a wagon that stood abandoned in a sunny corner, one axle propped up on a stone because the wheel was missing. The wheel itself was propped against the wall near the forge, waiting for the smith's attention.

"Wulfston said you eat vegetables raw," said Aradia. "Poor cook! I'm afraid he thinks his cooking hasn't passed approval."

"We always ate a very simple diet in the academy, but I understand that among those with an educated palate, a good cook is a precious commodity."

"Lenardo . . . did you never leave your academy?"

"I?" He decided she could learn nothing damaging if he told the truth, while he might be more closely guarded if she caught him in a lie. "Most Readers do leave, of course, when they have learned all they can. I was still studying, but I remained as a teacher."

"In that sheltered environment, what could you have done to be exiled?"

Lenardo again borrowed Galen's words. "I was taught to think for myself. Then, when I did so—I was exiled!" He was surprised at how easy it was to put bitterness into his tone.

Aradia studied his face. "You will find new ideas welcome here, Lenardo. However . . . I do not think you have told me your whole story."

How did she understand so much when she could not Read him? Again he decided limited truth was the best policy. "No, I have not."

"I hope you will tell me one day," she said. "Perhaps I can help you."

Although he expected to be far away from Aradia soon, Lenardo gave an answer to fit the role he was playing. "Perhaps. It is clear that you have power among the savages."

She grinned, this time without malice. "If you would ever Read past the end of your nose, you would find we are not savages. Then we may find a way to cooperate. I want you to trust me, Lenardo."

"Keeping me prisoner does not inspire trust."

"I know," she replied, quite serious now. "Yet how am I to trust you? You are a traitor to your own people. Until I know a great deal more about you, I can only assume that if it seemed the expedient thing, you would betray mine."

For a moment, he was tempted to tell her the ostensible reason for his exile, but he hesitated. "Then what do you plan to do with me?"

"For the time being, observe you, and allow you to observe. You have agreed to help me with healing, once you are well yourself. Perhaps we shall find other ways to work together."

Such as my directing your powers against the empire, thought Lenardo, glad he had not spoken but wondering if she knew anything about Galen. As an Adept, and clearly one with considerable power, Aradia should have supplied troops for the battle at Adigia—perhaps have been there using her mental powers to cause the earthquake. But now he realized that here in Aradia's castle he had Read none of the grief he had encountered in and around Zendi. He suddenly recalled picking Aradia's name from the mind of the young officer. Had one of those blasted shields in the forum once borne the image of the white wolf?

Lenardo ate in silence, trying to sort out his thoughts. Wulfston rode in through the open castle gate, a huge white dog loping along beside his horse. As Wulfston got down from his saddle, the stable boy ran to take the horse. The black man started over to where Aradia and Lenardo were sitting, but the dog ran ahead, bounding joyfully to Aradia, paws on her lap to lick her face.

She laughed and pushed the animal down, giving him a piece of meat and scratching his ears as she said, "Where've you been, boy? I haven't seen you in months."

The creature wasn't satisfied with having its ears scratched and began trying to climb into Aradia's lap, waving its plume of a tail. She put her arms around the animal to hug it, and as it turned yellow eyes toward Lenardo, he realized it was not a dog at all but a wolf—the white wolf!

"He's real!" exclaimed Lenardo, and Aradia looked up at him curiously. "I thought it was a hallucination," he explained. "When I was left to die by those bandits, this animal came and watched me. He acted as if he wanted me to follow him."

"Indeed?" Aradia said thoughtfully. "Another sign. I wonder why you have been sent to me, Lenardo?"

"I met the white wolf in the woods," Wulfston said as he joined them. "The watchers report he's been seen twice this month."

"We missed you," Aradia told the wolf, who was grinning like a dog praised by its master, looking unutterably silly with its tongue hanging out one side of its mouth. It made a whining sound and pressed its head against Aradia's knees. She went back to scratching its ears as she said to Lenardo, "You need not fear the white wolf. He would never harm anyone."

"I wasn't afraid. But how did you tame a wild creature like this?"

"Oh, he's not tame!" she said. "He loves Wulfston and me because we saved his life two years ago." She chuckled. "I know he's acting like a spoiled lapdog right now, but he's a wild animal in the woods. He'll bring down a deer if he can get one, but he never harms people. If we lose an occasional sheep to him, people feel that the white wolf is a good omen, well worth such a small cost."

"How can you be sure he won't attack someone if you let him run wild to hunt?"

"The command is well planted in his mind," explained Wulfston. He leaned down to pet the beast, and the wolf licked his face like an overeager puppy. "Hey! I know you're happy to see us again. We're happy to see you too, boy."

The wolf ignored Lenardo, the stable boy, the blacksmith. After a few minutes at Aradia's feet, he got up again and disappeared out the gate.

Meanwhile, Wulfston reported to Aradia, "The watchers say there's a good cloud bank to the west. We can have rain tonight if we want it. The farmers say we need it."

"Fine," said Aradia. "Take care of it, Wulfston."

The watchers, Lenardo thought. A spy system? Would they know Galen's whereabouts?

That night, he was wakened by the sound of rain. Going to the window, he peered out into the black night. Two torches flared under passageway roofs, reflected in the puddles in the courtyard. Was Wulfston controlling the rain? Lenardo Read for him, scanning superficially through the castle, and found him in the great hall, with the blacksmith and three people Lenardo did not know. He could Read only externals; all had the blocks of Adepts.

Reading visually, Lenardo saw that they had chalked a five-pointed star on the stone floor. Each sat cross-legged at one point of the star, relaxed, breathing slowly and steadily. Lenardo was reminded of the state of a Reader's body when he left it behind. Was that how Adepts did it? Did they project themselves from their bodies to—?

No—if they could do that, they could Read, and a Reader could Read them. There was a physical similarity, but clearly the real difference lay between what Readers and Adepts did with their minds.

As Lenardo watched, Wulfston opened his eyes, stretched, yawned, and climbed to his feet, rubbing his legs. As the others did the same, he said, "Nature will take care of the rest. Come and eat now, and then we'll all sleep well tonight."

His words were greeted by laughter, and the small group headed for the kitchen. Eating again! Lenardo was amazed at the amount of food he had seen Aradia and Wulfston consume—and now other Adepts as well. Could the energy to perform their feats come from their own bodies? As he had seen no fat Adepts, that seemed a likely theory. On the other hand, how could an Adept—or even several working together—produce enough energy to shake a mountain? He stored what he had seen as unassimilated fact, to be reexamined when he had more information.

It was not yet midnight. Lenardo had been asleep for two hours, and now he did not feel tired at all. After his brief time up and around, he had slept the afternoon away—but it was a beginning. With more exercise each day, he'd soon have his strength back.

And what good will it do me if I can't get out of this room? It was a perfect night to escape. The rain would keep people indoors, the sound of it masking any noise he made. If he could steal a horse, the fact that he hadn't yet regained his full strength would not matter.

He stared at the frustrating door. How could a door be charmed so it would open to every person but one?

The things Aradia and Wulfston had said suddenly fell into place. They worked with nature. "It is the nature of the body to be healthy," and Lenardo's body healed itself of infection. It was the nature of the rain to fall—the Adepts merely directed where and when it did so.

It was the nature of the wolf to kill . . . but the white wolf ran free, unmolested because it did not harm *people*. The *direction* of its antagonism was influenced, but no effort made to stop the drive itself. "The command is well planted in his mind."

Lenardo walked over to the door, tried it again. Still locked—but the kitchen maid could open it with one hand.

It's not the door they've bewitched! Lenardo realized. *It's me!*

The thought sickened him. That they should have such power over his mind—!

Is that what they did to Galen?

Staring at the door, he began to seek into his own mind, his own beliefs. He discovered a disturbing tendency to trust Aradia. He had been taking what she said at face value—Wulfston, too, perhaps the more so because the black man made it clear he did not trust Lenardo. Being unable to Read the Adepts was more of a disadvantage to him than to a non-Reader; Lenardo was too used to Reading people's motivations to remember the clues non-Readers used. Probably he had never learned them.

He also discovered that he had rehearsed his "treason" so often that it now had the ring of truth. He had almost blurted out to Aradia that afternoon that he thought Readers and Adepts could work together. But how could they, when the Adepts had the power to control the Readers? *Aradia didn't kill me because I was too weak to be dangerous. She used me as an experiment. If she didn't know about Galen, she has found out on her own that an Adept can control a Reader. I must prove her wrong . . . but then she'll kill me. Unless I prove her wrong by escaping clean away.*

Sifting through his thoughts and beliefs in the calm of deep meditation—the most complex meditation he had ever done—Lenardo finally found the alien, implanted belief that the door would not open. He *knew* it, as surely as he knew the sun would rise.

The dual perspective within his own mind was terrifying. That door would not open; it was solidly locked. There was no lock on the door; it would open to a touch. Both statements could not be true, but in Lenardo's mind they *were* true, "knowledge" battling with what his Reading of the door plainly told him.

He had once observed two personalities battling so within the mind of a madman. He must cast out the untruth—almost as painful as driving the violent manifestation from that poor man's mind. Lenardo had not done it; he had merely been an observer in his year at Gaeta. Two senior physicians, Master Readers both, had forced the patient to confront and evict the malevolent entity. But Lenardo, and all the other students who observed that rare treatment, had had nightmares for months afterwards.

Now he faced an intruder in his own mind, for he saw the belief not as his own but as Aradia's. Like the woman, it was both seductive and dangerous. Summoning the same strength he had used to deny her physical charms, he drove the alien belief out of his mind and flung the door wide— leaping immediately to catch it before it banged against the wall to rouse the castle.

He stood there, hanging onto the door, exulting.

I'm free!

He could be miles away by morning—back into those hills where the bandits had attacked him. The main road north was still his best chance to find some clue to Galen's whereabouts.

He dressed quickly, Reading through the door he had reclosed. From the kitchen, the five Adepts went their separate ways, Wulfston climbing the stairs and passing Lenardo's room to his own. Soon he was asleep. Aradia also slept, in a more elegant suite of rooms down the hall. Inside the castle, he could Read no one awake.

Lenardo crept down the winding stairs to the ground floor. He came out in the passage beyond the kitchen, Read storerooms lining it and a guard room where there were swords, shields, a jumble of equipment . . . and, hanging from pegs, a number of woolen cloaks. He slipped inside and selected a plain gray one with a hood, closely woven to keep out the rain and full enough to cover his easily identified clothing. He also girded on a sword, the lightest he could find but still heavier than he was used to. He had practiced with a savage sword occasionally, but in his present condition he wondered if he could even lift one.

Fastening the cloak over his gaudy outfit, he took bread and cheese from the kitchen, then walked through the connecting passage to the stables. The horses snorted restlessly in their stalls but calmed when Lenardo moved confidently, reading them, finding a strong bay gelding with enough spirit to carry him steadily through the night, but not enough to challenge a rider who was no more than an adequate horseman.

His Reading allowed him to find saddle and bridle, and soon he had everything ready. Except money. He could sell the horse once he'd put some distance between himself and Aradia's castle.

There was one last problem: the guard at the gate. He Read the man carefully. He was awake, and the gate was barred. As he could easily Read the man's thoughts, he knew he had no Adept powers. Nonetheless, Lenardo was in no state to overpower someone. How convenient now to be able to put someone to sleep—and how strange that Aradia should leave on guard someone who would succumb to that. Lenardo could Read no other guard.

He could not disable the guard, and he certainly could not ride past him unnoticed. He might create a diversion to get the guard away from the gate, but how without rousing the household? Fingering the wolf's-head pendant, he wondered what Quintus would do in this situation. Probably sneak up behind the guard and slit his throat. But Lenardo was no hardened warrior.

Then think like a Reader, he told himself, disgusted to be stalling here instead of acting. Again he Read the guard, seeking any clue to getting past him.

The man was being lulled by the soft rain, fighting off sleepiness by walking from one side of the gate to the other. Finally he gave up, sat down on a bench and nodded off to sleep. Lenardo caught his last defiant thought: //If anyone comes here in the pouring rain, they can just knock loud enough to wake me!//

Only then did Lenardo realize that the man was not a guard but a porter. Aradia's castle was not guarded at all! Just as his room had never been guarded. . . .

Of course. No guard could hold an Adept—and Lenardo had just learned that when an Adept held a non-Adept, she found it more efficient to chain his mind than his body. The castle gate was barred against animals or thieves, but what good would bars or armed men be against other Adepts?

The drowsing porter was not comfortable enough to go into deep sleep. Even if Lenardo abandoned the horse, the noise of unbarring the gate would surely wake him. He still had no way out.

Wait! Were there other gates? He had seen none off the court, no other main entrance, but as he Read through the great hall, back to the kitchen, pantries . . . storerooms—there! A doorway wide enough to admit a wagon! It was heavy and well barred but unguarded; clearly Aradia was not concerned about keeping people *in*.

Now Lenardo's only problem was noise—the sound of horse's hoofs as they went through the door at the end of the stable, not out into the court but along the passageway. The clacking sounds rang in Lenardo's ears, but there were no sleeping rooms in this wing. In the storeroom, he closed the door to the passageway, unbarred the outer door, and shoved against it. Weeds had grown up at the base since it was last opened, and Lenardo was clammy with sweat before he got it open far enough to let the horse through.

Then he was outside, in the pelting rain. The horse whinnied and stamped in protest. Lenardo quickly soothed the animal, leaning heavily against his side to catch his breath, cursing the loss of his stout walking boots as the mud soaked through the house-shoes Aradia had provided. Then he shoved the door shut again and mounted the horse. They made little sound in the mud.

After his exertions, Lenardo was nauseated with weakness. He kept the horse to a walk, not only because galloping hoofbeats would carry in the wet night but because he feared falling off. He had hardly done anything, and he was so weak that he longed to go to sleep again!

He dared not rest until he was well away. Reading no pursuit from the castle, he followed the road for a while, knowing the rain would wash away hoofprints. When it became difficult to Read the castle—a pitiful fragment of his normal range—he left the road, carefully riding the margin between two fields. Then a patch of woods and a narrow road leading northwest. Good—he would take this diagonal and meet the main road north of where he had left it above Zendi. He was recovered from the sick weakness by now. With the horse to carry him quickly away, he would certainly escape Aradia's pursuit. She had no idea which direction he had gone, and no Readers with whom to search for him. The breath of freedom buoyed him up, and he urged his horse to a canter. A whole castle full of Adepts were no match for one sick Reader! He laughed aloud in triumph as he rode through the rainy night.

By morning, Lenardo was exhausted. Dawn sent the last clouds scudding off to the east, but the fresh breeze chilled him in the clothes that were by now soaked through. He shivered and sneezed, for once longing for a bowl of the hot soup from Aradia's kitchen. He took off the soggy cloak and wrung it out as best he could, laying it across the saddle in front of him. The rest of his clothes would have to dry on his body.

He wondered if he should stay with the road now in daylight, or whether he ought to ride cross-country. The chances were that he could stay well ahead of any pursuit, and he would be less conspicuous on the road. The soaking had even dimmed the colors of his clothing.

He Read back the way he had come, finding no one in range—but his capacity was even further diminished. *I've got to get some sleep!*

Off to his left he noticed a flash of light, then another. The sun sparkling off some rain-wet surface? There was a strange rhythm to it, and he watched curiously until he had ridden to an angle at which he could no longer see it. It was several miles away—far beyond Reading in his present state.

He soon climbed into hilly country, the patches of woodland melting into forest. If he could get to the rocky hills by nightfall, he could find a place to hide and sleep. But could he keep riding till nightfall? He was having difficulty Reading the road ahead while guiding his horse over the bad stretches. His concentration was faulty. He sneezed again. His head felt vaguely disconnected from his body.

This road was not well traveled; he had made a fortunate choice. How far did Aradia's influence extend? Would she alert other Adepts to a Reader at large in their lands?

She had called him *her* property. Had she been hiding his existence from other Adepts? He cursed himself for not asking Aradia or Wulfston more about how the savages were organized. Was there any kind of central leadership? The empire assumed on one hand that they were a mindless force—yet on the other that they all shared the single purpose of destroying the empire.

Granted, Lenardo had spent most of his time in Aradia's castle asleep; but still, she had asked him very little about the empire. She wanted him to work with *her*, she said, never *us*. Riding through her lands today, he had Read none of the squalor, hunger, or fear he had found in the lands near the border.

The information contradicted everything he knew—or was it just that he could not Read well now? His head was spinning. He pulled his horse off the road, found a sunny break in the wood, and almost fell off the animal. In moments, he was asleep on the soft grass.

Lenardo woke to the sense of someone staring at him. Three people, he found: a man of middle years and two youths enough like him to be his sons. All three wore nothing but knee-length tunics. They spoke, but while Lenardo recognized the savage language, their dialect was so different from Aradia's that he caught only a word or two. *I must have crossed a border.*

His head ached, he couldn't breathe through his nose, and as he leaped to his feet, a wave of dizziness made him stumble. He was caught, and the older man took his sword while the two boys supported him. All the while the man kept saying something that he finally recognized as "It's all right. You're safe here."

He had no strength to fight; it was easiest to believe they spoke truth as they half-carried him through the woods to a small house in a clearing. Here were a woman, a girl of perhaps twelve, and two small children playing in the sunshine. All were sturdy, healthy, cheerful.

In organized pandemonium, the family bustled about, putting Lenardo to bed in the one large room of the house, in the only bed. The noise of their chattering kept him awake long enough to drink the hot spiced cider the woman brought him and to look around. The house was simple, dirt-floored with clean rushes spread about. There was a loft overhead. A fireplace of plain brick occupied most of one wall—a sign of some affluence for peasants. A few iron utensils hung on the well-plastered walls. Everything was unadorned, efficient, yet they seemed to be in no want of life's necessities. Nor could he Read any hostility in them—curiosity, even pity, but nothing to indicate that he was not safe.

Since they had not removed his shirt, Lenardo knew they had not seen either the brand on his arm or the wolf's-head pendant—why had he not thrown that into a ditch somewhere along the way? His right hand was still unnaturally pale, but they didn't seem to have noticed. He remembered the bandits' fear of Aradia and the strange emotions her name aroused in Arkus—even if he was away from her lands, he might not have escaped her influence.

When the woman came to take his cup, Lenardo said, "Thank you. I cannot stay here, though. I have no way to repay you."

The woman shushed him with reassuring noises, of which he understood only one word, "sleep." Seeing that he didn't understand, she pressed his shoulders down onto the pillow, repeating, "Sleep."

Reading her, he found no hint of Adept power. He was too exhausted to go on. At least he was temporarily safe here. After a few hours in a comfortable bed . . .

He woke to the sound of hoofbeats and chattering. Before he could move, the door opened to admit Wulfston. The man and woman were with him, babbling in their strange dialect. He seemed to understand them, but he spoke to them in his normal language. "You have done well. This is, indeed, the man Aradia is seeking. She will not forget your service." He dropped some copper coins into their hands. "Now let me speak with him alone."

Wulfston strode over to the bed, where he stood looking down at Lenardo in disgust. "You are more trouble than anybody's worth. Ingrate. Horse thief. Is that what they turned you out of the empire for—stealing from your benefactors? I don't know why Aradia thinks you're worth salvaging. She should have let you go get yourself killed in Drakonius' lands. The best thing I could do would be to stop your heart right now and tell Aradia you died of exposure—except that I would not dishonor my liege lady."

Lenardo flared. "Aradia's not *my* liege lady! You took me prisoner when I was helpless, and you held me by . . . tampering with my mind!"

At the utter loathing in Lenardo's voice, the harsh anger in the black man's stance softened. But then he said, "We also saved your life—and your right arm. As to keeping you prisoner, how were we supposed to trust an exile when we know not what crime you committed? You could be a murderer, a molester of children, a torturer of the helpless."

"I am none of those things," said Lenardo. "My crime was treason against the Aventine government."

But as he looked into Wulfston's dark eyes, he saw the question that did not have to be asked aloud: "How can we believe you?"

Finally Wulfston shook his head. "Aradia wants you, and she shall have you. Are you in any condition to ride?"

"I suppose so," Lenardo lied, tired of feeling so wretchedly weak. He sneezed.

Wulfston laughed. "*That* I could stop for you with hardly an effort—but it would require what you call 'tampering with your mind.' So you can just suffer through your cold and enjoy it. I'll tell Hlaf we'll stay the night."

Lenardo Read as Wulfston went outside. He had come alone. Of course; one Adept could certainly handle a sick Reader. *Or a well one,* Lenardo thought in frustration. How had they found him? Not enough time had passed for one of the peasants to walk, or even to ride, to Aradia's castle and then for Wulfston to ride here. Aradia's man must have been only a few hours behind him. How did he know Lenardo's direction?

Frustrated, aching in every muscle, his throat sore, Lenardo lay in the strange bed and fought back tears. He was a failure. He'd never find Galen, because Aradia would never let him go. He was a rat in a trap—each direction that seemed to promise freedom only trapped him more securely.

And in his own plight he saw the fate of the Aventine Empire, fighting hopelessly against the inevitable. The savages would take the empire as easily as they had taken Lenardo. Resistance was a temporary show. The most he could do was refuse to cooperate . . . and the most that would do was put off the inevitable by a few months . . . or weeks . . . or even just a few days.

Chapter Four

What Is Treason?

They rode back to Aradia's castle in easy stages. Wulfston making no attempt to conceal his contempt for Lenardo. The third time the young Adept commented, "I don't know what Aradia thinks she can do with you," Lenardo lost patience.

"She *thinks* she can use me to spy on her enemies," he said sourly. "She is wrong."

"Aradia has few enemies," said Wulfston. "Those she has are Adepts, and you cannot Read them."

"That is true. Perhaps you can persuade her to let me go."

"Go where? To Drakonius?"

"Drakonius?"

"You wear his mark on your arm."

"The dragon's head is the symbol on the savage banners —that is why the empire chose it as a sign of exile. It's been used for hundreds of years. I should think he took his name from the symbol."

"It is an old family," Wulfston explained. "The name and symbol have been in use for many generations, and they have always been in the forefront of the fighting against the empire." He frowned. "How could you not know that? Surely empire spies have Read across the border often enough."

"There is a limit to how far one can Read," said Lenardo. "This Drakonius—he holds all the land along the border?"

"Yes, and may take all of Aventine before he's through. Then where will he turn?"

"What do you mean?"

"Drakonius puts all his strength into conquest. He strips and wastes and moves on. You saw the state of his lands."

"Yes," replied Lenardo, "and the city of Zendi. It was an empire city when I lived there as a boy, beautiful, clean, comfortable. Now it's filthy, overcrowded, run down."

"Exactly. Other Adepts, like Aradia, are beginning to defy Drakonius. We sent no troops to join his latest assault —good fortune to us, as the bulk of his army was destroyed in an earthquake of his own making."

"I know," said Lenardo, careful not to give away his emotional shock: If he could find Drakonius, he would find Galen! On the other hand, Aradia and the other Adepts were allies of Drakonius. Perhaps they had defied him once, but against a common enemy from the empire they would certainly close ranks. So he must appear not to be such an enemy. "I was still at Adigia at the time of the earthquake," he said. "It was the narrowness of our escape that led to my exile."

Wulfston eyed him suspiciously. "What do you mean?"

"If you savages can create earthquakes, what chance have we against you? You will destroy what is left of the Aventine Empire, unless we make peace with you. For suggesting that we seek a peaceful treaty with our enemy, I was exiled."

Wulfston was staring at him. "Is this true?"

"It is, but I have no way of proving it. I suppose you'd rather think I'm a child molester."

Wulfston ignored the sarcasm. "But it will be a matter of public record. I shall find out. You are quite right—your empire has no chance against Drakonius, once he builds back his army. Unfortunately, neither will he treat with you. He cares only for conquest."

"But he does not rule all the savages?"

"I wish you would learn that we are not savages!" Wulfston snapped. "Nor are we a single unit, like your empire. No. Drakonius does not rule Aradia or Lilith or Hron or other great Adepts—but he exacts their cooperation now, while in the future . . ."

"You fear he may conquer the empire and then turn on you?"

"Yes. We have spent years renewing the lands Drakonius' ancestors destroyed and abandoned. It is only too easy to predict the temptation to Drakonius. For that reason, we have begun our resistance now, and Aradia was hoping—"

"What?"

"No, I will let her tell you. I still do not trust you, Lenardo. I only hope Aradia will not be too quick to accept your story. Why did you not tell it before?"

"Does it seem likely to you that to suggest one's country seek peace before it is destroyed utterly would be regarded as treason? I did not think you would believe me." The intensity of his words after prolonged conversation sent Lenardo into a fit of coughing. Wulfston pulled their horses to a halt, and regarded him with concern.

"I don't like the sound of that. You could develop pneumonia. If you won't trust me to heal you, we'd best find a place to stay over another night."

"I never said I didn't trust you to heal my body," Lenardo gasped painfully. "You said you'd have to tamper with my mind—and I'll have no more of that!"

"I don't have to," said Wulfston. "If you can relax and let me work, I can set your body to dry the fluid collecting in your lungs and purify your blood of this new infection." He sighed. "If you continue to expose yourself to one illness after another, before you fully recover, you could easily kill yourself."

"If you do the healing, or Aradia, why am *I* so weak?"

"We must tap your strength—if we had to give our own strength to the healing of others, neither of us would be able to walk across the room!"

Wulfston spread Lenardo's now-dry cloak on the grass by the roadside and had him lie down. Lenardo was relaxing before the familiar manner of a healer until Wulfston said, "You will feel heat in your veins. Fire purifies the blood of its taint."

"Fever kills the organisms that cause the infection," Lenardo corrected.

"Organisms?"

"I have Read them," said Lenardo. "An infection is a living thing—many living things so tiny no eye can see them, thousands upon thousands, feeding on the person infected."

Wulfston seemed disconcerted. "Living beings?"

"Not beings, but alive, yes."

"Poisons, we knew, but not— You mean there are creatures feeding on you?"

"Yes. Heat kills them. We have drugs to induce fever if the body does not—but high fever is dangerous in itself."

"I know. You are already feverish," Wulfston said, touching Lenardo's forehead. "I must increase your body heat, direct the blood flow to your lungs, and decrease the flow to your head, where excess heat might damage your mind. If you become sleepy, it is not because I willed it. Would you not rather sleep through the procedure? In my training, I had to experience it waking. It is not painful, but the first time it is very frightening."

"I've felt it before," Lenardo reminded him, "when Aradia healed my arm and my broken rib."

"Yes—a localized sensation is not so bad. However, she put you to sleep before she set your body to cleansing the poisons from your entire bloodstream. Tell me if the feeling becomes unbearable. There is no reason you should have to endure it."

"Why did you have to?" Lenardo asked curiously.

"How else would I know what I was doing to another? I cannot see within my own body or yours. I had to *feel* it."

What Lenardo felt was strange but not particularly frightening, not as fearsome as the first time he had Read his own body, watching the organs working, the blood pumping, certain that every strange thing he saw was a sign of some dread disease. Of course—to an Adept, this outlining of his veins with fire would be his first experience of his body's systems at work. Unable to Read, no wonder Wulfston had found it frightening.

Lenardo felt discomfort as his body temperature rose. His head ached slightly, and he wanted to pull his clothes off to let cool air touch his hot, dry skin. He tried to Read down to the microscopic level at which he could sense the organism the fever was attacking, but the effort was too great.

He let himself drift on the level of easy Reading, deliberately relaxing all his muscles. The headache subsided to a dull throb. Eventually Wulfston placed a hand on Lenardo's forehead, pleasantly cool on his feverish skin, and there was gentle concern in the young Adept's emotional presence as he said, "The worst is over now. I must maintain the heat for a time, but it will not increase. Do you find it disturbing?"

"No. I'm too hot, but I can stand it."

"Could you Read what I was doing?"

"I felt what happened, but not how you did it."

"I'm rather glad of that. If a Reader could learn Adept powers as well, he'd be invincible."

"Is that why you shield so carefully against Reading?"

"There is no shield. I'm not consciously doing anything to keep you from Reading me." He frowned. "This problem has always interested me. What is the difference between your mind and mine? We both have abilities most people do not, yet you cannot Read me."

"I can Read you physically," said Lenardo. "I just cannot get into your mind."

"That is interesting. I can affect your body, but— Tell me, Lenardo, how did you get out of your room at the castle?"

"Would you be satisfied if I said someone let me out?"

"None of Aradia's people would. You were able to break her control of your mind. We can affect each other's bodies but not minds."

"I can't affect anyone's body or mind," said Lenardo. "The idea of meddling with another person's thoughts, beliefs, is abhorrent to me."

"Yet you spy on people's most secret acts, fantasies, desires—"

"Never! The Reader's Honor forbids such a thing!"

"Oh, yes. I have heard of the Reader's Code of Honor . . . but does it bind an exile, Lenardo?"

"It binds a Reader, Wulfston. Wherever I go for the rest of my life, I shall never cease to be a Reader. I shall never cease to honor the Code."

The intensity of speech left him gasping for breath. Wulfston said, "I'm sorry. Please relax—I should not say things to anger you while I am trying to heal you." He shook his head. "I want to trust you, and I dare not. Aradia thinks you can help us, but how can we know you will not turn on us?"

"You can't know," replied Lenardo, "unless I tell you so. Right now I tell you that if I thought I could overpower you, I would escape."

"Where *to?*" Wulfston demanded in frustration.

"Not to—from! I owe you and Aradia something for saving my life, but that does not make me Aradia's property or give her the right to restrict me when I have done her no harm."

"Aradia's powers give her the right," Wulfston said in a tone that suggested he was stating a natural law.

"Might makes right?"

"Of course. How can the world be otherwise?"

"Then why talk of trust? Either you can hold me and force me to work for you, or you cannot."

"That is the flaw in Drakonius' thinking," said Wulfston. "He rules entirely by power and must spend much time and energy in enforcement. Aradia finds trust and cooperation better tools—you see what she has done for her people. In her lands, no one starves or goes in rags. No one fears an unjust death. Do you not think people will be loyal unto death to such a leader?"

"Aradia took a place like Drakonius' lands, and turned it into this pleasant countryside?"

"Her father began it," said Wulfston. "If he could only know how far she has succeeded, he would be immensely proud of her."

Lenardo saw unshed tears in the Adept's dark eyes. "Aradia's father is ill and blind, she told me. Still, can't he be told what she is doing?"

"He no longer understands. Nerius is gravely ill . . . dying. That's why Aradia did not come for you herself—

she is the only one who can control one of her father's spells."

"Spells?"

"You remember that day when things began flying about in your room? That was Nerius. His Adept powers go wild, destroying things and at the same time draining his strength. If Aradia were not there to stop him, he would kill himself by draining all his energy."

Reading Wulfston's grief, Lenardo tried a turn of subject. "You said Adepts don't use their own strength—?"

"Not when they can guide the power of nature or put another person's energy to work for himself." Apparently relieved, Wulfston began to deliver a familiar lecture to an interested audience. "Healing is the easiest of an Adept's tasks. Once he starts the process back to health, the patient's body takes over. Other things . . . the rain the night you escaped, for example. The natural movement of the weather here is from west to east. All we had to do was guide the clouds slightly and encourage them to drop their moisture over the area that needed it."

"What if there were a drought and no convenient clouds?"

"We study nature for that very reason. There was such a drought here, eight years ago. I worked with Nerius and Aradia—the first time I was admitted as a full Adept to their circle. It was very difficult to create the conditions for rain, working against nature. Aradia thinks it might be the way Nerius expended his strength then that caused his illness."

Back to Nerius. Clearly the health of Aradia's father weighed heavily on Wulfston's mind. "You have an irrigation system now," Lenardo prompted.

"Yes, built since the drought—or repaired, rather. An old Aventine aqueduct. In case of drought, there would be enough water to raise moderate crops. We wouldn't starve. But an aqueduct is such an easy target for one's enemies."

"I suppose it wouldn't take much power to shift a support," Lenardo mused, "to cut off the water supply. But tell me, Wulfston—what kind of power would it take to cause an earthquake?"

The young Adept pushed up Lenardo's right sleeve and traced the dragon's-head brand with one finger. "Impossible power," he said. "Even a large body of the strongest Adepts could not produce such energy, unless—"

"Unless?"

"You did come from Drakonius' lands," said Wulfston, "yet the brand on your arm was so new that it festered. I have seen many infections—I know it was not an old wound. If you had escaped Drakonius—"

"Only in the sense that I wandered from his lands into Aradia's."

"Drakonius claimed to have a Reader to guide him. Aradia did not believe him . . . or did not want to. She does not want to leave her father so ill, and she has little interest in making war on the Aventine empire. She challenged Drakonius to produce his Reader, but Drakonius refused."

Lenardo remembered that he truly did not know what Galen had done. "I do not think any Reader, no matter how unjustly exiled, would guide savage Adepts against the empire." He looked straight into Wulfston's eyes. "And no, I am not the Reader Drakonius had, if he had one," *I wish I knew a way to ask directly where Drakonius would keep Galen.*

"They succeeded in causing an earthquake," Wulfston mused, "but it brought an avalanche that destroyed their own army."

"Wulfston, if they had captured a Reader and forced him to do their bidding by chaining his mind as you did mine—"

The black man nodded grimly. "A perfect revenge. You broke the command we placed in your mind—so could he. He could pretend to obey, then cause them to destroy themselves. In which case he is surely dead by now." He looked at Lenardo. "You are even more dangerous than I thought. What are we going to do with you?"

"Let me go."

"You belong to Aradia. Plead your case with her."

After a time, Wulfston released the fever. Lenardo broke into sweat and felt his temperature drop to normal. The nagging aches in his head and shoulders disappeared, and he sat up without vertigo. Soon he felt himself again.

It was evening by the time they could see Aradia's castle in the distance. Wulfston urged his horse to a faster pace, eager to be home.

Suddenly, without warning, Lenardo's horse screamed, reared, and collapsed, throwing him clear. He scrambled up, expecting to have to dodge flying hoofs, automatically Reading—but the animal had gone limp.

"What happened?" demanded Wulfston, fighting his own plunging mount.

"By the gods—he's dead! His brain is shattered!"

"An attack!" exclaimed Wulfston, as in the distance there rose shouting, accompanied by various bangs and crashes. He reached down a hand, and Lenardo vaulted up behind him on his horse as they galloped for the castle. "We thought Drakonius would be too busy rebuilding his army to attack us!"

They were approaching the castle from the front now. A number of houses clustered near the gate, and as Wulfston and Lenardo flashed by, one suddenly burst into flame, showering them with sparks.

"Wulfston!" Lenardo shouted above the noise, "the attack is coming from inside the castle!"

"Nerius? No—oh, no, not at such a distance! He'll kill himself this time!"

They leaped off the horse in the courtyard and ran into the great hall. Lenardo Read the frail old man now, convulsing in synchrony with each blow, Aradia already at his side, blank to Reading in her concentration.

Wulfston dashed up the wide stone stairs, Lenardo on his heels, down the hallway toward the entry to the tower stairs, past a display of spears.

Behind them, a spear suddenly lifted from its brackets and sailed toward them with a force far greater than if a human arm had thrown it. Lenardo, breathless, could do no more than leap on Wulfston in a flying tackle, bringing both men to the floor in a tangle as the spear sailed over their heads to shatter against the stone wall at the end of the corridor.

Wulfston was gasping angrily, already gathering to strike back at Lenardo when the sound of the spear hitting the wall made him realize what had happened. He glanced at it, then turned back to Lenardo. "Thanks," he said, with a quick grip of the Reader's shoulder. Then he was up and bolting for the stairs.

They came out into a scene of frozen calm—the calm of death. The old woman who cared for Nerius lay on the floor, her staring eyes already glazing over. Aradia still stood beside the bed, head bent in concentration. The old man was unconscious, even more emaciated than when Lenardo had Read him a few days before, his skin chalk white, lips blue.

To appearances, Nerius was dead too, but Lenardo Read a lingering spark of life in that frail frame. His heart beat sluggishly, and his breathing was slow and shallow. Somehow, he clung to life.

Aradia raised her eyes, her grief a palpable presence as she sought her father's pulse.

"He's alive," Lenardo supplied. "He's very weak."

Tear-filled violet eyes turned to him. "Thank you," Aradia whispered and bent her head again.

"Aradia—don't!" said Wulfston.

She blinked at him, as if hardly seeing him. "Our father—"

"He's dying, Aradia. Let him sleep away in peace."

"No!"

Wulfston took her shoulders, turning her to look at the old woman's body. "It's not just himself he's hurting any more. Nerius is killing now."

"No," she repeated.

"Yes. Look. Vinga is dead. He's striking living things, Aradia. He killed Lenardo's horse, and he almost killed me."

She looked up at him. "What?"

Wulfston nodded grimly. "Nerius hurled one of the spears in the lower hall. If Lenardo hadn't been Reading . . ."

"What am I to do?" Aradia asked sadly.

"You know what you must do," Wulfston replied with gentle firmness.

Reluctantly, Aradia nodded. "He must never regain consciousness." Tears flowed down her pale cheeks.

Wulfston drew her against him, stroking her hair. "He's not really conscious. You know Nerius would never hurt Vinga or me. He doesn't know what he's doing, Aradia."

"I know," she said, pushing away from him and turning deliberately to look at her father. Then she went to kneel beside the body of the old woman, closing her eyes. "Poor Vinga. No, Father would never turn on you. He knew how you loved him."

"I'll carry her down," said Wulfston, "and send someone up to watch Nerius. Go and rest."

Aradia rose and saw Lenardo by the door. "You," she said flatly. "Now what am I going to do with you?"

It was the wrong time to ask to be let go, so Lenardo stood silently, feeling the false strength of excitement deserting him, wondering if his knees would give way before the pressure of her emotionless gaze.

"He needs to sleep," said Wulfston. "So do I."

"You saved Wulfston's life?"

"I knocked him out of the way of the spear."

A tired smile barely curved her lips. "Wulfston is very precious to me. He is my brother. Lenardo, need I send for the carpenter to bar your door, or will you give me your word not to leave your room until someone comes for you?"

He realized it was a major concession, made in a moment of emotional exhaustion. If he hesitated, she would think again and bar the door or set a guard. He was too tired to try to move tonight anyway.

"You have my word."

Perhaps it was that concession, along with the fact that Lenardo Read no second-thought guard outside his room in the morning, that made him less resentful toward Aradia the next day. Or perhaps it was the way sleeplessness had imprinted purplish bruises in the fair skin under her eyes. It was almost noon when she came to Lenardo's room; the kitchen maid had brought his breakfast some hours before.

"Did you sleep well?" Aradia asked politely.

"Indeed," he replied truthfully, "but you did not get much rest, I see. How is your father?"

She glanced upward. "If you really cared, you could—"

"No, Aradia, I could not. That is, I *would* not Read your father merely to satisfy my curiosity. Readers respect the privacy of non-Readers."

"I'm sorry," she said. "I didn't know. My father is still alive, in the same state I put him into last night. I must leave him so, to die." A tear escaped her control, sliding down her cheek. She made no move to wipe it away but set her chin determinedly to avoid further emotional display. "We must talk about . . . you."

"Aradia," he said, "would you like me to Read your father?"

"Read him?"

"I can at least tell you if he is in pain; and sometimes knowing the cause of an illness allows one to find a cure. Please—don't get your hopes up. I fear that all I shall find is a mind worn out with great age—"

"Age! Father is not yet sixty!"

"I'm sorry," he fumbled. "He looks so very old—"

"His illness. Lenardo, do you think you can discover why my healing powers have no effect?"

"I can try. But from what I've seen of your powers, I doubt I'll find any way to help that you haven't tried."

"Are you recovered enough?"

"For such Reading, yes. It won't require great effort, or extreme precision."

"Then come upstairs with me," she said eagerly.

Aradia dismissed the woman seated at Nerius' bedside, telling her, "Go and rest, Yula, and come back in—half an hour."

When they were alone, Lenardo stood beside the bed, closed his eyes, and began to Read. Nerius' heartbeat and breathing were steadier than the night before. His mind was unReadable, but Lenardo feared it was that no thought or dream crossed it, rather than the fact that the man was an Adept.

Somehow, despite being bedridden for months—years?
—Nerius' body was functioning. Everything was precariously balanced, no single part allowed to atrophy so that
the patient might die of failure of the kidneys, heart, lungs.
He retained a grip on life so fragile that it seemed the least
shock would cause all to collapse together. How had he
survived yesterday's convulsions?

Finally, Lenardo examined Nerius' nervous system. In
his present state, he could not reach the finest details, but
he could get an overall picture—

Then he found it.

Gross and ugly, hideously obvious the moment he began
a superficial Reading of Nerius' brain: a tumor. It was a
massive growth, compressing the normal brain tissue within
the confines of the skull, putting pressure on nerves—no
wonder the man had convulsions!

Gratefully, he withdrew, only to find Aradia's violet eyes
fastened on his with intense hope. "What did you find?"
she asked.

"There is nothing to be done," he replied. "I can tell you
why your father is dying, but I know of no way to cure
it."

"Tell me!"

"There is a growth in his brain. I've never seen one so
large, Aradia, but every one I've seen was a sentence of
death."

Her fair skin had gone transparent, and for a moment he
feared she would faint. Her eyes were immense. "I made it
grow! My efforts to strengthen his body were also strengthening that thing, feeding on him—!"

"No!" Lenardo said sharply. "Such tumors grow, no
matter what we do. Only your efforts have kept your father
alive this long, and if he has not suffered great pain, it can
be due only to you. Aradia, nothing more could possibly be
done for him."

"His brain," she murmured. "Oh, why *there?* Anyplace
else . . ."

Anyplace else, and it could be cut away. Readers did
such surgery in the empire, although Lenardo himself had
only minimal training in surgical techniques.

Aradia stood silently for a time, until Yula returned. Then she turned and left, Lenardo following her down the stairs, uncertain of what to do or say to her.

In the hall below, they met Wulfston, just coming out of his room. "I overslept," he said, although his face had the puffy look of someone wakened long before his need for sleep was satisfied.

"You didn't get to bed till dawn," said Aradia. "Have you appropriate clothing to lend Lenardo for Vinga's funeral? Or," she turned to the Reader, "would you rather not attend? You didn't know her."

"I should learn your customs, including those of sorrow."

So Wulfston took Lenardo back to his room and rummaged through a chest, bringing out a long tunic in dark green and a shorter one in brown. "That should do. No display of vanity—we recognize ourselves to be a part of nature as we return Vinga to the elements."

Lenardo noticed that for the first time Wulfston did not display the wolf's-head pendant, although when he looked for it he could see the shape of it under his clothing.

"Would you like a bath?" asked Wulfston.

"I certainly would, but I don't want to put anyone to the trouble."

"If you don't mind cold water, we won't trouble anyone. I need it to wake me up. Come on."

They went down only one flight, to a room just above the kitchen. "The cistern is full after the rain," said Wulfston. "We have drain pipes to collect all the rain from the roof, for bathing and washing. Most of the time we don't have to carry large amounts of water from the well."

Lenardo was used to bathing daily in hot, warm, and finally cold water. *I'll just pretend the first two steps are done.*

They doused themselves thoroughly, getting clean, but not wasting the water. There was a pile of linen towels—another small luxury like the mild and pleasant soap. The few luxuries he had seen here all had to do with personal comfort except for the beautifully embroidered tabard

Aradia had given him. Except for the wolf's-head pendants, he had seen no jewelry in Aradia's lands.

It reminded him of life at the academy, where Readers owned nothing but their clothes and a few personal possessions. A Reader's skills guaranteed him welcome anywhere, and in his age he would return to an academy, to pass his final years under the loving care of teachers and students.

But what did Adepts do? "Wulfston, you've said you're Aradia's apprentice. Is that the only way to learn to use your Adept powers—to be apprenticed to another Adept?"

"It's the best way. I was partly trained by Nerius, before he fell ill, so I benefit from Aradia's experience, Nerius', and all that he knew, passed down through generations of Adepts. One Adept alone will not learn nearly so much through trial and error, although there are those who succeed well enough even though they cannot find a master who will take them who is also a master they can trust."

"Then there are no academies of Adepts? In the empire, every Reader is trained to the best of his abilities in one of the academies. He doesn't have to go out and seek a teacher."

Wulfston was adjusting the belt of his gray tunic. Now he looked up at Lenardo. "You know that all your secrets will be laid bare before the teachers at this academy—people you do not know? How can you turn yourself over to them that way?"

"The Reader's Honor. Not that eight- or nine-year-old children could have many secrets, but the privacy of even the youngest and least trained is scrupulously maintained. As one grows older, one learns to protect one's own thoughts."

"Well, I'm glad Adepts can't be Read. I remember very well, carrying you home that first night, how you blurted out everything on the minds of the men with me."

Lenardo said guiltily, "I don't remember it. I was delirious. It should not have happened and I must accept responsibility for violating the Code . . . but the state of the body affects the mind."

"Yes," said Wulfton, "you've said that your abilities are

impaired . . . yet Reading does not tire you or aggravate your physical condition."

"Of course not. I am far beyond the stage of the child who squints his eyes and grits his teeth when he attempts a new Reading. The body has nothing to do with it."

"But you just said it has. When your body is afflicted, your Reading is impaired."

"True—but it is not Reading that afflicts one's body."

"The effects are directly opposite!" said Wulfston. "No amount of physical deterioration affects an Adept's powers —you've seen what Nerius can do, still—but Adept activity affects the body. That's why I'm so tired today, after healing you yesterday and then not getting enough sleep. Aradia's going on sheer nerve—I don't think she even went to bed last night. Are you ready to go?"

Wulfston's clothes fitted Lenardo loosely. The Reader was taller than the young Adept, so the undertunic came just to his ankles. His outfit was completed with a leather belt that hung loose on his hips and a pair of brown felt slippers that stretched enough to accommodate his larger feet. Although the clothes did not fit well, he felt less conspicuous and therefore more comfortable than in the outfit that had been designed for him.

Lenardo was hungry again, and surprised that Wulfston was not. "There will be a feast after the funeral," the Adept explained. "It is considered honor to the dead to eat heartily. I don't suppose you'll have any trouble with that today, but I must warn you that no one but Aradia and me knows you're a Reader. If you reveal yourself, you will undermine people's trust in Aradia. That may not concern you, but perhaps the fact that you would be killed immediately will."

"I won't betray myself . . . or Aradia."

When they gathered in the courtyard, Lenardo saw Aradia dressed formally for the first time. She was all in gray, her dress a slender column of fine cotton, the bodice fitted to her body, the skirt a mass of tiny pleats falling gracefully to the ground. The sleeves were also pleated, and so full that they fell from her wrists almost to her ankles, seeming to mingle with the pleats of her skirt. The vertical lines of the dress made her look taller than she was, and stately—no trace of mischievous village maiden today.

Her hair was covered by a veil of sheer gray material, a second veil attached to it in front of her ears, hanging under her chin, over her breast, so that her pale face looked out as from a closely drawn hood, the rest of her features merely background to her luminous eyes. Like everyone else, she wore no ornament.

Lenardo fell in with the crowd as the funeral procession moved out the gate. No one took particular notice of him. They went a fair distance from the castle, to a field grown up in wild grass, uncultivated. In the middle of the field was a large but shallow depression, the center of it a huge flat rock surface showing signs of charring. A huge mound of firewood lay ready to one side, and the cleanness of the flat rock, the grass along its edges cut back to form a perfect circle, bespoke careful preparations.

The cart bearing the body was placed in the center of the rock surface. The people moved into a circle, then one at a time moved to the center to say something about the dead woman. Not everyone spoke, and many who did said little more than, "Vinga was a good woman. She will be missed."

Wulfston spoke of Vinga's motherly kindness to him when he was an orphaned child. Lenardo noted one more fact about the mysterious Nubian Adept with the peculiar name—for all the talking they had done, he had learned precious little about Wulfston.

Finally Aradia spoke. "For the past five years, Vinga attended Nerius with great devotion. Like a soldier in battle, she gave her life in performance of her duty. Her memory will live as long as Castle Nerius stands, in the hearts of her children and her children's children."

Then the dead woman's family stepped up to look at the body once more. When they returned to Aradia's side, the circle of mourners began to file past the firewood, each placing a stick on the growing pile surrounding, then covering, the cart.

When the pyre was built and the circle again complete, Wulfston picked up a small jar that had been under the pile of wood and sprinkled its contents over the funeral pyre. Water? That was what Lenardo Read. When the young Adept went to the edge of the stone circle, scooped up a handful of earth, and sprinkled that on the pyre as well, Lenardo understood—earth, air, fire, and water. Wulfston had said they would return Vinga's body to the elements.

Again Aradia stepped forward. "Nature brings life," she said. "The elements themselves are eternal. We are not. But life is! Of all living things, only man passes more than mere life from one generation to the next. All that has been learned, all that has been created, we pass on—language, knowledge, song. Vinga exists in me because she taught me things. When I teach someone else, a part of Vinga is passed on, as well as a part of myself.

"Even more, Vinga exists in her children and grandchildren. The pain of parting is grievous now, but in the future it will be forgotten, and only Vinga's life remembered—a good life, a model anyone might honorably take for his own."

She moved a few paces from the funeral pyre, and the pyre burst into flame! It roared into consuming heat, the flames shooting straight up with the noise of a whirlwind.

Lenardo stared, astonished. Aradia was causing it, of course, possibly with Wulfston's help, but he had never seen such a fire before! The fires the Adepts started in their attacks were easily put out with a few buckets of sand or water. But what if they sent a conflagration like this one? Before anyone could put it out it could consume an entire building, just as this fire had already consumed wood, cart, and body, and was dying down to soft ashes—no charred remains to disturb the family.

The fire flickered out, leaving nothing but a scorch mark on the flat rock surface and a drift of powdery ash . . . the gray of mourning.

"Vinga is dead!" cried Aradia. "We live! In her honor, let us celebrate life!"

A cheer went up from the circle, and there was a sudden rush back in the direction of the castle. Now there was no procession; people broke up into groups, laughing and talking as if on the way to a party.

Lenardo caught Wulfston's eyes on him, and Read the black man moving in behind him in the throng, probably to see that he made no move to escape. *I'm not going anywhere until I get my strength back.* But Wulfston couldn't know that.

And not until I find out how you caught me the first time, Lenardo added to himself. Now he knew where Galen was, if he was still alive. How much at odds were Aradia and Drakonius? Would they spy on one another? If he could gain her confidence, he might even volunteer to Read for her into Drakonius' lands, playing his role fully. It would give him all the more chance to get at Galen, to find out if the boy were truly traitor or no.

Wulfston had independently drawn the same conclusion Lenardo had: Galen had broken a command implanted in his mind and turned the earthquake back upon the Adept army. Lenardo had to believe that. And if the boy had learned his lesson . . . then, if Masters Portia and Clement could get Lenardo readmitted to the empire, they could bring Galen home as well!

Home. Home with the news that only one Adept with his followers was attacking the empire. With the fact that others, like Aradia, might be willing to make peace—

But that was the treason for which both he and Galen had been exiled.

He pushed that thought aside. It would not be regarded as treason if the senate knew there really were Adepts who wanted peace. Galen's theories had been speculation, but now Lenardo knew they were truth. There was a chance to put an end to the constant warfare.

His step grew lighter than it had been in many a day as he followed the funeral party back to Aradia's castle to join the feast.

Chapter Five

The Quarry Sighted

In the days that followed, Lenardo set out to discover everything he could about Aradia's alliance with Drakonius. At the funeral feast he had found some curiosity concerning himself.

"You are the man the watchers were seeking, are you not?" asked one man.

"Uh . . . yes. The watchers," Lenardo replied. He had heard the term before—the watchers had reported the rain clouds.

"You look well enough now," said a red-haired woman. "They said you was an exile Aradia took in, and you was sick and lost your way."

Lenardo knew his accent would identify his empire origins, even if the brand on his arm was covered. "Yes . . . I got lost," he said uncertainly.

Wulfston, who was seated not far away, put in, "Aradia has asked Lenardo to stay here now. He has useful skills."

Feeling someone staring at him, Lenardo looked down the table to find Helmuth, the old man who had been with the rescue party that first brought him to Aradia. *You wear Aradia's sign.* Even though Lenardo was Reading only superficial emotions, the old man's suspicious thought came through clearly. Deciding to brazen it out, Lenardo smiled at him and said, "I have not had the chance to thank you for your kindness. I do not believe I have been told your name."

"Helmuth."

"Well, thank you, Helmuth. I owe a great deal to you, and Wulfston, and Aradia. I must find a way to repay all of you."

As he hoped, the man seemed to accept that. After all, Lenardo was accepted into the company at Aradia's table.

Not exactly at Aradia's table, as she was seated in the ornate chair behind the permanent table, with the family of the dead woman. Trestle tables had been added down either side of the great hall to accommodate the large number of guests. Lenardo suspected that Wulfston belonged at the high table but had taken his present seat to keep an eye on Lenardo. He soon found out why.

The red-haired woman was looking him over. "They're afraid of Adepts in the empire, I hear. Was that why you was exiled, a fine-looking man like you?"

"Lenardo has . . . unusual abilities," put in Wulfston. "I'd not advise you to try your wiles on him, Jenna."

"Someday a woman will tempt *you*, me black beauty," she replied.

"Probably so," said Wulfston, unperturbed, "but not you, unless all you are seeking is Wulfston's wedding right!"

That puzzling exchange, which was greeted with raucous laughter, reminded Lenardo of the fact that Aradia claimed virginity was necessary to keep her powers intact, yet her father was supposedly a more powerful Adept than she was. The next day, he asked Wulfston about it.

"Aren't you more likely to have Readers born of Readers than of non-Readers?" Wulfston asked curiously.

The two men were in Wulfston's room, Lenardo under orders from Aradia to keep the young Adept occupied in conversation so he would rest physically. He didn't mind, as he had many questions to ask—except that Wulfston had the annoying habit of answering questions with new questions.

"Yes," Lenardo told him, "but the very best Readers remain celibate, virgin, so as never to impair their powers. I take it you, as well as Aradia, are 'virgin-sworn,' as she puts it, for the same reason?"

"True. However, both of us owe it to future generations to pass on our powers. As a man, I can wait for a long time yet, and of course a man's part in the production of a child is quickly done. Nerius regained almost all his abili-

ties, by maintaining celibacy once Aradia was conceived."
He gave a sad smile. "He says it took over two years to
regain the strength he has now, and that he can—could—
sense distinct limitations. I just hope that one day I might
attain the power Nerius had before his illness!"

"And Aradia?"

"Her powers were approaching her father's when he fell
ill. It is possible she will exceed his abilities, but she owes
her people an heir. One day she will have to sacrifice her
powers, unless she can find a younger Adept her people
will accept as her successor."

"You?" suggested Lenardo.

"I am only five years younger than Aradia. Perhaps my
child one day, once our lands are safe from attack. If it
destroyed my abilities permanently, I would do it to save
Aradia from her mother's fate."

"Aradia's mother . . . died in childbirth?"

"No. Terrible as that is, it would have been preferable."

As Wulfston did not seem to be inclined to continue,
Lenardo suggested, "If it's a secret—"

"No. Everyone knows. Aradia's mother was an Adept,
of course—two Adepts always produce an Adept child. Is
that true for Readers?"

"Yes, although we test all children because sometimes
Readers are born in families where both parents are non-
Readers."

"You test *every single child?*"

"Of course. Readers are precious, and all are academy-
trained to their highest level of ability."

"That is something to consider—a system for reaching
and training every Adept . . ."

Lenardo noticed that Wulfston was only too eager to
change the subject. "What happened to Aradia's mother?"
he prompted.

"A woman's part in bearing a child is long and difficult.
She could not regain her powers after her child was born.
When Aradia was two, she killed herself."

"How terrible for Aradia," said Lenardo.

"They say—servants' gossip—that she claimed Aradia
stole her powers and that she tried to kill the child."

"Her own baby? Surely she was mad."

"Aradia was already showing Adept abilities."

"At two years old?"

Wulfston nodded. "There are legends of great Adepts who emerged from the womb and proceeded to heal their mothers, but those are fancy, I think. Two is early but not impossible. I was three."

"You don't really believe a child could steal her mother's powers?"

"I don't know," said Wulfston. "The very act of sex limits the powers of both parties, even if no child is conceived. It is the only instance of the state of the body affecting Adept abilities. It is a mystery, Lenardo—the passing of life from one generation to another. It is best not to question such things too deeply."

"Why not?" asked Lenardo, who had been taught to seek knowledge above all.

"People who become obsessed with that mystery become depressed and may even . . . abandon life." Wulfston's tone, and the euphemism, suggested that suicide was unacceptable here.

"Wulfston," said Lenardo, "do you not believe that a person's life is his own, to do with as he sees fit?"

"No! My life, for example, is pledged to Aradia. I would give it in her defense, but I have no right to abandon it, no matter what grief or pain I suffer."

"But there are circumstances . . . What about Nerius? He is dying, and while he lives he is a danger to those around him—"

Tears brightened Wulfston's eyes. "He's alive! Yes, he will die, but from that tumor in his brain, not from. . . ." The man shuddered at the thought. "Suicide!"

Lenardo waited while the young Adept regained control. "Wulfston," he said gently, "we have differing beliefs in this matter. In the Aventine Empire, suicide is not acceptable as a coward's way of avoiding debt, pain, or punishment. When a situation is hopeless, however, why should a dying or dishonored man continue to endure? We have no Adepts to stop the pain of the grievously ill.

Nerius' situation is even worse—he is hurting, even killing, the people he loves. He doesn't know it—I can Read that. If he did know, don't you think he would expect you to stop him?"

"Yes, of course," said Wulfston. "But we *have* stopped him, Lenardo. We didn't have to take his life to do it."

"What value is Nerius' life to him now?"

Wulfston stared at him. "Life is the greatest value. Without life there is nothing."

Lenardo recalled yesterday's funeral service, with no mention of deities or an afterlife. "Wulfston, what do you think happens to you when you die?"

"To me? Nothing. When life ceases, that is all."

"The body dies, but the person, the mind, the . . . individual must continue."

"That is superstitious nonsense, like the gods you swear by," Wulfston scoffed. "If the mind survived, Adepts would certainly make their presence known. Why, a powerful lord could go right on ruling after his body was returned to the elements! There are fantastic stories of that very thing, but everyone knows they are fairy tales. I suppose you believe in the winged folk of the wood, too?"

"If I ever Read one, I would believe!" Lenardo replied impatiently. "Wulfston, every Reader knows the mind—the personality—is a separate thing from the body. We *experience* it! And if it is separate, then there is no reason for it to die when the body dies."

"Have you . . . Read the presence of someone . . . after his body has died?"

Lenardo could sense Wulfston's desire to be told yes. But he could not have the man's confidence in him built on lies. "No, I myself have not—but others have."

"They told you they had. It's all superstition to chain your mind."

"You accuse Readers of chaining minds? You, who casually implant suggestions—?"

"Clean and simple barriers against pain," said Wulfston, "or to hold prisoners as we held you. Would you rather have been chained in a dungeon?"

"It would have been more honest!"

"Honest!" Wulfston glared at him, but then his fury subsided. "That will always be the crux, won't it? How can either of us judge the other's honesty?"

And why do we care so?

Lenardo's Reading abilities approached normal as his strength returned. He ate the huge meals Aradia provided, slept all night and part of each day, and on the third day woke on schedule at dawn, feeling completely rested. Having given his word not to leave his room, he lay still and Read beyond the castle, finding the flat rock where the only sign left of the funeral pyre was a bit of ash drifted by the morning breeze.

In the nearby fields, people planted and cultivated with the same instruments he had seen farmers use at home. Lenardo knew little about agriculture—Readers didn't need such skills.

Before the castle, people were rebuilding the house that had burned down—the ones on either side were only scorched, although they should have all gone up like torches. While Wulfston and Aradia were occupied, what Adept had miraculously contained that fire? This notion of stray Adepts among the common people, untrained . . .

He watched, focusing in on the carpenter in leather apron, gnarled hands carefully placing support timbers. Then he expanded his view, moving along the road, finding girls carrying food and water to the workers in the fields, and beyond them, on the grassy hillside, a flock of sheep tended by three young boys and a dog.

Satisfied that he could Read over a normal distance once more, Lenardo was about to test his limits when the kitchen maid appeared with his breakfast. "Beggin' yer pardon, my lady asks that ye attend her in the great hall at yer earliest convenience."

So he didn't linger over breakfast, but ate the bread, fruit, and cheese, and left the meat—time to return to a normal diet to bring his abilities back to peak efficiency. "Normal" was still far short of Lenardo's usual powers.

In the great hall, Aradia was receiving petitions. She was dressed more splendidly than Lenardo had ever seen her. Over a rose-colored dress similar in design to the one she had worn at the funeral, she wore a surcoat of rich blue velvet, with panels of gold embroidery. For the first time, too, she was wearing jewelry: gold pendant earrings, and two bracelets of gold on her left wrist.

Before Aradia knelt a man in tan trousers and a homespun tunic. Lenardo half-Read, half-recognized that this was the owner of the house that had exploded in Nerius' unconscious attack.

"Rren," Aradia was saying, "you are kind enough to allow me to make reparation without petition. You and your family were fortunate to escape from your burning home unharmed. You lost everything, however, through my fault."

"Nay, m'lady, you couldn't know—"

"I knew my father's seizures. He never before reached outside the castle, though, and never struck a living being. He never will again—I guarantee it."

"Aye, m'lady. No one doubts that."

"But you must have your home restored. I have ordered the carpenter to rebuild for you."

"Aye—he has already started."

"Good," she said. "But once you have your house again, you will want furnishings, and you will wish to repay your friends who are putting up your family. There—" she took one of the gold bracelets from her left arm, "—that should cover the value of anything you might require."

"Oh, my lady, this is of far greater value—"

"You must not refuse me, Rren."

"Uh . . . no, m'lady. Thank you, m'lady."

Still staring at the bracelet in his hands, he continued to mutter thanks as he made his bow and left.

"Now," said Aradia, "bring in the prisoner."

Lenardo remained on the steps, wondering if Aradia had sent for him to Read her prisoner. A Reader's testimony was not admissible in empire courts, but it could be used to discover concrete evidence. When Aradia did not call him forward, he sat down on the steps to watch the proceedings.

Two of Aradia's guards brought in a third man, shackled hand and foot. Although his outward attitude was defiant, Lenardo could not shut out the fear that radiated from him. Whatever he had done, he did not feel guilty, but he was in an agony of terror at being brought before Aradia.

Fighting to restrain his curiosity, Lenardo did not Read the man until Aradia demanded, "You are one of Drakonius' watchers?"

The man did not answer, but Lenardo Read that it was true. And that set him free to Read, to probe deeply for Drakonius' whereabouts—for Galen's!

What Lenardo Read was that this man was looking for him. The description was too good—it could only have come from Galen. The one thing the watcher didn't know, however, was that the man he sought was a Reader.

Aradia, meanwhile, was questioning the frightened prisoner and getting no response. "Were you coming into my lands or leaving them when you were captured?" she asked.

"Coming in," he replied sullenly—a half-truth. He had indeed just come in, discovered that Aradia's watchers were also searching for Lenardo, and started back across the border lands to report what he had learned when he was captured. He had not managed to make his report. Lenardo was confused by the fact that the man seemed to think he could have made his report without crossing back into Drakonius' lands or meeting anyone. Try as he might, he could not Read how the watcher thought to do so. The man's mind was darting like a wild bird in a cage, battering against the bars.

Aradia did not know how to question the man to bring to the surface of his mind the information she wanted. Lenardo considered going down to offer help, but she didn't want her men to know he was a Reader. The fact that Drakonius had not let his watchers know was further evidence that he was indeed in danger if so exposed.

"You will tell me what you were doing in my lands," Aradia was saying, the dangerous-wolf look in her eyes.

The watcher panicked. Hideous images flickered through his mind—pain, dismemberment, flame; an Adept could keep a tortured prisoner alive and in agony indefinitely. He had seen Drakonius do so!

Lenardo had no idea what Aradia intended to do to the man, but whatever the threat, it was the wrong move. As the watcher cowered before her, his psychic presence suddenly went blank—as blank to Reading as an Adept's! He realized that this was one of those men with some minor Adept power—like the young soldier he had met in Zendi —and that he had been driven by terror of Aradia to use it . . . on himself.

As the man collapsed before her, Aradia knelt at once beside him. His heart had stopped, but Lenardo Read it forced to start again when Aradia concentrated. But it didn't take hold. In the bare moments it took for Lenardo's long legs to carry him across the room, he realized that an Adept always had the means of suicide at hand by stopping his heart—but that it was ineffective before a stronger Adept, who could reverse the process. He Read, though, that this man was irretrievably dead. His power was not to move things—it was to create fire. And he had done so, to his own brain. It was cooked through.

The smell of burnt flesh was rising as Lenardo reached Aradia's side. She rose, staring in honest horror at what had happened. Although her thoughts were as unReadable as always, her nausea matched his own. She closed her eyes and turned away, saying, "How could he be so desperate? I had to know, but I wouldn't have hurt him—"

She squared her shoulders, becoming the calm leader again. "Remove the body," she instructed the soldiers. When they had gone, she turned to Lenardo. "Drakonius has watchers in my lands."

"They are looking for me," he replied.

"You Read him?"

"That is all I could Read—except that he did not report to Drakonius before he was captured."

"Then why didn't he *tell* me that? There was no need for him to die."

"Aradia . . . do you treat your prisoners as Drakonius treats his?"

Her lips thinned. "I should have known. Father would not have made that mistake. He would simply have implanted the desire to speak truth before the man was brought before him. But, Lenardo, if you were Reading him, why didn't you warn me?"

"I didn't know what he was going to do. And if I had known, and shouted it across the great hall. . . . Wulfston has warned me that your people would kill me if I gave myself away."

"Wulfston has told me a great deal about you, too," Aradia said. "You frustrate him."

"Frustrate?"

"He knows what great value you could be to us, and how dangerous you would be working against us. He wants to trust you . . . as I do, Lenardo."

"Don't," he said, not ready to discuss even a truce until he had had time to think over the scene he had just witnessed.

"There—you see? That is frustrating. You appear to be a man whose word we could take—if you would give it."

"What do you want from me, Aradia?"

"Your loyalty. If you were my sworn man, you might use your powers openly. No one would dare question your motives."

"Why should I give you my loyalty?"

"Because we have the same ideals. Wulfston told me why you were exiled. I can protect you from what you fear."

"What I fear?"

"Lenardo—do you not fear pursuit? Leaving here and running northward while you were still so weak—that was not the act of a rational man. Do you expect retaliation? Would the Readers send someone after you, to kill you lest you join with us?"

At this rate, how long before she figures out I am in pursuit of Galen? "Why should they? They know the savages will kill anyone who shows the ability to Read."

"But I did not kill you, did I? And Drakonius did not kill the Reader he used to attack Adigia, although he may have been killed since. I wonder." She took off the remaining gold bracelet and tossed it into a chest by the wall. When she lifted the lid, Lenardo caught a flash of brilliant metal.

Gold, silver, jewels, coins—an immense treasure! *And I thought there were no ornaments worn here.* Aradia still wore the small gold pendant earrings, but nothing more except the rich embroidery of her surcoat, a far cry from the many rings, bracelets, and necklaces a wealthy woman of the empire might wear.

Aradia clapped her hands sharply, and a man entered from the inner hallway. "Pepyi, have the treasure chest shut away."

"Yes, m'lady."

Aradia started up the stairs. "Are you going to leave the chest there, unguarded?" asked Lenardo.

"The lock can be opened only by an Adept. Would you care to try to lift the chest, Lenardo? It will take six strong men to put it away—and I do not believe six of my men at one time would conspire against me."

"The value of the items in that chest might make them consider it."

"Why? They want for nothing. Also, the punishment for theft would make them think twice."

"And what is the punishment for theft?" The memory of the tortures he had seen in the watcher's mind made his skin crawl.

"Years ago, my father found an excellent solution for nonviolent crimes. The criminal is simply struck dumb."

"What?"

"He cannot speak. That does not prevent him from making reparation. It is, of course, a handicap, a great embarrassment, because everyone knows why he cannot speak. Since it is difficult to communicate with others, he must commune with himself—and by the time the command is lifted, and they can speak again, most such people have reformed their ways."

"That's a terrible thing to do!" Was there no limit to the ways these Adepts manipulated people?

"It is painless. It does not separate the criminal from his family or make him incapable of honest work. He cannot run away, for he carries his punishment with him. Furthermore, only once, since my father instituted this method of punishment, has someone who suffered it repeated his crime."

"And what about the poor creature who is born dumb? He will be taken for a criminal under punishment."

Aradia stared at Lenardo in shock. "To be without Adepts—how horrible! You actually allow a child to grow up with such handicaps, deaf, dumb, blind—?"

"You can cure all of those?"

"Almost always in an infant. You saw Pepyi below? He was born blind, but my father cured him when he was just a baby—as soon as his parents discovered he couldn't see. It took over a year, but he sees."

"I have a friend who is blind," said Lenardo. "The optic nerves—the nerves from the eye to the brain—did not develop normally. Could you . . . ?"

"Is he a grown man?"

"He's seventeen."

"No, I don't think anything could be done now. When a baby is developing and growing, it is relatively easy to correct such defects. I am sorry for your friend."

"Torio would laugh at your pity. Fortunately, he is a Reader—one of the best I've ever known. One day he will be far better than I am."

"And how good are you, Lenardo?"

They had stopped at the top of the stairs. "What do you mean?" asked Lenardo.

"There are degrees of ability among Readers just as there are among Adepts, Wulfston tells me. What is the level of your skills?"

As he hesitated, not wanting to tell her he had just been admitted to the highest rank, she said, "No—your ratings would be meaningless to me. Come into my study."

She led him through her bedroom, where she paused to

remove her earrings and exchange the velvet surcoat for a worn and ink-stained robe, and into a smaller room with large, many-paned windows of clear glass. The walls were lined with books and scroll-cases—as many, it appeared, as in the academy library! So here was one savage who could read and write.

"You are a scholar?" he asked.

"One cannot go everywhere and experience everything. Books bring knowledge one could never gather in a single lifetime. But of all these books, Lenardo, many of them from the Aventine empire, not one explains the techniques of Reading."

"It cannot be taught by books," he explained. "One learns to Read by demonstration and experience."

"Very well. I want a demonstration."

"If you have not the talent—"

She smiled. "No, I did not mean you could teach me to Read. I want to find out how well you can do it." There was a table by the window, stacked with books and papers in uneven piles, a wax-encrusted candlestick holding down one stack. There were a tablet and stylus, quills, ink—all the supplies of a scholar, in deplorable disorder.

Aradia picked up the wax tablet and, holding it so Lenardo could not see, said "Tell me what I am writing."

"I, Aradia, daughter of Nerius, heir to—"

She stopped, turned the stylus, and rubbed out the words as she said, "I suppose that's an easy trick."

"Yes, but it's not the easiest. The first sign of Reading ability is to pick up another person's thoughts. I cannot touch yours, so I had to do a visual Reading of what you wrote."

"Let's try something a bit harder. You see the large red-bound volume in the middle of the top shelf?"

As there was only one book bound in red, he said, "Yes."

"Look at the first page—I mean, Read the first page to me."

"I can't."

"Oh," she said disappointedly.

"It's not that I can't Read it," explained Lenardo, "it's that I can't read it. Although I speak your language, I have never learned your alphabet."

"Here," she said urgently, thrusting the wax tablet into his hands, "copy it down! It doesn't matter if you don't know what it means!"

The tablet's surface did not show the rub-marks of the stylus; it was as smooth as if the wax had been remelted. Concentrating, he began to copy the characters in the book, letters made up all of straight lines, intended to be carved, not written.

Aradia watched avidly, until he had copied three lines. "That's enough," she said and went to the bookcase, stretching up on tiptoe for the book. Just as Lenardo was about to go reach it for her, it conveniently tilted forward and fell into her hands.

Eagerly, she opened it to the first page and compared what was written there with Lenardo's version. "You write with the precision of a scribe," she said. "It's perfect."

She looked up at him, her face flushed. "Lenardo, if we could only work together . . ."

"We can," he said, pressing his advantage. "Aradia, Drakonius is looking for me. I assume that that means danger to you if he finds out where I am. I *know* it means danger to me."

"How did he find out about you?" she asked suspiciously.

"His Reader knows me."

"Have you been in contact?"

"No. I've been too ill to search for him . . . and I do not know whether Galen is working freely for Drakonius or is being forced to do so."

"Of course," she said. "How stupid of me. You came here seeking this other Reader, Galen." She tilted her head, studying him. "To join him? Or to remove him from your enemy's arsenal of weapons?"

"Whatever my original motivation," he replied, "I now see that he cannot be left in Drakonius' power, even if he is there willingly. And that means I need your help, Aradia. I will Read Drakonius for you if you will help me remove Galen from his power."

"You realize that I am trying to extricate my people and myself from Drakonius' power?"

"I had surmised as much."

She searched his face, and he could feel empathically how her longing to trust him deepened. Then she said, "I am powerless to move against Drakonius. He knows that. I dare not leave my father for more than a day at a time. I cannot lead my army, even in defense . . . unless you will help me."

"To do what?"

"To cure my father!"

"Aradia, there's no way—"

"You can Read the exact location of his tumor, and I can remove it!"

"No, Aradia. My surgical skills are good enough for emergency measures, but even the finest surgeon dare not cut into the human brain. It would kill your father at once."

"Cut into—? What are you talking about?"

"Removing the tumor."

"By cutting? *No*, Lenardo! I am an Adept. I shall just— remove it! You must draw it for me, or make a model in wax. It must be exact—even more precise than these letters —but you can do it, can't you?"

"I . . . don't know," he replied, caught up in the idea. "I said I would help you with healing—but *this*. If you were off by a hair's breadth, you would kill him. The shock might kill him anyway."

"He is *dying*, Lenardo! If we do nothing, he will be dead within the fortnight." She lowered her eyes. "For three days I have been strengthening his body again, hoping you could do . . . what you have proved today. You are fully recovered, are you not?"

"No. You don't understand the precision required. I would have to fast and meditate—"

"How long?"

"At least two days."

"Then start now!" Her eyes were glittering with tears. Lenardo saw his chance of gaining Aradia—and Wulfston—as allies.

It was not mere selfishness, though, he realized; he *wanted* to use his abilities in this strange new way to save a life, but he wondered what Aradia would do to him if he failed. She looked so frail and delicate, and she commanded such power. He could circumvent any command she planted in his mind, but he could do nothing against physical attack. He remembered Wulfston saying, "The best thing I could do would be to stop your heart right now."

Dared he risk his life now that he knew where Galen was?

Then Aradia said, "Lenardo, if you save my father's life, I will grant you your freedom. I will form an alliance with you, to our mutual advantage, to remove Galen from Drakonius' power."

It was everything he could have asked—unless he failed. But he could not consider the possibility of failure.

"Very well," said Lenardo, "I will do it. You understand that while removing the tumor may allow Nerius to live, I cannot predict whether he will recover his faculties."

"I understand," she replied. "His life is all I ask of you. Now, as I have your word, you have the freedom of the castle—within reason. Do not enter anyone's private rooms uninvited . . . although I suppose you could Read anything you wanted, right from here."

"First, the number of dresses in your chest does not interest me," said Lenardo. "Second—and more important —it is forbidden to intrude on another's privacy out of mere curiosity."

"But if you were spying on an enemy?"

"For the time being, Aradia, I shall not consider you my enemy. Drakonius, however, may be enemy to both of us—and you know he is spying on you. Aradia, as I do not know Drakonius' specific location, I cannot Read from here, cannot contact Galen to find out if he is Drakonius' ally or prisoner. If you could show me on a map where Drakonius is—"

"I don't know," she said. "He moves constantly, but I can tell you the general area. He will be somewhere in the Western Hills, probably along the river."

"I cannot Read that far from here—not in my present condition, and even if I were at peak performance I could not do so without a specific location."

"I too would like to know exactly where Drakonius is," Aradia mused, "and exactly what he is doing. We can get nearer by riding out to the border tomorrow. Would that help?"

"Yes, indeed. At least I'd have a better chance."

"Then go and rest. We'll have a long ride tomorrow. Is there anything you need?"

"There's something I *don't* need—any more meat with my meals. Otherwise . . . could I have some different clothes?"

"Of course. The tailor is working on others already."

"I mean . . . could I have something less . . . exposed? I've noticed that Wulfston's clothes are of much the same design, but they're cut fuller, the tops longer."

Her smile became wolfish again. "Wulfston gives his own instructions to the tailor. But very well, Lenardo, I'll take care of it."

"Thank you, Aradia."

"You're welcome. One thing more—in public, your proper form of address to me is 'my lady.' "

"Yes, my lady," he replied, aware that the title was to remind people of her power. But he could give her that now. It was part of a pact that would soon be fulfilled— and then he would be free and have help in his quest for Galen.

Aradia and Lenardo set out at dawn the next day— alone. Lenardo was momentarily surprised, until he realized that an Adept required no guard. So he was surprised again when Aradia took him into the guard room and girded on him the same sword he had taken the night of his escape.

"I trust you know how to use it?" she asked.

"Of course. I instructed novices at the academy. However, could you not defend yourself better than I?"

"The sword is a symbol that you would defend me if you had to. You would, wouldn't you?"

"Yes. I would."

It was a beautiful day, warming as the sun rose. Aradia had apparently issued orders quickly yesterday, for this morning Lenardo had been provided with a new outfit in blue and green, with the more modest cut he had requested. He had also been given boots of softest leather, that molded to his feet and clung to his calves like a second skin.

Aradia pointed out the new extension of the irrigation system and, a little further on, an iron works. "It would be preferable to have our weapons made further from Drakonius' border, but this land is useless for anything else, and there is a good road northeast to the forest, where charcoal is made for smelting."

"An Aventine road," said Lenardo.

"Probably. Drakonius certainly didn't build it. He never builds anything except defenses."

"Then you took this land from Drakonius?"

"My father helped Drakonius win some battle long before I was born. When Drakonius asked what he wanted as reward, he asked for these lands that had been abandoned. Drakonius thought my father a fool, but he granted his request. Now the lands are ours . . . as long as we can hold them."

"That's the way everything is here, isn't it? Yours for as long as you can hold it."

"That is the way of nature," Aradia replied. "The nature of people, though, is such that they can work together, protect one another, so that a man is not torn between working his land and defending it. My people know I will defend them; thus they are loyal to me."

"I wonder," Lenardo mused, "if there will ever be a day when people can live peacefully, without fear of attack?"

"I don't know," Aradia replied. "Perhaps if no one were hungry or cold, or lacked a roof over his head . . ."

"Is that the world you want, Aradia?"

"Yes. Since I made the treaties with Lilith and Hron, Drakonius has not diverted his efforts from trying to take the Aventine Empire to fight three strong Adepts. For three years there has been peace in our lands—and no beggars in our lanes. Everyone has honest work, and the old and infirm are cared for."

"What of those who don't want to work?"

"Such people find themselves out of place, so they go off to join the hill bandits or cross over into Drakonius' lands."

"Exiles," Lenardo observed.

"Yes. If all the world were peaceful, where would such people go? Perhaps we would have to set aside a land for them and let them contend with one another."

"Then you believe some people are evil by nature?"

"Evil? In general terms, we would say that someone who inflicts pain for his own pleasure is evil. Yet that person exists by nature, as do storm and drought and flood. Evil to one person is good to another; the best we can do is work as closely as possible with nature."

"But . . . what are your values, Aradia?" Lenardo was deeply puzzled now. "How do you decide right from wrong?"

"Life is the highest good. That which prevents death contributes to life—hence peace is better than war. But it is not simple. Sometimes one chooses one life over another —just cultivating a field, the farmer kills the plants he calls weeds, so the food crops will grow. We kill and eat animals. How do you decide right from wrong, Lenardo? Or does your Reader's Code cover every possible choice?"

"No human law could do so. But we do believe that right conduct has a higher authority than simply what men can observe—what you call nature. There is a higher, sentient force, usually personified as the gods, although that simple belief has fallen into disfavor. The powers ascribed to those ancient manlike gods are painfully close to the powers of Adepts."

"Then what do you believe in?"

"A higher authority, the force that created the world."

"Nature," said Aradia.

"Wulfston tells me you believe that when life ends, the person—his consciousness, his personality—ends as well."

"Of course. We do not believe in ghosts, Lenardo."

"Then what is the point of living?"

"Life! It is all we have!" she said vehemently. "I shall live my life to the full, until it is taken from me by force!"

Remembering what Wulfston had said about Aradia's mother, Lenardo tactfully shifted the subject. "We believe that the point of life is to please the gods. However, that philosophy does not solve the problem of good and evil, any more than yours does. Even today, it is possible to get a debate going as to whether something is good because it is pleasing to the gods, or pleasing to the gods because it is good."

"And what good does it do to please the gods?" asked Aradia.

Lenardo was stopped cold. In ten years of teaching, he had fielded every possible question on the subject—he had thought. But Aradia approached from a different direction, attacking the question instead of seeking an answer. He thought about it for a moment. "Presumably it does the same good to please the gods as it does your people to please you."

Aradia laughed, then said, "Here is the best place to stop. A bit further on is the trail into the borderland, where you were attacked by the bandits. This is the closest we can come to Drakonius' lands and remain within my borders."

A small spring flowed from a rock into a pool the size of a hand bath—a natural fountain. Grass and a few trees grew where they could reach the moisture, forming a tiny park. Someone had placed small rocks to form a fireplace, but Lenardo and Aradia had no need of a fire this warm spring day.

"Tell me how to search for Drakonius," said Lenardo. "He was not in Zendi when I was there, but it is a place to start, as I can Read it easily. I once lived there."

"You have to have been there?"

"No, but it is a great help in Reading over long distances. An even greater aid is to have someone to contact at the other end."

"Try your powers. Read to Zendi. See how far recovered you are."

It took a slight effort, but Lenardo knew the exact location of the city. In a few moments, he was in the middle of the town, "looking" around at the milling crowds, the beggars, the filth—it was exactly as he remembered. He was grateful he didn't have to smell it.

The sun darkened for a moment, and Lenardo "looked" up to see a cloud passing, other clouds piling up in the west.

To Aradia, he said, "It's going to rain in Zendi by evening, and the clouds will reach here by tomorrow."

"You're better than the watchers!" said Aradia. "They won't know until tomorrow. Did you see anything interesting?"

"No—nothing but the same overcrowded conditions I saw in person. How do I find Drakonius from here?"

"He's got a string of fortresses in the Western Hills that he built as he forced the walls of the empire back. If you can find him, try to Read how far he has progressed in rebuilding his army. And whether he has other Adepts with him."

"You think he may be preparing to strike against you?"

"I know it must come. Had Drakonius won at Adigia, he would have been able to say to us, 'You see? You'd better come in with me next time!' But as he lost, he will try to force us to join him, to prove his strength. And if he finds out where you are, my lands will be his first target."

So Lenardo Read back to Zendi, then allowed his perceptions to rise, heading west, finding the hills with ease, although details were blurred. Following the river southward, he began to feel stretched, tenuous, as if his connection with his body might snap. It was pouring rain here, making visual Reading difficult.

When the river took a turn directly west, increasing the distance he was trying to Read even more rapidly, Lenardo almost gave up. He was beginning to wonder if he would be able to Read anything smaller than a river or mountain anyway—when suddenly a cluster of human minds drew his attention.

There were twenty or more people, spread through a warren of caves in the cliffside. Below was a large stretch of beach, where an army might camp—but there was no army there now, although defenses had been built along the beach.

Aradia wanted to know how many Adepts were here; that would mean attempting to Read everyone, to see how many could not be Read. It was getting harder and harder to focus. How could he—?

Suddenly, a lighthouse in the fog, there was the touch of a compatible mind. *Galen!*

//Yes? *WHAT?* Who's there?//

//Galen—are you well?//

//Lenardo!// All the joy of the boy's enthusiasm welcomed him. //Magister Lenardo! You've come at last! How did you find me? Where are you?//

Something behind that final question, a certain tension of hidden motives, made Lenardo recklessly drop contact with his body. He'd pay when he returned with cramped muscles and pinched nerves, but now he could Read freely . . . and Galen could not follow him back to Aradia, even if the boy could Read that far.

//I'll come to you, Galen,// he temporized. //Are you well? You haven't been hurt?//

//Where are you?// again, with an edge of desperation.

Maybe the boy *was* hurt. He was certainly frightened. //I'll find a way to get you out of there—// Lenardo began.

//No!// A burst of panic, followed by enforced but tenuous control. //Why should I leave? I'm never going back to an empire that locks Readers up in the academies and out of the senate, an empire that's afraid of us. Come join me. I'll prove I was right, Lenardo. I'll show you what our powers are for.// But the boy did not believe his own words.

//Galen—can't you see what they've done to you?

You've broke one of the commands they implanted—you can easily cast out these thoughts. They're not your own.//

//They said you were exiled! I've been Reading all over the land for you. They told me you had come to see things our way, that you were in Zendi, and then you disappeared. Where are you?//

Lenardo tried another approach. //Galen, you were right; it is possible to make peace with the savages. Everyone will know you destroyed Drakonius' army—//

//*You* destroyed them!// Galen raged suddenly. //I felt you touch my mind, distracting me! Now they don't trust me, because of you! I should have killed you when I had the chance!//

Beneath the boy's ramblings, Lenardo caught thoughts, suspicions: the Code a hypocrisy . . . Lenardo trying to keep Galen from achieving rank as a Reader . . . betraying him in his testimony at the trial . . . jealous of Galen, refusing to admit he was becoming the better Reader . . .

It was all nonsense—but how had Drakonius found these strange thoughts, to knit of them a snare for Galen's mind? Or was it possible they were not of Drakonius' invention, but rather the result of Galen's exposure for two years to the Adept's manipulations, transferred to his own disappointments?

At that moment, Lenardo could have wished for an Adept's skill to force Galen to calm down. The boy seemed not to have grown up at all—if anything, his adolescent mood swings had gotten worse. //Galen, I want to help you—//

//You! You coward! You let me be exiled—branded! You said you'd stand by me, and you didn't. You hate me because I'm a better Reader than you are. Everyone who's the best at something is hated. Now you want to trick me into going back to be executed. It won't work, Lenardo. I know you now, and I hate you!// Lenardo's mind flinched, but he could not avoid the intensity of the boy's hysteria. //I hate you! I'm going to find you and kill you, Lenardo, so you'll never betray me again!//

Chapter Six

The Wolf Stirs

When Lenardo's consciousness returned to his body, he was almost glad of the pain in his back, knees, and ankles, competing with the pain of his confrontation with Galen. He had been sitting tailor-fashion, not the proper posture from which to leave the body.

After the onslaught of aches, his next impression was that someone was touching him. He opened his eyes to find Aradia kneeling before him, holding his wrist with a finger on his pulse, concern in her violet eyes. "Are you all right? You slumped—I thought you'd fainted, but I was afraid to move you."

"I'm glad you didn't," he replied. "I'll be all right in a moment." He stretched his cramped legs, rubbing them, then stood up to stretch his back.

"Was it too far? What happened to you?"

"It was too far for a closely focused Reading, but I found Drakonius' stronghold. There is no army there now. As for Adepts—I'm afraid I couldn't concentrate enough to separate them from the others. There weren't more than thirty people in the entire stronghold."

"Are you sure that's what you found? Not just a castle?"

Oh yes. Galen would not be anywhere but in Drakonius' stronghold.

"It's not a castle. Drakonius has expanded some caves in a cliff, and built fortifications along the river's edge. It seems to be a new place that he's still working on."

"Did Drakonius' Reader detect your presence?"

"Yes," he admitted.

"Has he followed you here? Is he Reading us now?"

135

"No—I saw to it that he couldn't follow me, and besides, he can't Read this far. I fear Drakonius has chained his mind."

"Wulfston thinks—"

"What I thought: that Galen broke the commands implanted in his mind and bided his time until he could bring that avalanche down on Drakonius' army."

"But you don't think that now?"

"I don't know what to think, Aradia. Galen is young—only twenty—and his training as a Reader was cut off when he was exiled at eighteen. I don't know how far he may have progressed, but certainly not as far as if he'd stayed at the academy. I could not have Read so far at his age. I don't know whether he can break a command planted in his mind by an Adept, because I have no example but my own. It was easy enough for me once I knew what you had done. In Galen's case . . ."

"What?"

"First, it's possible he has truly come to hate the empire. Second, if Drakonius implanted that hatred in Galen's mind, how do I get Galen to *want* to break the command? I wanted that door to open for me, but suppose you had implanted in my mind the suggestion that I simply wanted to stay there?" He frowned. "Could you do that?"

"I could have. I would not."

"Why not?"

"I want your true loyalty, Lenardo, of your own free will. That is what Drakonius wants of Galen too. If he implanted false loyalties, he certainly learned his lesson at Adigia. If Galen were working against his true feelings, a 'mistake' such as bringing the avalanche down on Drakonius' troops is exactly the kind of thing to be expected. He wouldn't know, consciously, that he had done it deliberately."

Lenardo smiled in relief. "Thank you. I did not want to think Galen a traitor."

"Unfortunately," she replied, "I cannot think Drakonius so great a fool. He did not conquer many lands by making that kind of mistake. An unwilling army is a weapon for one's foe. I fear your friend truly believes whatever he told you. I'm sorry." She paused. "Does he know you're with me?"

"Apparently not. He kept asking me where I was."

"Could he tell anything to lead Drakonius to you?"

"No. But if I was observed after I left Zendi . . ."

"Yes—it won't take Drakonius long to find you. I don't suppose you thought to lie to Galen—to suggest that no one knows you're a Reader?"

"I didn't say anything either way, but if I hadn't been delirious when Wulfston found me, you *wouldn't* know. However, I can't be sure Galen credits me with common sense, or that he knows what sense is any more. Now what do we do?"

"Wait for Drakonius to act. Now lie down for a while, and then we'll eat before we ride home."

"Lie down? What for?" Then he laughed. "I told you— Reading doesn't use up energy. I'm as rested as you are."

But his real mood for the rest of the day was somber. Why would Galen feel such a personal hatred for him? They had been such good friends. . . .

As they rode home, Lenardo said, "I fear Reading for Drakonius was not a good idea. Now Galen at least knows I'm still alive, and so does Drakonius. I may have brought your enemy down upon you."

"You found out that he was already looking for you. At least we can be prepared. He will find you eventually; his watchers are as good as mine."

"Those people—the watchers. They watch the weather, I know, and I suppose some go over and mingle among Drakonius' people to bring you information. But it's half a day's ride even from here to your castle, and more in bad weather. How do you get news through so fast?"

"Heliograph," she replied.

" 'Sun-writing'? Is that an Adept trick?"

She chuckled. "You mean you've never played with a mirror, flashing light around a room?"

"Of course," he said, still puzzled.

"Well, the watchers use the same thing, or a lantern at

night, to flash messages from one hilltop to another. It takes only a few minutes to get a message from one end of the land to the other."

"Then that's what I saw the day I escaped! And how Wulfston found me so quickly."

"Of course. We sent out your description, and Wulfston was on the road soon after dawn. For as weak as you were, you got quite far, actually. You crossed the border into Hron's lands, but he is my ally, and so his people returned you."

"Your system is as effective as having Readers, it seems —and almost as fast. We must relay messages too, when they have to go beyond a single Reader's range."

"But Readers can do it without the rest of the world knowing," said Aradia.

"If you sent out my description that day . . ."

"Drakonius may already know where you are."

"Galen didn't know."

"Drakonius may not trust Galen, and Galen cannot Read an Adept." She rode silently for a few moments, then said, "Lenardo, how well do you know his capabilities as a Reader?"

"Very well. I was his teacher and often tested him."

"I know you want to think he deliberately caused the avalanche—but can you assume for a moment that he didn't mean it? Suppose he was truly intent on destroying Adigia. Is he capable of misjudging, of making that kind of error?"

"Yes," said Lenardo. "I could have made it myself. I was Reading the fault and the stresses flowing through it. The vibrations spread in both directions through the mountain. I didn't know myself which way it would go. I remember standing there helplessly, willing it to go the other way. . . ."

"And you feel responsible."

"I told you. I was his teacher."

"But the teacher must let the students grow up," said Aradia. "We hope it is when we feel they are ready, but sometimes they make their own decisions. And sometimes they're wrong. But we cannot stop them from making their own mistakes." She smiled ruefully. "Nor can I stop you from making yours. Come on—if we hurry, we'll be home by dark."

Lenardo spent the next two days resting and meditating. The third morning, feeling securely himself again, he ate a light breakfast, bathed, and joined Aradia at her father's bedside.

As she had promised, Aradia had strengthened Nerius' body. He was still a very sick man, but his heart beat strongly and he breathed evenly. If they could remove the tumor without doing further damage, there was a good chance he would live. But in what condition?

Presumably, Aradia's values reflected her father's. "Life is the greatest value." Lenardo had to assume that Nerius would want to live, even if the damage the tumor had already done left him blind, paralyzed, or otherwise crippled.

Aradia provided Lenardo with wax to make a model of Nerius' brain. Such modeling was part of a Reader's training, precisely for showing to non-Readers the things they could not see. Never, though, had he done work so delicate, so impossibly precise. He worked for hours, superimposing what he Read upon the softened wax in his hands, molding, carving, despairing of achieving the accuracy he had to have.

When he finished he was cramped with tension and fearful that he had missed something, somehow. He set the model down and leaned back in his chair, rubbing his eyes.

"Are you finished?" Aradia asked with mingled hope and fear.

"I don't know," he replied, pushing his hair back off his forehead—he really would have to cut it, as it was becoming an annoyance. "I don't think I can make a more accurate model, but I fear it's not good enough to guide you."

"Show me."

He had made the model in three parts, so he could take it apart to show the tumor, which he had stained with ink.

"It's close," he said, "but there is a limit to the accuracy human hands can achieve. If only you could Read it as well as destroy it . . ."

"Do you not know how frequently I have wished that these past few days? But I cannot Read. You must guide me. I'll get Wulfston, and then we can begin."

They started successfully enough, the two Adepts concentrating their powers on the center of the tumor. The bulk of the growth slowly but surely began to evaporate.

"Stop!" cried Lenardo, as Nerius' healthy brain tissue began to relax from its compression to fill the vacuum.

Violet eyes and brown stared at Lenardo from drawn faces. Both Adepts were breathing hard, their hearts pounding as if they'd run a long distance.

"What happened?" Aradia asked warily.

"You are succeeding, but the contour of the growth has changed." Hastily, Lenardo remolded his wax model, saying, "This is not as accurate, but—"

"We've removed that much? And not touched normal tissue?"

"That's right—but now the shape is changing even as I try to model it. You mustn't destroy normal tissue."

"Lenardo . . . can you Read the purpose of various parts of the brain?" asked Aradia.

"What do you mean?"

"A head injury may mean death, paralysis, blindness, palsy . . . or no harm at all! I healed a man once who had a spear-point in his head. All I could do was draw it out, stop the bleeding, and prevent infection. In three days he came out of the healing sleep and walked away as if nothing had happened!"

"It had entered the front of his head?" asked Lenardo.

"Yes—fortunately well above his eyes. But how did you know that?"

"We've never been able to Read precisely how the brain works, but over many years of study we have gathered some information, especially the peculiar fact that a very large area of the front does not have a function we can identify. However, your father's tumor is near the back, between the area which controls sight and that which controls muscular coordination. Hence his blindness and convulsions. Now the compressed tissue is moving back into place, blood flowing normally again . . . but I cannot Read what damage the nerve fibers have suffered. I have warned you that even if we save Nerius' life, I cannot predict what mental or physical function he will recover."

"Perhaps we should not try to remove the rest of it," said Wulfston. "If we caused bleeding . . ."

"I know," said Aradia, "but I cannot leave it half done. Lenardo, show us the contours of the growth now."

It had shrunk considerably as they talked, compressed by the brain tissue trying to expand to normal. It could not expand completely, of course, having atrophied. At last the movement seemed to stabilize. Lenardo worked on his model again, and Aradia said, "These are the difficult parts —where the growth is entwined with normal tissue."

"Also, you've been simply cutting off the blood flow as you removed the growth," said Lenardo. "You can't do that indiscriminately—you could cut off a vessel nourishing healthy tissue."

Aradia chewed on her lower lip, studying the model again. "Wulfston—"

"Aradia," the young Adept said, "I haven't that much control. I cannot trust myself to focus on such a small area!"

"Then strengthen me," she said. "I have to do it, Wulfston, or the tumor will grow back again. See that I do not falter."

"Yes, my lady." It was the first time Lenardo had heard Wulfston address Aradia in that fashion.

Aradia now took the wax model in her hands, looking from it to her father, studying carefully. *If only I could Read what she was doing,* Lenardo thought. But he could Read only the effects.

Lenardo watched the cells disappear as Aradia worked her way into one of the tendrils entwined with the healthy tissue, murmuring, "More to the left . . . higher . . . no, you missed some . . . back to the right—left! Slower! There . . . that's it."

He could Read the toll such slow, steady effort took

from Aradia's body, even with Wulfston supporting her—yet each time she speeded up, a few cells of her father's healthy tissue would be destroyed. It seemed to take forever, but they were determined to leave no alien cell to regrow.

Finally there remained one patch of tumor, twined around a pulsing artery. It was the most dangerous and difficult, because it moved with every pulse. By now, Aradia's pale skin was transluscent. Sweat beaded her face, and the pupils of her eyes were dilated. "Rest," said Lenardo. "You've got to be—"

"No." She was breathing in shallow gasps. He saw her force herself to take a deep breath. Wulfston was still as a statue, lost to them. "If I stop now, I'll collapse."

Lenardo explained, "It's the last bit of tumor, and the most recent growth. With the constant motion, I don't know how you can destroy the growth without breaching the artery wall—and that would kill Nerius at once. And you can't just seal off a main artery to the brain."

She pressed the fingers of one hand to her forehead, frowning. "At once," she murmured. Then, "No—it's not immediate. Every Adept has saved lives when people's hearts have stopped. A brief few minutes—but the heart can be restarted."

"Aradia! You're not suggesting—?"

"Stopping his heart will stop the motion. Here—model just that portion left around the artery, as it is between pulses."

"This is madness!"

"It is the only way," she said. "If I leave it, the tumor will regrow right there, choking off the blood and killing him. Do it, Lenardo."

Helpless to oppose her will, he hastily reworked the model—so little of the ink-stained wax left now. Had they performed this operation at Nerius' first symptoms, how easy it would have been! Just this healing technique alone would convince the senate that the empire and the savages could cooperate—and if Aradia could learn to trust one Reader, she could trust others.

There was no time to ponder such things now. Aradia

was doing the same deep-breathing exercise a Reader used before a difficult Reading. So much they had in common.

He handed her the reworked model. She looked from him to Wulfston, who was still deep in concentration. "Wulfston. Wulfston!"

"Yes, my lady?" He didn't look at her.

"I must stop Nerius' heart. When the last of the tumor is removed, you must stop supporting me and support Father. If I fail, you must restart his heart. You can do that—you've done it before."

"Yes, my lady."

Lenardo wasn't sure if Wulfston understood or was answering by rote. Aradia seemed satisfied, though.

He Read in fascinated horror as Aradia first speeded her father's pulse and breathing for a few moments, then quickly dropped them to normal, slowed, and then stopped them. Nerius was dead, although Lenardo could possibly revive him with the techniques he and Galen had used to revive Linus when he was struck by lightning.

But now he had to concentrate on the present, Reading Aradia as cell by cell she destroyed the last of the tumorous growth. Again he guided with words, fearing they were taking too much time, fearing to go too fast, until, "Stop!" he said. "That's it, Aradia. We've got it all."

Her eyes lifted from the model to his—and then fluttered closed as she fainted.

Lenardo caught her and laid her on the bed, panic shooting through his nerves. "Aradia! Nerius' heart!" Instantly, he turned to the old man, trying to pump his heart as he had learned at the academy—but he wasn't breathing either.

"Wulfston! Wulfston—start Nerius' heart!" Lenardo straddled the still form, dealing swift blows to the old Adept's breastbone, feeling the effect dissipated through the softness of the mattress. "Wulfston—start his heart—or help me get him to the floor!" He was futilely willing the heart to start beating again when Wulfston finally came through. The old man's heart fluttered, thumped wildly, and then settled into steady rhythm. Almost at once his chest moved under Lenardo's hands in a deep breath.

Lenardo backed off, Reading his patient, then Aradia—and then Wulfston, who staggered to his side, looking down at them.

"They're not both—?"

"They're alive. Aradia fainted, that's all. Thank the gods you were able to start Nerius' heart again. Here—" he pushed the black man to a seat on the edge of the bed, "put your head down before you faint, too."

Reading Wulfston and Aradia, Lenardo was astonished at their state of debilitation. Once, when he had been at Gaeta for the medical training required of every Reader, a galley slave had been brought in; the man's master had expected him to die and so had dumped him off the ship and bought another. Months of starvation, beatings, and work beyond his strength had brought him to the same state Aradia was in now—and Wulfston was not much better. Lenardo fought down panic as he Read the Adepts —all they had been able to do for the Galley slave was ease his death with opiates.

"Wulfston," said Lenardo, determinedly keeping his voice level, "why are you so weak?"

"Working against nature. Couldn't fight it with Nerius' own strength—actually had to destroy." He struggled up, looking gravely at Aradia.

She stirred. "Father?" weakly—then, in panic, "Father!" as she tried to sit up. "His heart!"

"It's all right," said Lenardo. "Wulfston started his heart again. Nerius will live, Aradia." *But will you?*

"I must . . ." Aradia whispered, "change his state . . . from unconsciousness . . . to healing sleep."

"Not until you've rested yourself," said Lenardo. "If you try to get up now, you'll faint again."

"But—"

"No 'but's.' Nerius is already starting his own natural recovery. If you want to speed the process later, after you've rested, fine. Use the healing sleep on yourself."

She smiled weakly at him. "Thank you, Lenardo." She slept.

Wulfston asked, "How can you not be tired?" His voice was flat with fatigue.

"I was only Reading—you two were doing the work." There was a deep, comfortable chair with a footstool before it, where Nerius' nurse undoubtedly napped away many hours. Lenardo installed Wulfston there and watched him, too, fall into deep sleep.

What a time for Drakonius to attack, he thought. *Both Adepts completely helpless.*

But fortunately Drakonius didn't know that. That night, Lenardo lay down and left his body. It was a dangerous move to attempt to reach Drakonius' stronghold from here, with no Reader to contact there, for this time he would avoid Galen, who could not Read him on this plane unless Lenardo willed it.

Lenardo had a strong foreboding about Drakonius. No clear flashes of precognition had come to him, but he had long since learned to heed this feeling of danger.

So, if the Adepts were out of commission, the Reader ought to be doing something. Traveling without connection to his body, he moved faster and more easily than a few days before. The dark of night was no obstacle to a Reader in full possession of his faculties—how absurd that mere rain had obscured his vision before!

He was even farther away now, and thus in greater danger of dissipating his consciousness if he could not find a focus. By the time he reached Drakonius' stronghold once more, he needed someone as the object of his attention. Anyone would do—he merely let his consciousness be drawn to the first person he encountered, a guard watching the river from atop the cave-riddled cliff. He was an old warrior, alert and prepared. Even while his eyes scanned the river continuously, though, his thoughts were on his off-duty time tomorrow and a certain farmer's wife whose husband did not question where the extra shares of food and occasional jug of ale came from as long as he shared them when he came weary from the fields.

Lenardo left the man to his fantasies, having learned that Drakonius' men were making no battle preparations. He then sought within the stronghold, an encampment with a very temporary flavor. In the long passageways, Drakonius' personal troops slept in bedrolls, a few guards at their posts. Despite the relaxed atmosphere, the guards were guarding, not conversing or napping. Clearly, Drakonius expected his men to maintain discipline.

He found Galen, also asleep, not merely not Reading but with an alert shield guarding his dreams. So . . . the boy was defended against him, for who else could Read him here? Not waking him, he thought for the first time to Read the boy's health, finding him not ill but underweight and on the thin edge of nervous collapse. His nails were chewed ragged, and there was a rash across the backs of his hands that Lenardo had seen before, each time Galen had had to stand for examination. *I thought he had learned to control his nervousness.*

The entrance to the cave in which Galen slept was blocked with a slab of rock. It was not too heavy for one man to push aside, but the "door" had been "locked" by driving an iron ring into the rock on either side and simply running a stout rope over the slab of rock between them. So Galen was not trusted. Lenardo felt a new appreciation of the fact that he could now walk out of his room—out of the castle if he wished—any time he wanted to.

He left Galen, found other small caves with one or two people in them—some not asleep, whose activities he deliberately did not Read.

It was only in the room-to-room search that he found Drakonius, for although the Adept was awake, his mind was unReadable.

At least Lenardo was fairly certain he had found Drakonius. The man was definitely an Adept, awake, and busy. Reading visually, Lenardo saw a broad-shouldered man in his fifties, black hair and beard streaked with white, skin tanned and leathery. His chair was actually a box containing a supply of arrows for his bowmen. Not even a stool to spare—on campaign everything must do double duty.

His table was a case lid set across two other boxes. On it were a candle, ink and quills, and a pile of papers, written over in the savage alphabet that Lenardo could not read. There were four messages . . . no, the same message four times. Lenardo was sure all the papers said the same thing, although Drakonius definitely did not write with the precision of a scribe. He studied it, so he would be able to reproduce it for Aradia.

The Adept called in the man standing guard at his door. "Get the messengers."

Drakonius folded the four papers and sealed them with wax, impressing each with his seal: the dragon's head, the same mark Lenardo bore on his arm. Meanwhile, the guard went to a room where four men were wiling away the time by gaming. They put away their dice at once and came to get the papers. Lenardo carefully noted the names Drakonius told them: Trang, Yolo, Hron, Lilith. The last two he had heard before. Aradia had called them her allies.

Lenardo was up at dawn, Reading as he dressed that the three Adepts in the room above his were all alive and all deeply asleep. He wanted to tell Aradia about Drakonius, but he feared to wake her or Wulfston. How long must they sleep to recover?

When he went down to the kitchen for breakfast, though, the cook stared in surprise. "Ye be up early. My lady left orders for a large meal for three at noon. Were ye not working with my lady and Lord Wulfston all yesterday?"

"They were working," he replied. "I was . . . observing." The cook suspected he was an untrained Adept. How else explain the interest Aradia and Wulfston took in him?

The aroma of baking bread permeated the air, and Lenardo had the pleasure of eating some still warm from the oven, with fresh sweet butter. There were fresh-picked berries this morning with thick cream, and hot cereal.

"Now, lad," said the cook, "I've been feeding my lady and her father before her these many years, and I know a proper diet for . . . those who need to keep strength up. Ye must learn to eat meat, son—'tis the fastest thing to rebuild your blood."

"I haven't lost any blood," Lenardo replied amiably. "This is the best bread I've ever tasted."

"Nay, don't try to turn me aside with compliments. Ye must eat properly, or ye'll never learn . . . what 'tis ye've come here to learn," he ended conspiratorially.

"Why don't we let the Lady Aradia judge that?" Lenardo suggested. "She and Lord Wulfston will certainly do justice to your fine dishes. I'll take the meal up to them at noon, if you don't mind."

Carrying the heavily laden tray up the twisted stairs to the tower room was not easy, and once at the top, Lenardo wondered what he ought to do. Both Aradia and Wulfston were still in deep, motionless sleep, while Nerius . . .

Interesting. The old Adept lay in the same position, on his back, head straight on the pillow . . . but his arms had moved. His hands were clasped, not tightly, just relaxed across his rib cage.

Setting the tray down, Lenardo went to the bed to Read Nerius deeply. He found two areas of the man's body hot with the painless flame of Adept healing: the portion of his brain from which the tumor had been removed, and the area beneath his breastbone, where Lenardo perforce had badly bruised him. He had gone from unconsciousness to healing sleep—by himself? Or had Aradia wakened in the night and done it?

There was still some distortion of Nerius' brain where the tumor had been—permanent damage, Lenardo judged, but nothing like the horrible compression of the growth. Only time would tell the effect of the lingering damage.

Aradia's father already looked better. His skin still had the pallor of someone who had not been out of doors for many months, but there was a hint of healthy color in his cheeks, lips, and fingernails. His face was relaxed but no longer slack; he looked more like a healthy man sleeping than like the dying man he had appeared yesterday.

Aradia still looked exhausted, the dark smudges back under her eyes, but the transparent look was gone. No sooner did Lenardo begin to Read her physical state, though, than she woke with a start, crying out, "Father!"

"He's much better," Lenardo quickly assured her. "Just look at him."

Aradia sat up cautiously and looked at Nerius. "Did you move his hands?"

"No—he's in healing sleep. I've already Read him."

"He did it himself! And he moved!" Pure joy lighted her eyes. "Oh, Lenardo, Father hasn't moved by himself, except for convulsions, since midwinter! He's going to be all right!"

"He's going to live," cautioned Lenardo. "Please . . . don't get your hopes up that he will recover fully. I cannot promise that."

"I don't ask it," she replied, but her elation told him she expected it. "We must let him sleep and recover now. I smell food, and I'm ravenous. Wulfston," she said as she saw the young Adept still sound asleep. "I must wake him."

"Don't get up," said Lenardo. "I'll wake him."

Aradia gave him a puzzled frown. "How did you know how to wake me? Cook had orders to bring our food up. Actually, I thought you'd be asleep too—or rather, I didn't think. I keep forgetting that Reading doesn't weaken you. I should have shown you how to waken an Adept."

"I didn't wake you," he replied. "You woke up on your own just as I started to Read you."

She put the pillow behind her back and leaned against it. "I wonder . . . Try Reading Wulfston and see what happens."

He did, finding the black man closer to recovery of his strength than Aradia but still profoundly asleep. "He'll be all right after some food and more rest."

"But it didn't wake him." She shrugged. "Coincidence. I can never tell when you're Reading me."

"Do you want to?"

"I can't stop you, and you can't Read my thoughts anyway." Turning the subject, she said, "Usually we just let someone sleep out the time he needs to heal, but without nourishment, that will leave him weak as you were for a few days. Wulfston and I cannot afford such weakness, so we must eat. Just touch him on the forehead, between the eyes, very lightly. Try to wake an Adept any other way, and there's no telling what he might do to you if he's startled."

"I'll remember that!" said Lenardo as he went to touch Wulfston.

The young Adept opened his eyes reluctantly. "Oh, Lenardo," he said in annoyance. "What is it?" Then he focused on the room and forced himself awake. "Nerius?"

"He's much better," said Aradia. "He went into healing sleep by himself, Wulfston—unless you did it?"

"No." Wulfston shook his head slowly, as if trying to clear it. "I was sound asleep. The last thing I remember is Lenardo hitting Nerius. Did I dream that?"

"No," said Lenardo. "I was trying to restart his heart. You finally did it, Wulfston."

"I did? I don't remember. I was just trying to stay conscious long enough to be sure Aradia and Nerius were both alive. It's like trying to remember a dream."

"Did you really hit my father?" asked Aradia.

"I'll show you sometime how a non-Adept can pump a heart from outside the body. It sometimes works. I suppose it's possible I restarted Nerius' heart, but it's more likely it was Wulfston."

"Then I have both of you to thank," said Aradia. "Now, let's eat before I fall asleep again."

As soon as they had finished, before the two Adepts could get sleepy again, Lenardo said, "Aradia, I have broken a promise to you."

"What?"

"I entered your private rooms, to write this paper in your study. I think you will agree this is important enough to warrant doing so when I could not ask your permission."

He had spent over an hour copying Drakonius' message from memory.

Aradia read it and handed it to Wulfston. "Where did you get this?"

"Drakonius sent that message out last night to four people: Trang, Yolo, Hron, and Lilith. What does it say?"

"You *know* what it says!" Wulfston exploded angrily. "It's a trick!"

"No," Aradia said quickly. "Lenardo *speaks* our language, but he can't read it. Besides, we'll have confirmation soon enough—Hron and Lilith will come to me for a denial of Drakonius' accusations. Unfortunately, they are partly true."

"Drakonius has found out where I am?" asked Lenardo.

"Or he's guessing," Aradia replied. "He says I am harboring a Reader, planning an attack on him. He further charges that the empire is infiltrating our lands with Readers, who are to ingratiate themselves with the Adepts and then betray them, as Drakonius was betrayed at Adigia."

"Aradia," Lenardo asked, "are you betraying Drakonius?" He recalled the blasted shields in the forum at Zendi. "Did you make an alliance with him and then break it?"

"No," she replied. "The alliances I have made with Lilith and Hron are something new among our people—Adepts swearing loyalty to one another as equals, rather than one person becoming the sworn man of a stronger. Nor am I sworn to Drakonius in the old way, as my father was until Drakonius granted him these lands. I break custom, Lenardo, but I do not break my word."

"Do you believe I have come here to betray you, as Drakonius accuses?"

"No," she replied, looking straight into his eyes. "I believe it was Galen who betrayed your empire. Now you have found him, Lenardo. What are you going to do?"

"If I can, I shall get Galen away before Drakonius kills him."

"Then you admit—?" gasped Wulfston.

"Yes. But I shall go home—if I go home—with far more than I came for. Aradia, the empire thinks all the savages are like Drakonius. But you are not. You took me in when I was helpless, healed me, and showed me the way you live. I got myself exiled by publicly espousing peace with the savages—but I was lying. I didn't think anyone in the savage lands would make peace with us. But you agreed to help me, and you have much to offer the empire. Just the healing power of an Adept and a Reader working together —think of it! That alone is worth a treaty."

Aradia smiled sadly. "You are an idealist, Lenardo. Your government is made up of non-Readers. How will you make them understand?"

"I don't know, but Readers are respected—"

"Readers are feared," said Wulfston. "Lenardo, I'm too

tired to argue, and Aradia must rest too. What are we going to do with you?"

"I have no intention of breaking my promise. I said I'd aid you against Drakonius, and if my Reading can do you any more benefit, I will use it so."

"You have already foiled Drakonius," said Aradia. "He knows that I never leave my father for more than a day at a time. Now I am free to move if he threatens. And if it takes long enough for him to gather other Adepts and their armies, he may be shocked to find he has the strength of Nerius to contend with once more."

"We don't know—"

"We *do* know. My father's Adept powers were never impaired. If his mind is clear, no matter what physical problems linger, he will be able to use his strength against Drakonius. Even if he remains blind . . . he is alive and can be guided," Aradia said firmly. "Lenardo, I must go down to my room now, and Wulfston should rest in his own bed. Will you please go downstairs and send Pepyi to me, and ask Yula to come and keep watch over Father?"

"Yes, my lady."

She smiled. "That form of address is not necessary in private—in fact, it is inappropriate until you are willing truly to accept me as your lady."

Lenardo spent the rest of the day Reading the castle while he let everyone assume he was asleep, as Aradia and Wulfston were. Life did not stop in Aradia's absence. The carpenter was putting the finishing touches on Rren's new house. The blacksmith was working in the courtyard—but in the middle of the afternoon he put away the farm implements he had been repairing and had the stable boy bring the horses out one by one, changing any worn or imperfect shoe.

Meanwhile, two other men began to inspect the tackle, while a man and a woman started checking gear in the guard room. Soon a fletcher set up shop in the courtyard. By evening, men were bringing wagons of vegetables and carcasses of deer, sheep, and swine. The cook added two men and another woman to his staff and fired up another fireplace, even larger than the one that was always kept going with a roast on the spit.

Preparations for war. The first troops arrived near midnight, collecting their arms from the guard room, being fed even at that hour, and setting up camp on the grassy slope behind the castle.

When Lenardo woke at dawn, there were over a hundred men in the camp, now armed and going through drills. He found breakfast laid out in the great hall, everyone helping himself as Aradia's staff hovered to replace each empty dish with a full, fresh one. Lenardo encountered Helmuth, herding a group of young men into the hall, telling them, "No more than half an hour, and then I want you all back at the east end of the field. And if we have to drill all day, you're going to work as a *unit!*"

He turned to Lenardo, grumbling happily, "These youngsters today—don't see the point in practice or precision. They all want to be heroes."

"It's hard to work together, once battle is joined," observed Lenardo, noticing that Helmuth was standing straight and looking considerably younger as he strove to be a model soldier for his troops.

"You're an experienced soldier, are you?" he asked Lenardo.

"I've fought my share of . . . battles."

Helmuth laughed and slapped him on the back. "Fought your share of savages, you almost said. Well, now you're a savage yourself, lad, and if you survived those other battles, we'll be glad to have you on our side."

"You trust me?" Lenardo asked in surprise.

"Aradia trusts you," said Helmuth. "I need no more than that."

Aradia herself soon appeared, Wulfston at her side, and called for all troop leaders to join her. Helmuth went off with them to another room. Lenardo did not Read their conference but went back to his room, where he could Read without trying to carry on a conversation at the same time. At the west end of the field, archers were practicing —but never had he seen such consistent accuracy! During the flight of the arrow from release to target, the bowmen became unReadable, yet they were not Adepts. It was just that one skill, to direct the arrow. Apparently it was required of Aradia's bowmen . . . and women, he noted.

Just before sundown, what appeared to be an entire army came marching along the road from the north. When they came into the courtyard, Lenardo went to the window and looked down at them. Heralds blew a tribute on trumpets hung with the sign of the blue lion. A woman rode in, surrounded by men in blue livery. Aradia came out to greet her as she dismounted, the two women bowing to one another. Then they went inside.

This must be Lilith, one of the Adepts Aradia called her allies. Burning with curiosity, Lenardo forced himself not to Read the women, although not long afterward he heard them come up the stairs and go into Aradia's chambers.

A few minutes later, Pepyi knocked at his door. "If you please, my lady asks that you attend her."

The two women were alone in Aradia's anteroom. As Lenardo entered, Aradia said, "And this, Lilith, is Lenardo, the reason my preparations for battle are so far advanced."

The other Adept looked him over, and he had the strange feeling she could tell as much about him as if she had Read him. If Aradia was like the wolf she chose as her symbol—cunning, dangerous, sometimes deceptively playful—Lilith was indeed the regal lion. Her skin was golden, her eyes a golden brown, looking out at him from under a noble brow. She was slightly taller than Aradia, and a headdress of blue veiling gave her additional height, hiding her hair except for a dark widow's peak that accentuated the smooth planes of her face. While Aradia's face was mobile and expressive, Lilith's was aloof, secretive.

"So," said Lilith in a dangerous voice, "this is your mysterious exile."

"Hron told you?"

"Yes. He said his people returned a man of this description to you—one who bore the mark of an Aventine exile." The loose sleeve of Lenardo's shirt moved of its own accord, to reveal the brand on his arm. Annoyed, he tugged the sleeve back into place and had the satisfaction of seeing Lilith blink. She had been working against gravity to lift it in the first place; they both knew it was not worth the waste of strength to work against Lenardo's muscle as well.

Watching Lilith's expression, Aradia said, "Lenardo does not take well to being treated as a possession. On equal terms, however, he is of immense value."

"Equal terms? How can you trust him, Aradia?"

"You have just confirmed my trust in him," she replied. "Lenardo, the Lady Lilith has brought me this." She handed him Drakonius' message—one of the originals, bearing the now broken dragon seal. "And, Lilith, yesterday Lenardo gave me this." Lenardo's version. "I received Drakonius' message before you did."

"He must have known I would bring it to you."

"Hron did not," Aradia pointed out.

"My watchers report troops massing at Hron's castle," said Lilith.

"As do mine," agreed Aradia, "but he has made no move in this direction."

Lilith paced to the door. "Hron has always had doubts about our alliance—he fears Drakonius' retaliation and does not wish to believe Drakonius will turn on us if he succeeds in taking the empire."

"The fool! Does he think Drakonius will trust him now?"

"Oh, come, Aradia," said Lilith, "we all know Hron is loyal as long as he thinks he's on the stronger side! You sought his alliance too soon. You expect everyone to act on reason and honor."

"Hron is a Lord Adept—he has his people to think of."

"Drakonius gave him his lands," Lilith replied. "He did not give you yours," she added significantly.

Aradia drew herself up to her full height. "If you are suggesting that Drakonius gives power only to those he can manipulate, I might remind you that he gave these lands to my father."

"I'm sorry," said Lilith. "I did not mean that Nerius could be intimidated—in fact, I believe Drakonius gave him his own lands because he feared that Nerius had the power to take them." She paused. "Your father still lives?" she asked gently.

"Yes," replied Aradia. "But let us not discuss Father now. I have brought Lenardo here to demonstrate the use he can be to us."

Lilith looked again at the paper in her hands. "Indeed— most useful. Lenardo, how did you intercept this message?"

"I was Reading Drakonius when he wrote it."

"Reading Drakonius? But his stronghold is two days' hard ride from here! Can you Read that far?"

"Not right now, standing here and telling you about it. I must . . . seek a trance state," he equivocated. "I could not communicate with you at the same time. Normally, I would have another Reader to relay my message to you."

"His powers decrease with distance, as ours do," said Aradia.

"Can you Read Drakonius' Reader?" asked Lilith.

"Yes, I can, unless he shields his thoughts from me."

"And will he know you are Reading him?"

"Yes. However, that is not how Drakonius found out about me."

Her eyes snapped to his. "Are you Reading me?"

"No, Lady," Lenardo replied.

At the same time, Aradia laughed. "Give Lenardo credit for following a train of thought as easily as you or I. He cannot Read an Adept."

"Ah," said Lilith, "but you would Read me if you could?"

"You are the Lady Aradia's guest," Lenardo replied. "I would not attempt to Read you unless she requested it."

"Yes," murmured Lilith, "I am Aradia's guest. What are you to her, Lenardo?"

"We have . . . an agreement," he replied. "If you understood the Reader's Code, you would not fear my betrayal."

"Lilith," said Aradia, "I hope before we leave here to show you that an Adept and a Reader can work together for a common good. But for now . . . Lenardo, will you please Read Drakonius' stronghold again and tell me whether he is ready to move out?"

"Yes, my lady."

He bowed and left the room, half hearing Lilith's question to Aradia, "*Are* you his lady?" Deliberately, he did not Read them, and so did not hear the answer.

Drakonius, Lenardo found, was not yet ready to move. In his stronghold Lenardo could locate only one other Adept, a young woman—twenty at most, he judged. As he had learned that Adepts, like Readers, did not come into their full powers until midlife, this could not be one of Drakonius' powerful allies. An apprentice, perhaps—he could have overlooked her on the other Readings. It was only too easy for a Reader to miss an Adept amid the clutter of other thoughts. Avoiding Galen, he Read room by room through the entire stronghold.

When he reported his findings to Aradia, she asked, "Was Drakonius making preparations to feed and shelter an army?"

"No—in fact, even using the beach as part of the camp, he doesn't have room for as many men as you have already gathered."

"Then he plans to meet them elsewhere," said Aradia. "If only I could have a Reader there in his ranks, to inform you if anything happened . . ." She sighed. "Have you Read my father today?"

"This afternoon. No change. I will check again before I sleep."

"Thank you, Lenardo." She reached for his hand, and he forced himself not to withdraw as a Reader normally would. He was getting used to the way the savages touched each other constantly, meaning nothing by it.

But Aradia's hand was warm on his, and he felt a pleasant tension between them. *The wrong time*, he thought, and then was surprised at the thought—no time was the right time for a Master Reader. Something in Aradia's eyes held him, a puzzled longing . . .

He mentally shook himself. *I'm flattering myself. I can't*

Read her, and so I imagine she desires . . . No. Aradia had made no overt advances since the day of the infamous bath. Now she was simply grateful for his help. As if to confirm his interpretation, she merely squeezed his hand, saying, "You won't regret helping me, Lenardo. I promise —you won't regret it."

In the morning, Lenardo found things much the same with Drakonius. The camp was designed to move at a moment's notice; he could detect no sign that notice had been given. He decided to Read Nerius before he went down to breakfast.

In the room above his, the woman Yula was sleeping soundly in the comfortable armchair. But Nerius—

Lenardo ran down the staircase to the great hall. Reading for Aradia, he finally found her inspecting a new contingent of troops at the lower end of the back field.

He was breathless by the time he reached her side. "Aradia—my lady—it's Nerius. He's sleeping." At her puzzled look, he added, "He's *just* sleeping."

Her eyes widened. "Karl, take over here! Where's Wulfston?"

"At breakfast," said Lenardo as they ran back toward the castle. The back door was propped open now, the path between field and castle already well worn.

"Wulfston, come with us, please," called Aradia as they hurried through the great hall and up the stairs. The young Adept left his place without question and followed them to Nerius' room.

Aradia was first in and went directly to the bedside. Lenardo heard her gasp "Oh," halfway between a laugh and a sob. Nerius was curled up on his side, in a perfectly normal sleeping position, snoring softly.

Aradia extended a trembling hand toward his face, then stopped, turning to Lenardo and Wulfston. "Whatever happens," she said softly, "whether he sees, whether he knows us . . . it makes no difference in my gratitude to both of you." Then she reached up to Lenardo's shoulders. He almost ducked away as her hands touched his neck, but then he realized what she was doing as she found the chain of the wolf's-head pendant and pulled the amulet out to hang on his breast, as Wulfston wore his. "Now, if Father can see you, he will know at once that you belong here."

Lenardo stepped back then, letting Aradia and Wulfston stand before Nerius as Aradia reached out to touch her father's forehead, just between the eyes. He turned away from the touch, onto his back, stretching and frowning as he came awake.

His eyes opened—the same violet color as Aradia's—but they were blank. Only for an instant, though. He winced, as if the morning light were painful, and when he reopened them he focused on his daughter. "Aradia," he whispered.

"Oh, Father!" she cried, hugging him. "You can see me! You know me!"

"Yes, child, but—" As she let go of him he tried to sit up and fell back weakly on the pillow. "What has happened?" he asked plaintively. "I can't remember. I was blind, and then—"

"It doesn't matter!" Aradia said quickly. "You've been very ill, but you're well now. You've had a long, hard healing, Father. You must rest."

"My dear child," he murmured with a smile, then looked at Wulfston. "My boy . . . but you're not a boy any more, Wulfston. You're a full bearded man. Aradia, how long—?" Lenardo could Read his fear, even though his thoughts remained shielded.

"You're alive, my lord," said Wulfston, his voice choked with tears.

"That's all that matters," Aradia reassured him. "You'll remember, and what you don't we'll tell you, Father. Don't waste your strength now. You must eat and sleep some more. Yula. Yula!"

Lenardo stepped aside as the nurse woke with a start, wide-eyed with astonishment to see Nerius awake. "It's a secret, Yula," said Aradia. "I don't want anyone bothering Father until he gets his strength back."

"Yes, m'lady."

"Now run downstairs and bring up some soup. Hurry!"

"Oh, my lord! I can't believe it!" Then she glanced at Aradia, muttered, "Yes, m'lady, I'll be right up," and scurried out as Aradia called after her, "Tell no one!"

"Daughter . . ." Nerius tugged at Aradia's hand. "What has happened?"

"We'll tell you everything, my lord," Wulfston answered for her. "You'll be up in a day or two." Tears rolled down his cheeks, unnoticed.

But Nerius noticed, looking from Wulfston to Aradia. "I remember this," he said. "No one could heal my blindness —not I, not you and Lilith working together. And I remember pain, and gaps in time. How did you heal me, daughter?"

"I found someone . . . someone sent to us, Father. No Adept could heal you alone . . . but with Lenardo's help—"

Lenardo stepped forward. Nerius' eyes widened. "You!" he gasped. "How dare you wear my sign?"

Aradia said, "Father, this is Lenardo. He—"

"I know this—traitor! You would steal my daughter's powers!"

"No, Father!" cried Aradia. "Lenardo healed you. Don't you understand? You would have *died*, Father. Lenardo saved your life!"

But if Nerius heard, he was not listening. Weak as he was, he managed to prop himself up on one elbow and point at Lenardo. "You are the foul beast of my dreams, who would ravish my daughter. Did you think I would trust you because you have stolen my symbol?"

The wolf's-head pendant jerked, and moved toward Nerius' outstretched hand, the chain cutting Lenardo's neck. As he reached to lift it away, he was paralyzed, helpless as pain drove into him until the chain broke and the pendant flew into Nerius' hand. Released, Lenardo staggered, but remained standing as Nerius gripped the pendant, falling back on the bed.

"Thief!" he growled. "You'll not steal my powers, nor my daughter's. Throw him in the dungeon!"

"Father, you don't understand," Aradia pleaded. "You're alive only because Lenardo—"

"I said take him from my sight. To the dungeon!"

"Lenardo, you'd better go," Aradia said softly.

But the moment he turned, Nerius cried, "Stop! Whom do you obey, daughter? Who is lord in this castle?"

"You are, Father," she whispered.

"And I will have this evil creature in the dungeon. Take him, Wulfston—or have you, too, forgotten who is your master?"

"No, my lord," the young Adept mumbled, but his face was contorted with pain. "Come on, Lenardo," he managed, and started out of the room, remembering to push the Reader in front of him only when they reached the door.

Chapter Seven

Attack of the Dragon

Halfway down the winding stairs, Wulfston stumbled, blinded by tears. Lenardo took his arm and guided him the rest of the way, then took him into his room, knowing they could not negotiate the crowds below until the young Adept got control of himself.

"He's mad," Wulfston said. "We thought he might be blind or crippled, but never that his mind . . . What can we do?"

"I don't know, but if anyone can help Nerius, it's Aradia."

Wulfston gathered control of himself. "I suppose you're right. Here—you're bleeding." Almost casually, he placed a hand on Lenardo's neck where the chain had cut him. There was a fleeting instant of healing fire, and the pain evaporated.

Then the young Adept sat down heavily on the stool by the table. "Now what?"

"I think," said Lenardo, "you'd better take me to the dungeon."

"But—"

"Nerius is more likely to listen to reason if his orders are carried out."

Wulfston fingered his pendant. "You're right. I must obey my liege lord. But at least we'll make you as comfortable as possible—you might be there for a day or two. Take your pillows and blankets." He picked up a candlestick and one of the stools and led the way.

The dungeons were underground, chill even on this warm day, and faintly damp. They were also empty. Wulfston tried several cells until he found one that was dry and lit by a tiny barred window at the top of the wall. A narrow wooden bed frame hung from the wall, rusted iron shackles dangling above it. "The best of a poor lot," said Wulfston, setting down his burdens. "We certainly won't be needing these!" he added, grasping the shackles and concentrating for a moment, then giving a tug. The bolts came out of the wall as if it were unfired clay.

Lenardo studied the holes in the wall. "You couldn't keep an Adept in here."

"No—only a stronger Adept can hold one, or sometimes two or three of lesser power working together. Think of everything you might need while I go get us some food." He left, closing the cell door.

"Wulfston," Lenardo called after him, "you forgot to lock the door."

"I don't know where the key is."

"You don't need a key—you're an Adept."

Wulfston's face appeared at the grill in the heavy door. "Nerius told me to put you in the dungeon. He didn't tell me to lock it. In the next few days almost everyone will be moving out of here. If you're not with us, I won't have you left here helpless. And unless Nerius regains his faculties, we have no hope against Drakonius without your help. If he does return to normal, then he'll understand what you've done for him and let you out. Either way, you're not going to stay in the dungeon for long."

"And if Nerius regains his strength but remains convinced that I am dangerous to him?"

"I don't know. You're the Reader—you tell me what's on his mind."

At that moment Aradia arrived; it was she who provided a tentative explanation. "I'm glad to find you really came down here," she told the two men. "Father is used to implicit obedience . . . and I'm afraid I've gotten used to it these past few years. I must remember that Nerius is my father and liege lord. While he lives, he rules."

"What if—" Wulfston began.

"He'll be all right," she said firmly. "I know what's wrong—starvation. Wulfston, you remember when we released those people from Verrik's dungeon, years ago? He was starving his prisoners to death," she added to Lenardo. "Those who survived were all mad with hunger, hallucinating, just as Father did today."

"But we cared for Nerius—" Wulfston protested.

"What food have we been able to get into him? Nothing but a bit of gruel now and then. The healing sleep must have used up the last of his reserves, but he's just eaten a bowl of good rich soup and is asleep again. We must wake him and make him eat every two or three hours. He can't take much at a time."

"Do you really think it will help?" asked Wulfston.

"It has to," she replied. "Lenardo—I'm sorry. Father is very confused about you. He's afraid you're going to hurt *me* somehow. You know how dreams often cobble together unrelated things from our waking life? Somehow, I think he's got his fear of leaving me unprotected confused with a tangible threat—and when he found a stranger in his room he simply identified you with that threat." She sighed. "I was wrong to have you wear the wolf-stone openly. Of course Father knew it should not be worn by someone he does not know."

"I have no right to wear it anyway," said Lenardo.

"I think you will earn that right," Aradia told him quietly.

Lenardo was left alone for most of the day, although it was easy enough to keep track of comings and goings about the castle. While Aradia's troops continued to gather and practice war games, Lenardo Read northward and found another army on the march—toward the west. When Wulfston brought him his evening meal, he gave him the information.

Wulfston nodded. "Hron. We were afraid of that. He'll have to go out of his way to avoid crossing Aradia's lands, but he could still be at Drakonius' stronghold in a five-day march. From what you've said, Drakonius will probably move out to meet him, so we have less time than that. Aradia won't want to leave Nerius."

"He's not going to die now, Wulfston. Or harm anyone."

He rubbed the back of his neck, where the cuts from the chain had healed over so he could barely feel them. "He didn't even do me any serious damage when he was afraid I might hurt Aradia."

"Have you Read him today?"

"Yes—he was sleeping again. His body is functioning normally, as far as I can tell. What I can't tell is how his mind is functioning, or the balance of elements in his blood. I just hope Aradia's diagnosis is correct—then he'll be himself soon."

At noon the next day, Aradia came to get Lenardo. "My father has agreed to speak with you. He is deeply concerned that I made a pact with a Reader, yet grateful that you saved his life."

"He no longer thinks I came here to harm you?"

"Let him tell you."

Nerius was sitting up in the armchair, a loose robe covering the thinness of his limbs. His hands, pared to skin and bone, showed the ravages of his long illness, but he was clearly a man on the way to recovery. The querulousness and petulance of his wakening mood were gone. He looked Lenardo over calmly and said, "Please sit down, Master Lenardo. If you will permit, let us begin our acquaintance from this moment."

Lenardo sat, taking the time to choose his words carefully. "I agree, Lord Nerius—but why do you address me as Master?"

"Only a Master Reader could be Reading Drakonius at such a distance and reporting his activities . . . unless, of course, you are lying."

"I am not lying."

"Perhaps withholding the truth. It is difficult for an honest man to play a false role. From what my daughter tells me, you have no reason to harm us. Indeed, I owe you my life. That fact is indisputable. And yet, when I look at you again in the full light of day, it is indisputably your face I saw in my dreams. I could not see you—I was blind—and yet you appeared to me as a danger to myself and a deliberate threat to my daughter. What do you make of that, Master Reader?"

Two pairs of violet eyes were fixed on Lenardo, Aradia's wide and wondering, Nerius' calm and demanding. All he could do was speak the truth. "Were you yourself a Master Reader, and given to precognitive dreams, I should say that you were right. As you are not a Reader, and as I know that I mean no harm to you or your daughter, I must say that I cannot explain how you could have seen my face. With all due respect, possibly the nightmares caused by your illness showed you a faceless danger . . . and when you first saw me, an intruder in your domain, you grafted my appearance onto your dreams."

The old Adept studied Lenardo dispassionately. "I owe you too much not to give you the benefit of the doubt," he said at last. "Further, my daughter trusts you, and I trust her judgment. Wulfston has argued on your behalf, and I must remember that he is no longer of an age to be swayed by a boy's enthusiasm for an exotic person with unusual powers." He smiled. "Has Wulfston told you how that enthusiasm brought him here, almost at the cost of both our lives?"

"Father, he was only a baby!" Aradia protested.

Nerius looked toward his daughter. "Yes, and now he is a grown man and has become your protector in my absence. I almost dread to see what else has changed while I was ill."

He turned back to Lenardo. "My daughter has made an agreement with you. My life for your freedom."

"That is correct," said Lenardo. "However, I agreed also to aid Ar—the Lady Aradia with my abilities." He hoped that the flash of annoyance he caught from Nerius was no more than a father's overprotectiveness. "I intend to fulfill that agreement," he continued. "Your needs and mine coincide."

"Indeed?"

"Perhaps the Lady Aradia has told you that I am here in search of Galen, a Reader, a boy I myself trained. I regret that my teaching was not entirely successful. Galen was unable to accept the empire's refusal to attempt to make peace with her . . . attackers. For publicly opposing government policy, he was exiled.

"Two years passed. When Galen was detected aiding the enemy, I volunteered to come for him, to get him out of the enemy's hands. In order to move safely here, I had to be an exile. So . . . I agreed with Galen, saying things I did not then believe."

"And now?" Nerius prompted.

Lenardo glanced at Aradia, and then back to her father. "The irony is that since my exile, I have come to Galen's point of view. You see, the empire knows nothing of you, your daughter, the Lady Lilith—Adepts who would be willing to make an honest peace. All they know is Drakonius . . . and you must admit that it would be impossible to make a treaty between Drakonius and the Aventine Empire."

"Not so long as Drakonius thinks he can conquer you," Nerius agreed.

"But other Adepts are now opposing Drakonius. If you had the Empire, the army, its Readers, aligned with you— if Drakonius has the intelligence with which the Lady Aradia credits him, he would not dare attack. There could be peace, and if there were peace between your people and mine, think what progress could be made with Readers and Adepts working together!"

"I, of all people, cannot argue with that," said Nerius. "How do you propose to bring this peace about?"

"First, I must remove Galen from Drakonius' influence. He appears to have adopted Drakonius' philosophy of violence. Then, when I return to tell what I have learned here, I will go to the senate and present my case. If I can take with me a statement of your willingness to negotiate . . ."

"Master Lenardo, you are a— No, you are my guest and my ally; I will not call you a fool. You are an idealist who has seen little of the world outside the walls of your academies. Don't you know what will happen if you appear at the gates one day, with or without Galen?"

"I must contact the Readers who sent me. Otherwise, as an exile, I would be driven away or killed if I tried to re-enter."

"Yes. You would be allowed to re-enter. They don't

want you out here, aiding the enemy. Let us suppose, for the sake of argument, that they would not execute you or throw you in prison, but simply return you to one of the academies."

"Of course I will eventually return to the academy," Lenardo said.

Nerius studied him. "It may be too late for you, raised against nature like a bird taken from its nest by children, that returns to its cage rather than flying free—"

"Lord Nerius—" Lenardo began in annoyance.

"No, let me explain. I grow tired, but I want you to think about this before we meet again. The reason the Aventine Empire cannot hold strong against our people is that those people who have the real power in your society are taught from childhood not to use it. Readers are barred from your government, locked up in academies, made the servants of the ungifted. Lenardo, you ought to rule! By nature, you have abilities that place you above other men —yet you do not exercise them to that purpose."

"Power corrupts—"

"Of course it does!" said Nerius. "Just look at Drakonius. But he has misused his power. His people hate and fear him, and if another conquers his lands and is a gentle and generous master, they will forget Drakonius and become loyal unto death to their new lord."

"You?"

The old man nodded. "You see no dissent in my lands, and my daughter will rule after me in the same fashion. Power can be for good or evil, Master Lenardo—and while one cannot do great evil without power, neither can one do great good."

"Then what are you advising me to do, Lord Nerius? Go back and try to take over the Aventine government— become emperor?"

Nerius laughed. "The people of Aventine would be better off if you did. And if you set your mind to it, you would have a better chance of becoming emperor than of persuading the senate to treat with me and my allies. But I don't think you have any desire to foment civil war."

"Nor to be emperor," Lenardo agreed.

"Then let me tell you how to get the Aventine senate to listen to you."

"I am a Master Reader—"

"All the more reason for them to fear you and therefore suppress you. You cannot negotiate from a position of weakness, and in the Aventine Empire society is structured so that Readers, without property, without money, without the right to hold office, are in the weakest position of all."

"What would you have me do? Threaten the senate? Suggest that the Readers could make public all their secret actions?" Lenardo said distastefully.

"I see you are well aware of your power," said Nerius, "even though you do not exercise it. No—I know as well as you that you cannot do such a thing, and if one Reader could, other Readers could not. I am aware of the Reader's Code. I respect it. One day, I hope there will be such a code binding upon all Adepts."

"Then what is your advice, Lord Nerius?"

"Do not return to the empire as a Reader, an Aventine citizen petitioning the senate's favor to grant a hearing. Stay here. Become my sworn man. Then approach the Aventine senate from a position of strength, demanding a hearing for the representative of a Lord Adept. Enter the empire surrounded by my guards, with an Adept or two. Demonstrate what a Reader and an Adept can do together . . . and offer peace."

"Change my loyalty?"

"You are an exile. The empire has disowned you. Consider my proposal. I am not asking that you swear loyalty to me today—you cannot yet know me well enough for that."

"Nor do you know me," added Lenardo.

"I know that I owe you my life. I also know that you could make a formidable enemy—and I would rather have you as a friend. Go now, and consider it. I must rest. Oh—one thing more: ask Wulfston how he came to be my apprentice. Learn something of the way the people of the empire react toward someone with power they have not themselves."

Lenardo was grateful to be back in his own room, to come and go at will—and especially to bathe and put on fresh clothes. Then he took a walk in the sunshine and fresh air. There were even more troops camped on the slope beneath Aradia's castle—were the Adepts responsible for keeping the weather so pleasant? Wagonloads of food were arriving from far-flung areas of Aradia's—no, Nerius' —lands, some escorted by men in Lilith's blue livery.

Feeling a need to take his mind off Nerius' proposal, Lenardo joined a group of swordsmen doing practice exercises. As he had lost his own sword, he wanted practice with the heavier type the savages used. Working himself breathless felt good, but after a rest they broke up into pairs to practice fighting. Lenardo defeated two opponents, then bowed out lest his apparent skill give away his Reading ability.

There were spectators, but Lenardo paid them little heed until he put his sword back in the rack and turned to find Helmuth approaching. "I see you are indeed an experienced soldier," the old man said. "Has the Lady Aradia assigned you a place in her army?"

"Not yet," he replied.

"I've got mostly raw lads from the village here, who've never seen a real battle. I could use your skill, if Lady Aradia is willing."

"I would be honored to fight at your side, Helmuth," Lenardo replied, "but I think the Lady Aradia has other plans for me."

Helmuth glanced around and drew close to Lenardo, speaking in a low voice. "Is it true, then, that you're an Adept, exiled from the empire when they discovered your powers? Everyone is saying that's why my lady and Lord Wulfston spend so much time with you."

"Is that what you think, Helmuth?"

"I have my own suspicions," the old man said, "and if I'm right, you know what they are."

Indeed, Helmuth did suspect Lenardo was a Reader. "There are . . . things I cannot speak of at this time," Lenardo said. "The reason for my presence is for the Lady Aradia to reveal, not for me."

"Very well," said Helmuth. "I trust her, as does everyone here. But anyone who betrays her trust . . ."

"I have no intention of doing so," said Lenardo, wondering if anyone else had the same suspicion. The rumor that he was an Adept he encountered everywhere; the rumor that he was a Reader might start a panic. But he Read that Helmuth had shared his suspicions with no one, and would not.

"Just take care, lad," said Helmuth, "that your actions live up to your intentions."

As Lenardo's intentions were to aid Aradia in the coming struggle against Drakonius, he went back to his room and Read the enemy stronghold again. Frustratingly, he came in on the very end of a meeting between Drakonius and Galen.

"You prove yourself to me this time," the Adept was saying as he got up to leave Galen's room, "and you'll have your freedom. Betray me again, and this time I'll kill you . . . and not pleasantly."

Galen was shielded against anyone Reading his thoughts, but Lenardo clearly Read the pain that suddenly lanced through the boy's right hand. Muscles convulsed, tendons and ligaments drawing Galen's fingers back grotesquely, while he screamed in agony. There was a snap, and then another, as bones broke—and then the hand went limp.

Galen fell to his knees, sobbing as he held his injured hand against his chest. Drakonius put a hand under his chin and raised his face up to look into his eyes. "You remember this lesson," he said. "If you betray me again, I won't do that to just one hand. I'll do it to your whole body, break every bone, and then I'll throw you into the forum in Zendi to die, where everyone can see what happens to the enemies of Drakonius."

"I did not betray you, my lord," Galen gasped through his tears. "I shall never betray you. You are my liege lord."

"As long as you remember that . . . Here." He took Galen's hand, and Lenardo felt the familiar healing heat flow through it as the bones began to knit. The pain disappeared. "Go to sleep now, boy—we'll have need of your skills soon enough."

For what? Lenardo longed to know, but he dared not try to contact Galen at that moment. So he followed Drakonius, who went down to the river's edge, walked out onto one of the fortifications, took hook and line from his pocket, captured a passing dragonfly, and proceeded to go fishing!

This was a general preparing for battle? It made no sense at all, as Lenardo told Wulfston when the two men, unable to converse in the hubbub of the great hall, took their evening meal up to Wulfston's room, where they could talk while they ate.

"He's waiting for something," said Wulfston, "or some-*one*. Our watchers report Hron's movements, and Yolo's, but not Trang's. On the other hand, Drakonius is far from stupid. If his Reader has told him that you Read his stronghold once, he's expecting you to do it again. Perhaps he wants you to find him fishing."

"I don't think he would have wanted me to find him torturing Galen," said Lenardo, and he told Wulfston of the scene.

"That is typical of Drakonius," said Wulfston. "We've told you he rules by fear. When he takes a new territory, he'll publicly torture a few influential people, then heal them and keep their loyalty through threats of further pain."

Lenardo's appetite had disappeared. Wulfston noticed his reaction and said, "No one here—not Nerius, not Aradia, not I—would harm somebody simply as an example."

"But as a punishment?"

"One might as well not have power if one is unwilling to use it. There is no need for gratuitous torture, but people must know that punishment will be swift and unpleasant, or some will not obey. It is always best to demonstrate justice early with light punishments—exactly the way one teaches a child."

To lighten the tone of the conversation, Lenardo said, "I suppose Adept children can get into a great deal of mischief."

Wulfston laughed. "Oh, indeed! I remember when Aradia and I decided we'd rather drink wine than milk, so we soured all the milk in the dairy for two days—and on the third day Nerius made us drink it anyway. And of course children can't resist spooking horses—or making them refuse to move. It's a wonder anyone was willing to live around here, with *two* Adept children playing pranks."

"But you never did anything really dangerous?"

"Oh, yes. The one time I remember Nerius actually paddling us with his own hand—when anything at a distance was unsatisfactory—was the time we set fire to the woods just west of here. We almost burned up with them."

Remembering what Nerius had told him, Lenardo asked, "How did Nerius come to take you in, Wulfston?"

"I was very young when he saw signs in me, which is why he knew I would be a Lord Adept. People who have merely one ability develop the talent at eight or ten."

"What happened to your own family? They were not Adepts?"

"No—although it seems my mother had one talent." He went to the mantel and picked up a bowl from the collection of pottery that lined it. Handing it to Lenardo, he said, "My mother made that."

"But it's Aventine."

Wulfston smiled sardonically. "I was born a citizen of your empire—a free citizen, although my parents had been slaves. They earned their freedom and citizenship, and moved from Tiberium to a small village near the border, where they made pottery. It wasn't easy for a black family outside the capital, but their work was the highest quality, and they made their way. My sister was born first, and I was born a few years later. I can't remember much except being happy there. I was only three when—"

"You began showing Adept powers," Lenardo marveled.

"Yes. At first it was great fun. I didn't know what I was doing, but I could make the birds and squirrels and rabbits come to me. The other children loved that—and no one associated it with Adept powers, which they always thought of as destructive. In fact, I think people thought it was an early sign of Reading."

The young Adept pointed to the design of fine lines in the bowl Lenardo held. "No one recognized that as an Adept skill either."

"I wouldn't," said Lenardo. "It's beautiful, the work of an artist—but why Adept?"

"Because it's all done freehand. My mother would just take a stylus and inscribe the design—but it has a precision an ordinary human hand cannot match. Nerius recognized it, but of course he didn't say anything."

"Nerius?"

"Our village was near the border, but not on one of the main roads. When Nerius wanted to come into the empire—"

"What! An Adept going in and out of the empire?" Lenardo was stunned.

Wulfston laughed at his dismay. "Lenardo, there is nothing to keep an Adept out of the Aventine Empire! If I want to go in, I can climb a wall in a deserted area, or enter through one of the gates, making the guards open it for me and then forget I'd ever been there—"

"By the gods," whispered Lenardo. "You could have been among us—"

"Yes. The only danger is the chance of encountering a Reader."

And he might not notice you, Lenardo realized, recalling how hard it was to find the Adepts in Drakonius' stronghold. "And even if you were recognized," he murmured, "no prison could hold you."

"However, we don't want the Aventines to know we walk among them."

"Then you should not have told me, Wulfston."

The black man studied Lenardo. "You won't go back," he said. "Certainly not back to your old way of life. You don't know how much you've changed in the time you've been here. If you go back at all, it will be as Nerius' representative."

"Do you still think you can force me to think your way?"

"No, and I never thought so. But you are an intelligent man. You already know that an honorable peace is the only chance for the empire to survive. What you have yet to accept is that Nerius is right about how to obtain that peace."

"You still have not told me how you came to be Nerius' apprentice, Wulfston. What did he do—steal you away from your family?"

"Not exactly. He saw the Adept skill in my mother's work, and so he watched her children. He knew the danger if either of us showed Adept powers—unless, of course, they were similar to our mother's. My parents, like all new citizens, were fiercely loyal to the empire. Nerius dared not reveal his identity prematurely. He could not come to our village often, either—perhaps once in three or four months, each time stopping with us on the pretext of buying pottery. He would play with my sister and me. I know now that his games tested our powers.

"In those days, Nerius wore the wolf-stone—the same one I wear now. I was fascinated by it, and even though I was only three I can remember very clearly that one terrible day. It was Nerius' first visit since I had learned I could call the animals. When he arrived, I wanted to show him my new game. My parents' wares were on display on a stand in front of our house. When Nerius rode up, I ran to him, all excited—but there were other customers, a man—I don't remember who—and a woman who was frantic because she'd just broken her cooking pot but didn't want to pay our prices for a new one. I remember her saying that she didn't care about fancy decorations, didn't we have a nice, plain, sturdy pot?

"I didn't care about any of that. I wanted to show Nerius my game, so I tugged at his cloak until he finally picked me up and set me on the wall beside the stand. He told me he'd see my game later, and he turned to wait for my father or mother to be free to talk to him.

"I sat there, kicking my heels, ignored. Then I noticed Nerius' wolf-stone. I had wanted it since the first time I'd seen it, and it occurred to me that if I could call the other animals, maybe I could call the wolf too.

"So I started to call it. Not knowing anything about Adept powers, I called out loud, the way I called the birds and animals. And it came to me."

"Everybody saw it?"

"I couldn't have been more conspicuous if I'd planned it. I started calling, and my father turned and told me to hush—and just as that drew everyone's attention, the stone lifted from Nerius' chest, pulled free of the loop sunk into it, and sailed into my hands. Here—" he showed the stone to Lenardo, "you can see the hole at the back where the metal loop was set in. It wasn't meant to take the force of an Adept! Now we put a hole right through the stone—you'd have to break the pendant to get it off."

"But a three-year-old boy was able to pull the pendant free from a metal loop," Lenardo marveled, "with his mind!"

"Yes. If Nerius had wondered about me, now he knew—but so did my parents, and the man and woman buying pottery. I was thoroughly pleased with myself for a moment, until both women screamed. My father was staring at me as if he'd never seen me before. Then the two villagers started shouting, 'Adept! Adept! Kill him!' and my parents started toward me from behind the stand. They would have pulled me over the wall and taken me into the house, I think, but Nerius knew that if they tried to protect me the people would turn on the entire family. He snatched me up from his side of the wall and ran for his horse.

"Of course I was scared and squirming, and the man and woman were shouting while my parents were trying to keep Nerius from kidnapping their son and at the same time to keep the others from killing us. And other people were running out of their houses along the lane, picking up stones to throw. A few hit us, and the horse, and with a rearing horse and a screaming child, it's a wonder Nerius ever got us out of there.

"He was able to stop the stones from hitting us—a good

thing, because by now some people were throwing knives and axes. We galloped off and rode hard for quite a distance before Nerius was sure we had eluded pursuit. Then he took a terrible chance—we hid out until dark and then rode back. Nerius said we were going to get my family to go with us. But we were too late."

Lenardo knew the dread terror inspired by the very idea of an Adept within the empire. Even now, surrounded by Adepts whom he had come to regard as friends, he felt the old fear stir at the helplessness of anyone, even a Reader, before their power. And so he didn't have to ask what had happened to Wulfston's family.

The young Adept told him, calmly and quietly, speaking of an old wound, long healed. "The villagers had killed my family and burned down our house. I suppose they thought we were all secretly Adepts—although they must have known that Adepts would not stand still to be murdered!"

"Mob frenzy doesn't stop for rational thought," said Lenardo.

"No," Wulfston agreed sadly. Then he straightened. "I have learned to be grateful that Nerius was there that day to steal me away, or else I would surely have shown my powers in some unmistakable fashion soon and been killed along with my family."

Lenardo wondered if it had ever occurred to Wulfston that Nerius might have planted the suggestion to try his powers in the little boy's mind. No—he surely would not have intended a public display that gave away his own identity.

"So Nerius brought me home," Wulfston was saying, "and raised me as his own son. I was very young. It didn't take me long to recover. And there was Aradia, who thought I was the best present her father had ever brought her."

"She does tend to take possession of people," Lenardo agreed.

"I'd been a nuisance to my real sister, who had to take care of me while our parents worked. Aradia, though, was starved for the companionship of another Adept child. That's why the difference in our ages meant so little, although it's certainly the reason she got me into so much trouble."

"What about your name?" asked Lenardo. "I understand why naming you after the wolf-stone that revealed your powers is appropriate, but you already had a name."

"An Aventine name," said Wulfston. "Nerius decided that it would be best for me to leave my old life behind completely, so when he adopted me he gave me a new name. Actually, it's a very old name—there are two legendary Wulfstons celebrated in song: Wulfston the Red, a non-Adept warrior king who ruled his people well despite his lack of powers, and Wulfston of Caperna, who subdued the ghost-king."

"The ghost-king?"

The young Adept grinned. "A fairy tale, to be sure. He's also the Wulfston of the famous wedding-right. I think I told you there were legends of Adepts who survived death and continued to rule their people. You will have many things to learn this side of the pale, Lenardo."

"Legends are interesting but not my highest priority. Two things I must learn soon, Wulfston: how to read your alphabet, and the code the watchers use to transmit messages."

"Better take them one at a time, or you'll mix them up," said Wulfston.

"No—if you will show them to me, I can commit both to memory overnight."

"Really?" Wulfston was clearly impressed. "Now there's a Reader's trick I'd like to learn!"

"I wonder . . ." said Lenardo. "It's not exactly Reading. There's no harm in trying to teach you—but first you teach me!"

As Lenardo absorbed the new knowledge, he pondered Wulfston's statement, "You won't go back." How could he not go back? He couldn't live here, cut off from other Readers.

Strange . . . now that he thought about it, he was not experiencing the deprivation he had expected from being separated from other Readers. He had expected to feel isolated, but ever since he had begun working with Aradia and Wulfston to heal Nerius, he had become so involved in their problems that he hadn't thought about his own, other than the immediate problem of Galen and Drakonius, which he shared with the Adepts.

Of course—that was why he felt so comfortable here now: they shared a common enemy. When Drakonius was defeated and Galen rescued, Lenardo would have to take Galen home. Deliberately, he shut out the fear that Galen could not be taken from Drakonius alive, and considered the problem of getting the boy back within the empire's walls. How much influence did Portia have with the senate? She was the one who insisted that the Readers take care of their own. But once Galen was stopped from working with the enemy, what would become of him?

He should be given over to the physicians at Gaeta. Can Portia and Clement arrange that? Or will Galen be imprisoned? Or executed?

Suddenly the idea of returning to the empire with Nerius' strength to back him took on new appeal. Nerius wanted Lenardo's help in negotiating a treaty, and in return Lenardo could ask him to protect Galen. An elegant solution —provided Lenardo could get back alive.

In the morning Aradia sought Lenardo out. "I do not think my father will be pleased that Wulfston taught you the watcher's code."

"You forget, Aradia—I can pick up my message directly from the minds of the watchers. I wanted to know the code in case I need to *send* a message."

She laughed. "Of course. Watchers never use the heliograph in sight of the Aventine walls for that very reason. And once we have made peace, we will have relays of Readers, and the heliograph will become obsolete."

"You expect that kind of cooperation?"

"It has to come. If it does not, one day the whole world will be in the hands of men like Drakonius. What can you tell me of him this morning? As you did not come seeking me, I fear there is no news."

"I could wish for those relays of Readers now," Lenardo replied. "Last night, all except the guards in Drakonius' stronghold were sleeping. This morning Drakonius was fishing again. But who knows what might have happened while *I* was sleeping? Or might be happening right now, while we talk? Your watchers report troop movements; I don't know where to look for them. To do a proper job of watching Drakonius' preparations, we should have at least ten Readers, strategically placed. Someone ought to be Reading Drakonius every moment, so we don't miss a message, a command, any clue to his intentions."

"We," Aradia said thoughtfully.

"Hmmm?"

"You keep saying 'we,' not 'you' anymore. Lenardo, why has the empire not kept such watch on Drakonius all along? How could his attack on Adigia have surprised a whole academy of Readers?"

"An academy is a school, not a spy system. To do what you suggest, Readers would have to be sent out into the savage lands . . ." Suddenly the words of Portia, the Master Reader, came back to him. *We must not make our own people mistrust us.* But they already mistrusted Readers— so much so that they feared using them as their best line of defense!

"Lenardo?" Aradia was looking up at him in concern.

He shook his head. "The strategy seems so obvious to me now. Yet . . ." He shuddered. "Look what Drakonius has done to Galen, and now he's looking for me, thinking he can use any Reader thus. Readers are human—you Adepts could break some and use them, and kill those you could not conquer. No, the empire dares not risk having their own weapon turned against them."

Aradia sighed. "Your loyalty does you credit, but your stupidity does not. Father is right: the Aventine people fear the Readers' powers, but the government fears most of all, knowing that they hold the positions *you* should have by right of nature. Never mind—you will come to it. We don't have ten Readers, only you, so tell me how we can best use your abilities."

"If I continue to keep watch on Drakonius himself, I can tell you when he leaves to join the assembled armies. I take it he will have to come close to you to attack?"

"Yes. Our powers decrease with distance, so even if Galen could Read my castle as you can read Drakonius', he could not attack from there."

"Is that why you have not suggested that I direct you in an attack on Drakonius from here?"

"That is one reason. However, I have obligations to my allies. We know perfectly well that we are Drakonius' target—yet there has been no declaration of war and no attack. Unless Lilith and I agree, neither of us would attack Drakonius, as that would bring him down on the other."

"Unless you succeeded in killing him."

"My powers have never been tested against Drakonius. He may be the more powerful. What he does not know as he goes fishing is that all the time he waits he is giving my father time to recover. Drakonius made one mistake in his climb to power: instead of testing himself against Nerius, he gave him these lands and made him his ally."

"That seems a wise move to me," said Lenardo.

"For Nerius to make, or Lilith, or me. But Drakonius rules through power and fear—and it is often said that he feared my father, that Nerius was the stronger Adept. Now Drakonius thinks Nerius no longer a threat—but I am. I am just approaching the height of my powers. He dare not wait much longer lest my strength be equal to his . . . or beyond it. I have been expecting his attack ever since Nerius went blind—hence my alliances."

"Drakonius also has allies."

"True, but not in the sense of sworn loyalty among equals. Not one of those Adepts is his equal. They're all at the height of their powers, and none is as good as Wulfston is already. Or Lilith. Four strong Adepts, maybe an apprentice or two, and a Reader. They are counting on having the advantage over Lilith and me. I suspect they underestimate Wulfston, and you are an unknown quantity."

"I don't think Galen would assume I was working for you freely. But then, I cannot predict Galen's thinking these days."

"What they do not know is that Nerius lives and is regaining his strength. If they give us but three more days, my father and I together will be invincible!" She smiled. "My father and I . . . and you, Lenardo. We have the better Reader, and he is working with us, unconstrained."

The next morning, Drakonius was gone. Lenardo Read his stronghold, all the soldiers still there, everything seeming exactly the same as yesterday . . . except that there was no sign of Drakonius, Galen, or the young woman he had decided was Drakonius' apprentice.

Aradia was in Nerius' room. Lenardo took the treacherous stairs two at a time and then at the top composed himself. Nerius was standing at the window, fully dressed, staring down into the courtyard.

Lenardo said softly, "Aradia, I have important news."

"If it is about Drakonius," she said, "you may tell my father. I have just told him all that is happening."

Nerius turned to greet Lenardo. He was almost as tall as the Reader, still too thin and too pale, but otherwise in apparent health. "Good morning, Master Reader. What news of Drakonius?" His voice was vibrant, robust, returned to what must be its natural timbre. Despite his white hair, he seemed ten years younger.

"Bad news, Lord Nerius," Lenardo replied. "I've lost him."

"What?" exclaimed Aradia.

"He is gone from his stronghold, as are his apprentice and his Reader. I Read along the river and the road, but could not find them. Trying to cover a large and distant area with a single Reader—"

"Do not apologize," said Nerius. "You bring us news we would have in no other way. So . . . he leaves his own troops behind, to travel in secret. Our watchers will not be looking for a party of three, but for an army. Aradia, advise our troop commanders that we move out tomorrow morning."

"But Father—"

"I am well enough to ride."

"No! Certainly not a day's ride or more! You will use up your strength and be of no use in battle!"

Lenardo was startled at Aradia's choice of argument,

until he saw that she was saying what would weigh heaviest with Nerius.

The old man frowned at his daughter, saying, "We cannot stay here, waiting while I eat and sleep as our enemy brings the battle onto our own lands. We must move out to meet him. If he is riding fast, he can join Hron's troops today, and tomorrow morning they will reach our lands. We must march toward them at the same time."

"Your strategy is not in question, Father," said Aradia. "Your health is."

"I am in better health than I have been in five years. Master Lenardo—tell my daughter I am fit to ride."

Lenardo Read him, marveling at the powers of Adept healing. "You are in perfect health, Lord Nerius—for someone who has lain in bed these past two years. There is nothing positively wrong with you—"

"You see?" Nerius said to Aradia.

"—however," Lenardo continued, "you are completely out of condition. Your muscles are lax, you have no reserve strength at all, and—a minor point but true—if you spend an entire day out of doors you will suffer a painful sunburn."

Not used to having his will opposed, Nerius stared at Lenardo incredulously. Aradia said, "You see, Father? We have time—"

"We do *not!*" Nerius said angrily. "Drakonius is no fool. He expects Lenardo to tell us he has left his stronghold. He expects us to think he will join Hron's troops at Zendi— but Hron's army and troops from Zendi may move today. They could meet at our borders tomorrow."

"Our watchers—"

"Will be hours in reaching a point where they can safely relay the news. If we do not want the battle here, destroying our castle and our best lands even if we win, if we do not want women and children caught in the midst of battle, we must move out no later than tomorrow morning!"

Aradia sighed. "You are right. The troops must move out. But you—"

"I shall go with you. Now that Drakonius has finished

his waiting game, he will strike quickly, thinking to surprise us. But what a surprise *he* will have when he finds I
am alive and well!" He grinned in anticipation, the same
dangerous look Lenardo had seen on Aradia's features.

"You won't be well if you ride all day," Aradia pleaded.

"So it seems," said her father. "While fatigue would not
diminish my powers, it could impair my judgment, so,
much as it may hurt my dignity, I will agree to be carried
in a litter like some fat Aventine senator. No more pro-
tests, daughter—that is the greatest concession you'll have
from me. I'm going to fight in that battle if I have to
walk!"

"It . . . may be all right if you sleep on the way," Aradia
said, defeated.

"It's settled," said Nerius. "Now, it's time I went downstairs to breakfast."

"You can't!" his daughter said.

"What? Am I a prisoner in my own castle?"

"No, Father—but you will start a riot if you simply
walk into the great hall. People will think the ghost-king
has returned!"

"You haven't told my people—?"

"Only Wulfston, Lenardo, and I know—and Yula. I did
not want them to know until you were well enough to
come downstairs and greet everyone—for every one of
your people will want to see you, Father. Yesterday that
would have tired you beyond your strength. Today—take
your meals here, and rest this one more day while I prepare a ceremony for this evening. Let me present you to
Lilith and then to your people, and in their rejoicing at
your recovery, they will accept what you tell them about
Lenardo—that he saved your life, that he is our ally . . .
and that he is a Reader."

Nerius nodded. "Good strategy, daughter. The news of
my recovery will hearten my people on the eve of battle.
That Lenardo is responsible will give them faith in him and
at the same time assuage their fears of Drakonius. It is
common knowledge that he has a Reader, is it not?"

"Common rumor," Aradia replied with a shrug.

"My people will accept Lenardo on my word," said Nerius, "but, Master Reader, you may expect them to fear you too."

"I understand that," said Lenardo. "They'll soon learn I offer them no harm."

Nerius slowly shook his head, studying Lenardo thoughtfully. "I believe it is true . . . yet every time I see your face I see again that nightmare figure sent to destroy my daughter—and I not here to protect her."

That evening the wardrobes and treasure chests were opened. Aradia insisted that Lenardo wear the green outfit she had first given him, with the addition of a dark green velvet robe—and since that covered all but a glimpse of the embroidered tabard, he did not object. *Perhaps*, he thought, *I will one day appear at such functions in the scarlet robes of a Master Reader.*

Aradia herself was in purple, which darkened her violet eyes. Dress, surcoat, and robe were all of the same color in different fabrics, all with designs embroidered in gold.

Wulfston was dressed like Lenardo, but in the same rich dark brown as his skin—an imposing figure of a sorcerer indeed. He wore the wolf-stone, of course, but Aradia also fastened a golden fillet about his forehead, gleaming richly against his black hair.

Lenardo noticed that Aradia wore a similar gold band across her forehead, worked into the elaborate coiffure that restrained her pale blond hair into braids and sculptured coils. "Nerius rules here," she replied when Lenardo commented on it. "Wulfston and I are his children."

Lilith, all in deep blue velvet, soon joined them. A ruler in her own right, she wore a small golden crown on her dark hair. Looking at the fillet on Aradia's brow, she asked, "What has happened? Nerius cannot have died—?"

"No," said Aradia, her eyes sparkling with joy, "Nerius is not dead. Come upstairs with us, Lilith."

Nerius was seated in his armchair, waiting—and did not rise even for Lilith, suggesting that, in some subtle way Lenardo did not comprehend, he outranked her. Lilith was not offended, but rather astonished and delighted. "Lord Nerius! Oh, my lord, you are well!"

Only then did Nerius stand, to clasp Lilith in his arms, saying, "Yes, child, I am well. Ah, Lilith, let me look at you. The last time we met, I could not see you."

"My lord—how have you been healed? Have Aradia's powers increased so—?"

"No," Aradia answered, "but I have learned how welcome an ally a Reader can be."

When they had explained to Lilith, it was time to go downstairs. Aradia had called all her troop commanders together in the great hall—temporarily cleared of food and trestle tables, although the good smells permeating the air told that the cook had not abated his labors.

Aradia, Lilith, and Lenardo went down into the great hall, a hush of expectancy falling over the crowd at their entry. They proceeded to the far end and turned to face the gathered officers.

"My people," said Aradia, "you march tomorrow in defense of our lands. Those of you come at the behest of Lady Lilith, our dear friend and ally, have our deepest gratitude—and with our thanks our promise that we of Castle Nerius will always be equally willing to join in defense of your lands."

A rumble of "Ayes" went up from Aradia's men. Looking out over the assembly, Lenardo saw a few familiar faces—Helmuth, the blacksmith, the fletcher—but he Read from every one of them an iron determination to die in defense of the way of life Nerius and Aradia had established there. He Read clearly, though, the expectation of death. They knew they were outnumbered, but like any good officers, they considered each of their men equal to any three of the enemy.

But the heart of a savage army was its Adepts, and there they feared they were outranked. Drakonius was the strongest Adept now practicing, and with him were three others: Trang, Yolo, and Hron. On Aradia's side were Lilith, a fine Adept but not a match for Drakonius; Wulfston, not yet come into his full powers; and Aradia herself

—maybe a match for Drakonius, but untried. And the rumor that Drakonius had a Reader spying on their movements . . .

Despite their full understanding of the apparent situation, Lenardo Read no thought of surrender or even regret.

"We move out before dawn," Aradia was saying, "against our common enemy. I know that you will fight to the last drop of blood . . . and I know what is in your hearts, my friends. Not fear—I need not be a Reader to know there are no cowards among you."

There was surprise at her choice of words, and several pairs of eyes besides Helmuth's fixed suddenly on Lenardo, distrust shoved aside for a sudden surge of hope—*Even the odds! A Reader of our own! Render back blow for blow—* as the evidence clicked into place.

Aradia smiled as if she could Read them. "Yes—you know I would not assemble you for a hopeless task. We have an advantage Drakonius does not know about. He does not understand your strength, your loyalty to me and to one another. But, even more, he does not know that the wolf stirs again in his lair. Behold!"

Surprised, everyone followed Aradia's gaze to the back of the great hall, where Nerius was slowly descending the stairs, Wulfston at his side but not supporting him. A gasp—then the total silence of held breath. Reality penetrated. As one man, the assembled officers sank to their knees, tears of joy misting the eyes of hardened soldiers.

Crowned with a circle of twisted gold, Nerius moved majestically through the room, Wulfston falling a pace behind him. When he reached the front, he turned and said, "Rise, my officers, and behold your lord, alive and well."

As Nerius began to speak to the assembly about his illness, something stirred at the back of Lenardo's mind. Sensing danger, he Read outward . . . not in the castle . . . not out among the troops on the grassy slope. He reached the limits of the circle in which he could Read outward from himself in every direction at once, and began to Read in a spiral pattern, seeking some clue to what had alerted him. Nothing. Was it imagination? Nerves? He was many years beyond that kind of error.

Then he felt it again: feather-light touch of a mind on his. Galen! Galen close enough to Castle Nerius to Read—and that meant Drakonius was nearby.

Knowing Galen could use him as a focus, Lenardo deliberately stopped Reading, eliminating Galen's easiest target—but giving them only a short time if he was on the move, for he would easily fasten on the army massed behind the castle.

"Lord Nerius!" he said boldly, interrupting the Adept's speech. Every eye in the room fastened on him in outrage, except for the four Adepts'.

"Why do you interrupt me, Master Lenardo?" One or two people understood the significance of the title; the rest were confused, surprised, but confident in Nerius.

"Drakonius is within your borders." *Or close to it—* Galen's range might have improved, but he was still only twenty.

A murmur of consternation, which Nerius silenced by raising one hand just as a man rushed in breathless from the courtyard, crying, "My lady!" Then, seeing Nerius, he gasped, "My lord!" and paled so that Lenardo was sure he would faint.

The Adepts, he surmised, lent the man physical support, for his color returned as he stumbled forward. Nerius said gently, "Yes, lad, it is I. Tell me your news."

"The watchers report an army crossing the border lands."

"Good work," said Nerius and spoke again to the assembled officers. "We move out tonight then. The battle will soon be upon us—but have no fear! Not only is your Lord Adept restored to health, but you have seen even now the great advantage we have over Drakonius: Master Lenardo.

"I know—you have heard that Drakonius has a Reader to guide him, and that strikes fear into your hearts. But Drakonius has a young boy whom he has bullied into serving him. I have a Master Reader who serves me of his own free choice!"

A murmur went through the crowd of officers—suspicion, superstitious fear. Lenardo had already stopped Reading, to give Galen no chance to find him, but at that moment he would have stopped anyway, by the Readers' Code, for in such a situation all a person's most guilty thoughts and secret fantasies rose to the top of his mind as if to fulfill the dread fear that a Reader would know the worst about him. He could see the fear in these men's eyes.

"Yes," said Nerius, "we have all feared the Readers of the Aventine Empire. We have killed anyone in our lands who has shown signs of knowing our thoughts. But I say we have been wrong! Drakonius has shown us how an Adept can use a Reader to destroy—but Lenardo has shown us how Adepts and Readers can work together to preserve life. *My* life. You marvel at my standing before you, alive, whole. Were it not for this man, this Reader, I would even now be dead or dying.

"Only because Lenardo could Read the disease within me could my daughter and my son destroy it. Now the disease of Drakonius' cruel ambition threatens us. With Lenardo's help, we shall destroy this infection! Trust Lenardo as I do, for with his help we shall win!"

Nerius held up the wolf's-head pendant Lenardo had worn. "I was wrong to take this from you, Master Reader. You have earned the right to wear my sign—and all who see it will respect it." The pendant floated from Nerius' hands, the chain spreading to form a circle and slipping over Lenardo's head to settle as if it had never left him.

Once more Nerius turned to his officers. "Go, now—move your troops out, and never fear. By nature, strength is with those who are in the right."

A cheer went up, and the men moved out quickly. The Adepts started for the stairs, but Nerius stopped Lenardo with a hand on his arm. "Master Reader, you can interpret dreams."

"Lord Nerius, it is difficult even for a Reader to sort prophetic dreams from those caused by anxiety. I simply do not know how to assure you that I mean no harm to Aradia."

"Nay." The old Adept smiled. "I believe you are right—the other dreams were brought on by my illness and fear of leaving my daughter unprotected. But today, a well man, sleeping merely to gain strength for the coming battle, I dreamed a new dream."

"What was it?"

"I saw the future, many years from now. There was peace throughout the land—not just the small land I now hold but a land reaching far beyond our borders, many lands joined into an empire as great as the Aventine Empire once was. And in my dream, I saw Aradia reigning over all those lands with you at her side, Adept and Reader together bringing peace to all the known world."

"I think," said Lenardo, "that your dream may truly be prophetic, for it is clear that Adepts and Readers can work together for a common good. I think that is what it means, Lord Nerius—not literally Aradia and me, but all Adepts and all Readers. And I assure you, I shall do all I can to make your dream come true."

Hastily, the Adepts doffed their cumbersome finery, then climbed up to the castle battlements. When Nerius appeared, a wild cheer went up from the army, already assembling into units to move out against the enemy. Lenardo felt hopelessly torn—Readers should be going with the army, some to lead, others to maintain an overall view and direct troop leaders. But this army would have to fend for itself, as it always had.

"You say Drakonius has gone out ahead of his army?" Nerius asked Lenardo.

"Yes."

"Then we will do the same. Where is he?"

"I have Read along the road from here to the border and found nothing. He must be in the hills."

"There is a steep back trail," said Nerius, "that a small party could take. You know where the trail from the borderland enters the main road?"

As they climbed down from the battlements, Lenardo quickly found the trail from Nerius' description. Someone had been over it recently, galloping along the treacherous rocky way with reckless abandon. In moments he found them: Galen, Drakonius, and three other Adepts. Galen cried, "My lord! They've found us!"

"Lord Nerius, I have found them, but Galen detected me," reported Lenardo. "Now they're stopping, letting the horses go, climbing the rocks—"

"Keep moving!" said Nerius as they hurried down the stairs to the great hall. "At that distance, they can't—"

A wall of flame leaped before them, blocking their way. They stumbled back.

"How did they locate us?" Wulfston asked.

"Galen is Reading me," Lenardo replied. The flames disappeared as quickly as they had come.

"Can't you prevent him?" asked Lilith as they moved cautiously between the scorch marks left on stone stair and stone ceiling.

"No. I can't Read without being Read. But neither can he."

"Where are they now?" demanded Aradia.

"Below a big anvil-shaped rock—"

"Can we bring it down on them?" Wulfston asked at once.

Lenardo Read it and replied, "Yes. Remove the earth at the forward part of the rock—it's baked clay—can you crumble it?" Even as he asked, the earth crumbled and the rock toppled—but Galen was warning Drakonius at that moment, and the Adepts guided the path of the falling rock harmlessly to one side.

As Lenardo relayed the news, the ornate wooden table at the end of the great hall burst into flame. The castle itself was solid stone, the basic structure fireproof.

"Spread out!" directed Nerius. "Lenardo, keep moving— you will be their primary target—without you we are blind. We must get their Reader!"

Kill Galen? As if she Read him, Aradia said, "Lenardo, he must be stopped!"

"With Drakonius," he began numbly. "To his right—"

What seemed to be a thunderbolt scorched the air just in front of Lenardo. As he leaped back by reflex, he realized that if he hadn't slowed his pace to answer Aradia, he would have been struck, and—

Even as he stood paralyzed for a moment—barest seconds—pain seared through his chest and down his left arm. Strong arms caught him and pulled him back, and he Read his heart returning to its normal rhythm as the pain faded and Wulfston said, "I'll support you—keep *moving!*"

"Drakonius is conserving his strength," said Aradia.

"Come on!" said Lilith, leading the way to the courtyard, where horses were being saddled for them. Men were already putting out the fire, but Lenardo had no trouble fighting off the sense that the castle was the safest place to be. Drakonius obviously knew Castle Nerius only too well.

"Drakonius is moving down the trail," Lenardo reported. "Galen with him—past a twisted tree, on further—no landmarks— Look out!"

Cement from the battlements rained down on them, and everyone surged away from that side of the courtyard, horses rearing as great chunks of stone toppled—but fell harmlessly near the wall.

Lenardo was used to Reading at a distance while doing some ordinary thing like walking, but he had never been in the middle of a battle of Adepts, trying to report the others' actions aloud. Galen was reporting Lilith mounting her horse near the smithy. "Lilith!" he shouted—no time for more, but she swung into the saddle and spurred her horse. It reared and lunged as another of those thunderbolts scorched the air where they had been the instant before.

Grabbing the moment, the others mounted and galloped out the gate, Lenardo trailing as he wondered how he could communicate while they were strung out along the road. Then they were off the road, Aradia in the lead, leaping fences and ditches as Lenardo clung to his horse for dear life, wondering how Nerius could ride so steadily.

The army was on the move, cavalry galloping along the road as foot soldiers fell into formation behind them at a brisk march. The Adepts kept pace with the front ranks, zig-zagging through the fields, avoiding landmarks. Drakonius and his Adepts remained gathered in their canyon as Galen reported the situation. Atop the highest bare rock on the canyon wall, a fire suddenly sprang up, winked, blinked—

Lenardo Read that the code was a signal to Drakonius' army to engage the enemy, for they began to pour through the border lands, more slowly in the rocky terrain than the army advancing toward them. As Nerius feared, the battle would take place on his land.

"Invasion!" Lenardo shouted over the galloping hoof-beats. "Drakonius' army has entered your land!"

"Then there will be no question about who attacked whom," Nerius remarked grimly. He spoke in a normal tone of voice, which Lenardo could not have heard, but he was Reading wide open and so "heard" him easily.

He was also wide open to the nerve-shattering pain of the thunderbolt that took down the first rank of cavalry, men and horses alike. He screamed with their death agony, but in an instant it was over. Four men and their horses lay dead, the others breaking ranks to detour around them, while Lenardo clung to his own mount, sweating and shaking as the animal plunged and reared in frightened response to its rider's emotion.

Wulfston grasped the bridle, and the horse calmed at once. "What happened?"

Lenardo was already regaining his composure. "When I'm Reading, I'm open to everything—including other people's deaths."

The black man winced. "How can you do battle then?"

"I don't know. Something happens in the actual fighting —men don't feel the pain. All a Reader picks up is the exhilaration of battle." He urged his horse forward, and they galloped to catch up with the other Adepts.

More troops went down—flames seared them or thunderbolts pierced them, leaving bodies scorched through the center, like lightning-blasted trees. Troop commanders directed their men to scatter, but death was coming thick and fast before they could reach sight of the opposing army.

"We can't let our people die this way!" said Aradia, as Lenardo and Wulfston reached the other Adepts.

"Drakonius wants a direct confrontation," said Nerius, "or he wouldn't be wasting power like that. Aradia—"

"This way!" She led them again, through a patch of woods and out into the last large area of cleared land before the rocky hills. They pulled up in the middle of a field—the middle of nowhere, Lenardo realized as he looked around. Fields stretched in every direction. How could Galen describe their exact location now?

With a surge of glee such as he hadn't felt since the last time he had fought sword to sword with the savages, Lenardo slid off his horse. "Good choice, Aradia—I wouldn't know how to pinpoint this place verbally."

"Where is Drakonius now?" demanded Nerius.

"He and Galen are off to the north of the trail, almost at the bottom of the slope."

The four Adepts joined hands, circling Lenardo, and as Galen cried, "Get down!" a mass of rock seemed to . . . explode! . . . showering Drakonius' party with debris.

"No one hurt," Lenardo reported. "Try south about fifteen paces." A burst of flame scorched Drakonius' and Galen's retreating heels. "They're moving southwest—"

"Where are the others?" demanded Nerius.

"One man about ten paces east—"

Another instant of pain and death while he was Reading fully sent Lenardo to his knees in shock. "You got him," he choked out, feeling unwanted strength pouring back into his limbs as the Adepts supported him. Climbing to his feet, he said, "The rest are all moving again. Galen says you've formed a circle. Drakonius demanding where. Galen trying—"

Off in the distance, a corner of a field burst into flame. Aradia turned her head to look at it, and the fire went out.

"They'll try to circle in on us," said Nerius. "Quick—destroy them before we must move again. Lenardo—"

"The other men are above Drakonius and Galen on the slope, coming toward them—"

Another fire, roaring through a group of soldiers just off the road, killing them more slowly than before, in wrenching agony that Lenardo shared until the last one died.

"Fire the entire canyon," Nerius said grimly.

"Father, it's against nature!" said Aradia. "There's nothing there to burn!"

"Drakonius and his minions will burn! Lend me strength."

"You're not well enough!"

But as another thunderbolt struck close by, Nerius was already at the task—not just a momentary burst of flame but a roaring continuous blaze scorching through the canyon with the white heat of a funeral pyre, the Adepts and Galen caught, trapped, screaming in agony—

Lenardo could not stand it, retreating to Read the power draining from the circle around him, through Nerius, taking his last reserves—

"No!" shouted the old Adept, "you'll not escape me!"

In their death throes, Drakonius and his Adepts were throwing flame, thunderbolts, explosions, all around the circle. Lilith's dress caught fire—a break in concentration as she put it out. Nerius sagged. Aradia cried, "Father!" as suddenly Nerius lunged sideways, knocking his daughter aside as one last thunderbolt tore through that very spot— tore through Nerius' frail body, burning out the core, leaving only a scorched shell.

Chapter Eight

A New Outlook

The last rays of the setting sun showed what Lenardo as easily Read: Nerius dead; Aradia, unhurt, bending over him in disbelief; Wulfston, also unharmed, kneeling beside her with tears stinging his eyes; Lilith, already starting to heal superficial burns along one arm and leg, looking sadly down at Nerius.

Aradia raised her head, a hard glint in her eyes. "Lenardo—did we get them all? If anyone is left alive, he'll pay for this!"

Reluctantly, he Read the scene in the canyon. At this distance he could not seek for the faintest signs of life unless he left his body—but there was no need to. There could be no life in those five charred forms still baking in the intense heat held by the rocks they lay among.

"They're all dead," he reported.

"Then we must go with our army. With no Adepts, the enemy troops will be easily taken."

"Aradia—" Wulfson began.

"Take Father home," she told him, "and then join us."

"You go home, Aradia. The rest of the fighting will be no more than cleaning up. We'll take Drakonius' troops easily, once they realize they no longer have Adepts."

Aradia shook her head. "My people must see that I am alive and able to lead them. If both Nerius and I disappear, they will fear we are both dead."

Weakened by the battle of Adepts, Aradia was clearly Readable at the emotional level. Lenardo felt her tense control as she put her duty to her people before her personal grief. He rode beside her, wondering if she would break under the strain.

Then he Read ahead. The two armies had met head on while the Adepts were fighting each other. Battle raged just this side of the hills where he had suffered, in a tangle of small valleys and rocky canyons. Reading the banners with the white wolf's head, Aradia's sign, he remembered seeing the wolf in his delirium and thinking it a dream. *Had I been able to follow, would he have led me to Aradia?*

A sense of destiny rode with him as he remembered Nerius' dream. Perhaps it was prophetic, after all. Perhaps he was meant to help Aradia unite the warring lands of the savages with the empire. Now that her father was dead, people would turn to her for leadership, and she would require counselors.

But he was getting ahead of himself. Up ahead, Aradia and Lilith's combined army was outnumbered, and although they fought valiantly, they were being pressed steadily backward. A standard bearing Lilith's blue lion went down, only to be snatched up again and waved tauntingly by one of her men.

He saw the golden boar, signifying the troops of Hron, who had betrayed Aradia, as well as a brown horse's head and a green spear adorning other banners, but the largest, most numerous, and gaudiest banners bore the head of a dragon, black, on a field of gold. Drakonius' troops fought on, ignorant that their lord was dead.

Don't they know? he wondered. Didn't they wonder at the absence of Adept tricks? But then, there was little magic on either side—they must think the Adepts were still busy fighting one another.

There was some Adept activity, however. On both sides horses stumbled, foot soldiers found their swords heavy and awkward, and small fires surged up in what little brush there was. Volleys of arrows flew, many swerving to find their mark—but others were deflected in midair. Minor tricks, all of them, Lenardo now recognized, although a few short weeks ago he would have trembled before any one of them, thinking it the work of an Adept lord.

The majority of the soldiers on both sides simply fought, well and bravely. When they came within sound of the

battle, Aradia spurred her horse. "Aradia!" Lilith called,
"we must climb up where we can see the fighting!"

"My people need to know I'm here!" Aradia shouted
back, riding harder.

Lenardo watched her in concern, and he saw the same
expression in Lilith's eyes. Adept or no, Aradia had just
lost her father and had exhausted a good deal of energy
destroying Drakonius and his minions. How much strength
could she have left?

He urged his horse closer to hers and said, "Aradia, your
people will know you're there when they start getting your
help. Lilith is right—let's ride up to the top of that hill—"

"You two go if you want to," Aradia replied without
taking her eyes off the road ahead. "I'm going to the aid of
my people!" And she kicked her tired horse again, spurring
him out ahead of her companions'.

By now they could see the torches moving in the valley
ahead, the flickering reflection of fire on metal. As they
galloped along the road, a sheet of flame suddenly flared
before them. Their horses reared, and in the scuffle of
regaining control Lenardo heard Lilith exclaim, "Who did
that?"

"Drakonius' apprentice," he supplied. "I forgot about
her." Indeed, he soon found the young woman on the
opposite slope, watching the battle from behind a rocky
outcropping. "Why wasn't she helping them before?"

"Conserving her strength," Aradia replied. "She won't be
much trouble—she's hardly more than a child. Where is
she, Lenardo?"

At the grim tone of her voice, he hesitated. Aradia
reached out to grasp the bridle of his horse, pulling them
both to a halt, the horses snorting at each other as their
riders sat eye to eye. "What will you do to her?" Lenardo
asked warily.

"Will you leave the dragon spawn to grow up and attack
us again?" Aradia demanded.

"You said she's hardly more than a child. Can't you—?"

"After she's been trained by Drakonius? Lenardo, she
knows that if I'm here, Drakonius is dead. But she doesn't

flee—she fights! That is a grown woman, loyal to death to her lord. Where is *your* loyalty, Lenardo?"

To the empire, but that was not the issue here. To his Reader's Oath, which forbade him to use his powers to harm others—except, of course, the enemies of the empire. And Aradia need not be such an enemy. "With you, my lady."

"Then point the Adept out to me."

"You can't see her from here, but she can see you." As if to confirm his words, another wall of flame shot out of the earth before them, singeing the flailing hoofs of Aradia's rearing horse.

"Get down!" cried Lilith, abandoning her own horse to dart behind some rocks.

Aradia scrambled down, and Lenardo followed her to shelter. "Drakonius' apprentice is almost directly opposite us now," he said. "Have you the strength between you to topple the rocks she's hiding behind?"

"It is simpler to create a fire than to move those rocks," said Lilith. "Even after we destroy that Adept, our armies are still outnumbered."

"Yes—fire," said Aradia. "Turn her own weapon back on her. I don't think she has the strength for much else."

"She's moved," said Lenardo. "There's a kind of trail—maybe just a rabbit track—and she's peering out just to the left over there—"

He was looking to where he was Reading. As he spoke, a blaze roared up behind the young Adept woman, trapping her, climbing the rock faster than she could. Her pain as the fire consumed her clothing, hair, flesh, was open to him as if she were non-Adept. Relief came only as the woman died, and there was nothing more to Read but continued charring of her remains. "You can stop," he gasped. "She's dead."

The blaze died, and both women slumped. Lilith sat down on the ground, panting. Aradia kept her feet, but Lenardo could Read her weariness. She took a few deep breaths, though, and said, "The rest will be easy. The few with minor Adept talents cannot harm us, and soon Wulfston will be here."

"Good," said Lenardo. "Then you can rest for a while."

"While my people die?" she asked in astonishment. "Lilith, we should separate."

The other woman nodded and climbed to her feet. "I'll go this way. I saw my banners over there. I'll circle around and join my troops."

Where do they get their strength? Lenardo wondered.

"Come with me," Aradia told him. "You can Read better than I can see. Tell me where I'm needed."

They descended into the fray on foot, their horses having strayed too far to chase without wasting precious time. For Aradia's troops were being slaughtered. At first Lenardo didn't have to say a thing; a horseman wielding a battle-ax collapsed and fell from his horse just as he was about to swing down upon one of Aradia's men who was engaged with another of the enemy. In another skirmish of three on one, two suddenly turned and began fighting one another, although both wore the black dragon of Drakonius' livery.

Unsure of how much protection Aradia would need, Lenardo drew his sword. Instantly, one of the savages was on him, hiding behind a stout leather shield as he hacked at Lenardo. The Reader thrust, his blade was knocked aside, and he stepped back—to feel his footing give way as his boot sole slid in the mud created by blood mixed with the dry earth. As if stout arms had caught him, he was set upright, able to skewer his opponent, who had dropped his shield to give his own sword arm free swing, thrusting at the man he expected to be down and floundering.

Pulling his weapon from the groaning savage, Lenardo looked up to see Aradia's wolfish smile. At that moment another man knelt, pointing at Aradia, sighting along his arm as if along an arrow. "Aradia," Lenardo warned, pointing, "what's he—?"

She turned swiftly, and the man groaned, clutched at his chest, and collapsed. "Had others joined," she said grimly, "a group of even these very minor Adepts could destroy a weakened Lord Adept. Thank you, Lenardo."

Then they were moving on, Lenardo finding himself fighting off those who tried to reach Aradia whenever she

paused to concentrate—and her pauses became longer and
more intent as she grew more tired. She became more and
more Readable, her panting breath roaring in her ears as
she expended her energy, not to win a decisive victory
through her Adept powers, but to even the odds so that her
troops could win for themselves. The word that she was
there was spreading rapidly; her soldiers redoubled their
efforts, and slowly the battle turned, the enemy driven
back.

Aradia moved off to one side, where several of her men
were crowded into a tight little circle, back to back, pre-
senting a bristle of weapons to a far larger force of the
enemy. Enemy troops began to drop, one by one, as
Aradia approached. Someone turned, saw her, and cried,
"Get the bitch!" Another man grabbed a pikestaff, and
flung it like a javelin, while beyond them several bowmen
heard the cry and nocked their arrows despite the poor
visibility. The rain of weapons was deflected as if an iron
shield were placed an arm's length before Aradia's face,
but Lenardo felt the effort drain her. She stumbled, then
sagged in a faint.

Lenardo leaped to her side, with one blow slicing off the
arm of a man thrusting at her. He snatched her up and
backed off as her own men broke their tight formation to
race to her rescue. As the enemy were concentrating on the
chance to kill Aradia, her men came up behind them,
killing several before they were aware. Lenardo dragged
the Adept's dead weight toward the rocky outcropping
where he could shelter her, hampered in using his sword
until he finally stumbled through the rocks and dropped
Aradia, turning to defend the narrow opening that could be
held by a single swordsman—for a while, anyway. He cast
about for Lilith, but she was in a distant part of the valley,
fully occupied.

Aradia's men were attacking from behind, but between
them and Lenardo were at least a dozen men who did not
care if they died if they could kill Aradia in doing so. They
were more skilled than Lenardo in the use of the heavier
sword, but he had the advantage of a Reader, knowing their

moves even as they did. In this position, he had to take only one at a time; it was possible he could hold out until help reached him.

By the time he had dispatched two of the men, however, the energy of excitement was beginning to fade. His muscles quivered, and rivers of sweat poured down his body. He stopped trying to Read whether Aradia was recovering, and concentrated on the new opponent coming up before him.

The force of the man's rush drove Lenardo back a step into the narrow passage between the rocks. A bit further, and he would trip over Aradia's still form—or give the man a chance to reach her with his blade!

The savage before him was taller than Lenardo and muscled like a bull—pure fighting machine. His swordplay was not skillful—he was trying to hack his way in on strength alone, butting with his shield as much as cutting with his sword. Against such tactics Lenardo's Reading was not nearly as much of an advantage as against technique.

The enemy warrior had forced his way to a position where he was buttressed behind his shield, his longer reach keeping Lenardo at bay, although the Reader was determined he should not get through the passage.

I should learn to use one of those shields, Lenardo thought, the weariness in his sword arm making him long for the lighter, swifter blade the bandits had stolen. And but for that one skirmish with Helmuth's men, he was a month out of practice. It was telling badly. *How often I drilled into my students the importance of daily practice!*

Forced back step by step, Lenardo finally reached the narrowest part of the short passage, too narrow for his opponent to get through without turning sideways, his sword arm unshielded. Quickly Lenardo engaged, swords sliding along one another until the crossguards met. He could not hold thus against the other's brute strength but had no intention to. He held long enough, he hoped, then let his arm fall as if all the strength were gone from it, gasping in feigned dismay.

The savage raised his sword to slash down on Lenardo, but the Reader swiftly brought his blade up beneath the man's arm, the warrior's own strength slicing through flesh, cutting to the bone, impaling his forearm on Lenardo's sword.

With a roar like a wounded bull, the savage warrior swung his injured arm, spraying blood, so swiftly that Lenardo was thrown off balance, forced to let go of his sword, which, caught between the bones of the man's arm, was flung with such fury against the rock wall that the blade shattered.

Disarmed, unshielded, Lenardo faced the wounded giant. Berserk with rage, the man did not know his life was spurting away through the severed arteries in his sword arm. When that arm would not obey him, although its fingers remained tightly clasped about his sword, He charged Lenardo with his shield, knocking the Reader back behind Aradia's limp form.

Even as he fell, Lenardo was twisting to scramble up, breathless, leaping at the savage giant as he stood over Aradia, raising his shield to smash her face. Lenardo threw his whole weight at the man's knees and was kicked off. As he picked himself up to charge again, he saw that the giant had abandoned his shield and was clumsily transferring his sword to his left hand. Loss of blood was beginning to tell, but he was determined to kill Aradia before he died. Other men were coming through the unguarded passage. It was hopeless—but Lenardo nonetheless flung himself upon the savage warrior, trying to wrest the sword from his fumbling fingers, succeeding only in making him drop it.

Lenardo dived on the sword, rolled, lifted the weapon, and with both hands awkwardly thrust it at the lurching giant. The savage tried to swerve, stumbled, and fell on the blade. Lenardo thrust the heavy body off him and scrambled to his feet to face the oncoming savages. Pulling the sword from the giant's body, he found it so heavy that he needed both hands to wield it. Five men were grouped before him, weapons at the ready. If Aradia did not wake now, there was no chance. But he would take some of them with him as he went to his own death.

"Aradia!" he shouted, Reading that she was deep in healing sleep. Not daring to let go the sword, he nudged her with his foot. "Aradia—wake up!"

The world exploded.

Lenardo was thrown head over heels, the explosion deafening him as he hit solid rock and collapsed, feeling the sharp pain of broken ribs. Unable to move, he Read the scene: Aradia groggily awake, what little strength the short sleep had restored spent in that defensive burst of energy; the five attackers sprawled as Lenardo was—but three of them already stirring. The other two were dead, one from having hit his head against the rock wall, the other gruesomely spilling his guts across the ground, his belly cut open by his own sword.

But the others were merely stunned, and they knew enough of Adepts to see that they still had a chance at Aradia. She could not even sit up—Lenardo Read clearly how hard she was trying.

One of the three climbed to his feet but fell back with a yelp of pain, nursing a broken ankle. The other two found their fallen weapons and advanced on the helpless Adept. Despite his pain, Lenardo bent for his sword and staggered toward the foe, dragging his weapon, then leaning on it as he faced them across Aradia's body. Weakly, she whispered, "I can't help you, Lenardo. Thank you . . . for trying . . ." and fell back into unconsciousness.

The two savages had the strength to raise their weapons. Lenardo tugged at his, but with the pain of broken ribs he could do no more than drag the tip along the ground. He struggled to stand between them and Aradia, waiting for an ignominious death.

Suddenly the two men before Lenardo burst into flame! He lurched back, coming up against Aradia, realizing she had not done it—and without turning he Read Wulfston half running, half sliding down the steep rock face from above them. The searing pain and agonized screams of the two burning men cut off as they died, and Lenardo managed to gasp, "It's about time you got here!" as he collapsed into Wulfston's arms.

When Lenardo woke, his pain was gone, and he realized

that what had wakened him was Wulfston's touch on his forehead. "Don't move!" the young Adept warned. "I haven't healed you, just stopped the pain. Is Aradia injured or just exhausted?"

"Exhausted," Lenardo replied.

"Yes—she must have used her last strength in that bolt to tell me where you were. We're safe for the moment. Our own troops are defending the entrance, and only an Adept could come up and over as I did. How badly are you hurt?"

Lenardo quickly Read his own injuries. "Dozens of bruises, some strained muscles, and three broken ribs."

"Show me."

Again Lenardo felt the healing heat as Wulfston's hands moved over his body. At his direction, the ribs were brought back into place and given strength to hold so he could move. "I can't let you sleep," Wulfston apologized. "Aradia must—I suppose she dared spend the last of her energy because she knew I was coming."

"She didn't know. It was my fault. I wasn't Reading beyond right here, trying to fight off those savages. When I was outnumbered I tried to wake her—and forgot how. I'm afraid I . . . kicked her."

"And you quickly learned *why* there is only one safe way to wake an Adept!" Wulfston gave a humorless laugh. "Fortunately, she didn't have the strength to kill you, and so the blow probably saved your life by telling me where you were. Do you think you can walk now? I need you to Read the battle for me."

"We can't just leave Aradia here!"

"Our own men are guarding the passage now. She'll regain enough strength in an hour or two of sleep to get along until we can all rest safely."

Once Wulfston, under Lenardo's guidance, joined the battle from this side of the valley, with Lilith and her troops moving in from the other side, the fighting was soon over. Then Wulfston and Lilith directed Helmuth to take the rest of their army and proceed into Drakonius' lands— Aradia's lands now, by the law of the savages, for as long as she could hold them.

By this time, Wulfston was able to waken Aradia with a proper touch on the forehead. She smiled sleepily at him. "Wulfston . . . my brother. You did come." Then panic filled her eyes as memory returned. "Lenardo!"

"I'm here," he said quickly. "Wulfston arrived just in time to save us both."

"But I owe you my life several times over," she said. "Both of you. Wulfston, you should have seen Lenardo fighting Drakonius' men—he certainly told the truth when he said he could use a sword!"

"The gods were with me. Wulfston," Lenardo added, "I notice you don't wear a sword."

"I'm an Adept," the black man replied, and Lenardo realized that any time an Adept's powers were so drained that he could not fight with them, he would be too weak to use conventional weapons.

Before they could return to Castle Nerius, there was still more to be done. The wounded had to be cared for, first their own, and then many more from the opposing army. Aradia insisted she was strong enough to help, and Lenardo Read astonishment among the opposing troops at being cared for instead of killed, and at Lenardo, a Reader, helping the Adepts to discover and heal their injuries. *Did Drakonius never think to have Galen help him at healing?*

The sun was up, the day promising to be the first really hot day of the summer. Aradia and Lilith doffed outer garments, and Lenardo stripped off his tabard, wishing for a cooler but more modest tunic. They were working with the last of the wounded now, the least serious injuries among the enemy troops. Lenardo Read someone watching him and turned to find Arkus, the officer he had encountered in Zendi. Despite his Adept talent, the man had received a sword wound through the shoulder. It was not serious—if it didn't become infected, he would be good as new in two weeks. With Adept healing, a day or two.

"Can you not heal that yourself?" asked Lenardo as he knelt beside Arkus.

"Then you do remember me?"

"Certainly. You tried to entice me into Drakonius' army

and displayed Adept power. Why can't you heal your shoulder?"

"I can move things, not heal. I'm not a Lord Adept, nor a Reader either. Would that I were—I'd never have let you leave Zendi had I known who you were. Drakonius' message reached us too late, and we couldn't find you again."

"Now you have," replied Lenardo, looking up as Lilith approached. She was beginning to show the effects of the night's work. Her golden brown eyes appeared to have retreated into her face, completely circled by dark rings. Although she did not seem to be troubled by her own injury, even her pale blue underdress was charred, one sleeve in tatters.

Arkus looked up at her. "You chose the right side, Lady Lilith."

"No, captain," she replied. "I remained with those to whom I had given my pledge, as did you. We have no quarrel now that the battle is done." She turned to Lenardo. "A clean wound?"

"Yes, Lady."

She touched Arkus' shoulder, and Lenardo Read the dull throb of pain give way to healing fire. "There are many who must be carried," Lilith said to Arkus. "I think you are well enough to walk to Castle Nerius, but if you grow weak or have pain, do not hesitate to ask for help."

The young officer's eyes spoke the incredulity Lenardo Read in him. "Why are you healing an army that has just opposed you?"

"An army is made up of men, captain, and men choose their loyalties. You are no longer bound by your oath to Drakonius, as he is dead. You commander—"

"Braccho is dead also," said Arkus.

"Then at this moment you have no loyalties. You are the property of the Lady Aradia, but I think you will choose to become her sworn man."

And what is my choice now? Lenardo wondered, knowing that he wanted to ally his efforts with these people who, instead of killing their enemies, healed them and turned them into friends.

The image of five charred bodies in a rocky canyon intruded on him—but that was self-defense. What else could they have done against Adept power? *But oh, Galen, why did you have to fall into Drakonius' hands?*

He pulled his mind away from the thought. Galen was dead. Lenardo's mission for the empire was complete.

And if he had managed to take Galen back? Once the senate knew that Galen had conspired with the enemy, what choice would they have had but to execute him?

Didn't I know that all along?

Nerius had been right. The only way Lenardo could make the senate listen to him would be to approach them as Aradia's emissary. There soon would be peace in all the lands along the border, the lands Drakonius had ruled. The time was right. As soon as Aradia had firm command of all the lands she had won, he would attempt to make a treaty with the empire. *May it be the will of the gods that there never be another night of savage destruction like the one just past!*

There was a mass funeral three days later for all the troops that had been killed in the battle . . . and for Nerius. One gruesome report that Lenardo heard, but that was kept from most of the people, was that the men who went to collect the remains of those who had died in the rocky canyon found that scavengers had got at the bodies, and nothing was left but scattered bones.

It was a very long funeral, beginning early in the morning, for there were many dead to be eulogized. Lenardo was surprised when Aradia found something to say even for Hron, who had betrayed her. When it came to Nerius, every person there except the survivors of Drakonius' troops had something to say. Lenardo had come to respect Aradia's father on just a few days' acquaintance; now he got a fuller picture of a strong, firm, honest, and entirely honorable man whose wrath was feared but who was deeply loved by his people.

Everyone was all in gray, and Lenardo noted that, as he had seen at the other funeral, no one wore any ornament.

Like Wulfston, he had hidden his wolf's-head pendant inside his clothing once more.

Yet both Aradia and Wulfston wore the gold fillets across their foreheads—the mark of children of the Lord Adept.

Lenardo was one of the last to speak, for once in his life finding words would not come to express his feelings. He stumbled through somehow, unsurprised and unashamed at the tears coursing down his cheeks—tears for Nerius, but also for Galen.

The mourners formed several circles about the flat rock. When the speeches were over, there was silence—suddenly broken by a mournful howling. Everyone looked up in amazement, to see the white wolf atop a nearby hummock, howling as if he too grieved that the lord of the land was dead.

Finally all was silence. The wood was already piled over the bodies, and Aradia and Wulfston performed the ceremony of earth and water. Then both removed their gold fillets and laid them on the pyre.

Everyone backed off, for when the huge pyre went up in roaring flames the heat bombarded them in waves of physical pressure. As had happened before, every trace of the bodies was consumed, the fire died back, and all that was left was a skiff of ashes.

This time Lenardo found it difficult to be cheerful at the funeral feast. It was far too large a gathering for the great hall, and so the slope behind the castle, no longer grassy after being an army camp for days, became the scene of an immense picnic. Soon pipes were playing, and people began to dance, as Lenardo watched with increasing glumness.

Finally Aradia asked him, "What's wrong, Lenardo?"

"I know it is your custom, but to me it seems completely *wrong* to—to celebrate Nerius' death."

"We celebrate his *life!*" she replied. "His life and ours. I am the child of Nerius' body—his life is in me, and I celebrate that fact."

"It all seems so pointless," said Lenardo. "We worked so

hard to save his life. He hadn't even recovered his full health yet—and then he died. What was it for?"

"Perhaps the day of Nerius' death was set in the stars," Aradia said. "There are those who say it is—it could be that if we had done nothing to heal him, he would have died that same hour. Do you not think, had he been given the choice, Nerius would have preferred to die defending his people rather than to sleep away helplessly?"

"I'm sure he would," Lenardo agreed, but he could not shake off his mood.

"Lenardo," said Aradia, "you should have spoken for Galen today."

"No one spoke for Drakonius, although his soldiers were there."

"I do not think any close friends were among those troops. They feel the loss of a leader, fear over what will happen to them now, but not the breaking of a personal bond of friendship, as you do."

"That is why you spoke for Hron today?"

"Aye, and why Lilith did too. Hron was a weak man, but not an evil one. Speak for Galen now, Lenardo. Tell me what was best about him."

The nervous, unpredictable, vengeful young man he had last Read was not the Galen Lenardo wanted to remember. He thought back to the boy as he had first known him. "He had intense enthusiasm. Each new lesson was a joy to him, and he made something I'd taught a hundred times fresh and new for me. He wanted to know everything at once, always eager to get on to the next lesson, the kind of student who breaks a teacher free of routine."

As he spoke, he felt better. Aradia smiled at him. "Are you glad you knew him?"

"Yes."

"Then celebrate that he lived, and that we all live yet to bring what good we can into the world." She took a brimming goblet of wine from one of the tables, handing it to Lenardo. "Let us drink together in celebration of life."

Lenardo took a sip, and Aradia took the goblet from him, raising it to her own lips and looking at him over the rim. When she had taken a swallow, she said, "You are free now, Lenardo. I have no more hold on you, the empire has none. All your promises are fulfilled. What will be your choice now?"

"I am a teacher."

"Are you? I need someone to teach us all what your powers can do. Think about what my father said before you go back to obscurity in your academy."

"Not at once," he replied. "First the negotiations—"

"You have decided to try to convince the empire to negotiate with us?"

"Yes."

"And what will become of you if you do, Lenardo? I care what happens to you. My people owe you their freedom. I owe you my life. At least accept my protection if you must return to the empire. If you go back unprotected, you will be accused of consorting with the enemy . . . and this time the sentence will not be exile."

"I accept your protection, Aradia. I will go as your emissary."

A warm smile lit her eyes, and suddenly she put down the goblet and threw her arms around him, kissing him. He made no attempt to avoid it. The embrace was over too soon—it was only when he found himself wanting more that Lenardo became disturbed at his reaction.

But as Aradia broke free, unconcerned, Lenardo told himself firmly that the gesture meant nothing more to her than when she kissed Wulfston—a sisterly caress.

"Now come and dance with me," said Aradia.

"I don't know how," said Lenardo. "In the girls' academies, dance is taught as exercise, but the boys learn swordplay."

So Aradia went off to find another partner, and Lenardo watched the dancing. He thought of the future, regretting that he would soon leave Castle Nerius until he recalled that he would be back—back and forth between here and Tiberium while the treaty was negotiated, and then—

And then . . . what?

How could he consider anything but returning to an academy—wherever Master Clement was rebuilding? But

Aradia wanted him here, and the treaty would include bringing other Readers over the border, teaching them to work with Adepts. That would be his task, certainly! The idea pleased him.

They said he had changed. Lenardo had to agree: now that he saw all there was to do in the world, he would never again be satisfied to live apart from it. The academies were necessary, but so would be the liaison position he would hold. *Best of both worlds,* he thought, smiling to himself. *You're as bad as the Adepts: all you want is everything!*

But it was in a cheerful mood that he left the celebration, returning to his room in the castle. It occurred to him that he ought to try to report back to the empire, to let Masters Clement and Portia know that Galen was dead. He thought he could reach Adigia from here—it was farther away than Drakonius' stronghold, but he had spent most of his life there. Perhaps Master Clement was still there.

The stone castle was cooler than the night outside. Lenardo was the only one indoors, except for the cook's staff bustling in and out lest anyone lack for one more bite of some delicacy.

He went up to his room, lay down, and left his body. He needed no landmarks to guide him to Adigia—a moment's concentration and he was "there," in his own room at the academy. The building was deserted. Unless he found a focus, he would have to retreat.

Reading through the town, though, he quickly found the active mind of the blind boy who was always Reading. Torio was in a room at the inn—safe enough now, as the innkeeper's daughter had long since married and grown into a plump and proper matron with three children. If it was hot where Lenardo was, it was even hotter in Adigia, and Torio was sitting at the open window in his nightshirt, contemplating going down to sleep in the plot of grass around the fountain in the square, where a number of people had already gathered.

//Torio—//

//Master Lenardo!// The leap of joy in the boy's mind

was almost painful in its intensity. //Are you all right? At least you're still alive.//

//I am alive. Galen is dead.//

//Oh.// Shock and sorrow, followed by hope. //Then you're coming home!//

//Not yet. Torio, are you the only Reader in Adigia? Why are you there alone?//

//There were complaints when Master Clement insisted I remain alone, but how else guarantee privacy if you contacted me? The people are afraid of further attack, here on the border. A single Reader can't help very much.//

//I know,// Lenardo replied. //I wish you could reassure them there is no danger of attack. It's true, for the Adept who was so determined to beat back the walls of the empire is also dead. But you cannot tell the people of Adigia that. Where is Master Clement now?//

//Tiberium. They've housed the academy in a villa there, and the last I heard the senate was refusing funds to build elsewhere.//

//Despite the women's academy in the same city?//

//They say, "You're Readers—avoid each other!" They claim the savages have taken so much land, and it costs so much to mount the army against them, that the money simply isn't there.//

//There will soon be a change in their attitude. Now, you have one final duty in this plan, and then back to your studies. You are at a crucial point in your education, Torio. I'm sorry it was interrupted, even for these few weeks.//

//I don't know,// said Torio. //Master Clement told me not to get my hopes too high—those who show promise at my age often fail dismally.//

//Torio—he was reacting to Galen's betrayal. You are the best Reader for your age that I have ever seen—and that means you have the potential to grow into a better Reader than either Master Clement or I. Come now—you're old enough to know that teachers are human, too, and sometimes say things in the bitterness of disappointment that they regret later.//

//Yes . . . I suppose I do know that. I'll be a teacher

myself as soon as I get back to the academy. Master Clement has let me keep the title of tutor and has promised me a class of novice swordsmen once my duty here is done.//

//It is done. But tell me . . . how is Decius?//

//Still healing. Master Clement says he is bravely facing his pain and has determined to turn all his energies to becoming a great Reader.//

Still in pain! Lenardo was certain Aradia could have saved Decius' leg, but even if she could not, she would have been able to take his pain away at once and heal the wound within a day or two.

//Torio, there are so many things I wish I could tell you. I will when I return. Now you must go tell Master Clement that Galen is dead, and the savage threat to the empire is over—permanently, if I can accomplish all I want to.//

//But when will you come home? Master Lenardo—are you a prisoner?//

//No—far from it. But it will be weeks, perhaps months, before I return to the empire.//

//Branded as an exile—how will you return unless someone is here in Adigia for you to contact? Whoever replaces me here will not know about you.//

//I cannot communicate with Tiberium from where I am now, but I can if I come near to Adigia on the other side of the border. Even if the academy moves, so you and Master Clement are not there, Portia never leaves Tiberium. You must not worry about me, Torio. I am safer than you can imagine, and if my plans work out, life in the empire will be much better in the future.//

//Master Lenardo—where are you? If Master Clement wants to contact you—//

Lenardo considered. //No, you had best tell him to wait until I contact him.//

//You're keeping something from me,// said the boy. //So is Master Clement. When he contacts me, I can tell there are things he's holding back. He's worried, Master Lenardo.//

//Of course he is—he's worried about me! But now you can tell him I'm safe. I'm with friends.//

//Friends? But how can that be?//

//Torio, you are far too good a Reader for your age, and that should tell you you've nothing to worry about on your exams. But you will have to accept that I cannot explain everything now. It will all be clear when I come home.//

//Please come soon. I miss you, Master Lenardo.//

//I miss you, Torio. I'll come as soon as I can. But for now you'll be happy to get back to your friends at the academy.//

//You've always been my best friend,// the boy told him.

//Then trust me.//

//Oh, I do!// Lenardo felt Torio's reassurance like the unReaderlike hug the boy bestowed on those he loved.

//Good. Then give Master Clement my message, and apply yourself to your studies—for I am going to have work for you as a Reader such as you have never dreamed of!//

It was with regret that Lenardo broke contact with Torio's mind. It would be so good to get back among Readers—

No. It would be so good to have daily contact with Torio and Master Clement, his dear friends . . . but he would miss Aradia and Wulfston. *I am going to have work for you,* he had told Torio. *I don't suppose there's any hope of persuading Master Clement to venture beyond the pale. I wonder if Aradia could ease his rheumatism?*

Lenardo lay back, hands clasped behind his head, contemplating the future. It looked good. He felt good. All his wounds were healed again, but the source of his sense of well-being was not physical. Rather, he felt satisfied with himself for the first time since his failure with Galen.

Lifting his right arm, he looked at the dragon's-head brand in the flickering candlelight. The mark of the exile— but he did not feel exiled. He felt at home. Readers were having problems in Tiberium; Lenardo would have the power to demand that their rights be recognized. The senate said there were no funds for a new academy? Suppose

it were built here, at Castle Nerius! No—better yet—
restore the academy at Zendi! It had been a female academy in Lenardo's childhood, but with the male academy
gone from Adigia—

Yes, he must speak with Aradia about Zendi! He longed
to see the city restored to its former glory, and what better
way than to make it the neutral ground on which Readers
and Adepts could meet and learn to work together?

Perhaps, thought Lenardo, *I was not well suited to the
cloistered life of the academy. Or perhaps being there on
the border, I Read without being able to accept it that we
should not be fighting one another.*

He had taken Galen's exile, Decius' wound, Galen's
death, all as his own fault. But they were all part of the
perpetual war between the empire and the savages.

He stroked his beard, thinking, *Now I'm part of both,
the Aventine Empire and the savage*— No, not an empire,
but perhaps one day an amalgam of alliances such as
Aradia had forged with Lilith. Their alliance had withstood
the power of Drakonius.

Filled with hope for the future, Lenardo slept the sleep
of deep contentment.

The next day everybody in and about Castle Nerius slept
late except Lenardo. He was up at dawn, as usual, and for
the first time found the kitchen not only deserted but in a
shambles—clearly even the cook and his staff had finally
joined in the celebration last night. He found fruit and
bread and met the bleary-eyed dairyman bringing in fresh
milk—cows, the man grumbled, had to be milked no matter how one had spent the night before. Lenardo helped
him pour the milk into the cool stone vats and earned for
his efforts a mumbled thanks and, "I don't suppose you can
cure a headache, Master Reader?"

"No, I'm afraid you'll have to ask one of the Adepts for
that."

"Aye, but they'll be too busy curing their own today.
Good day to ye!"

Apparently everyone knew who he was by now—even

the proper way to address him—but there was none of the
fear Nerius had predicted. Aradia's sworn man, wearer of
the wolf-stone . . .

When Aradia appeared downstairs, looking none the
worse for her night of revelry, Lenardo approached her
with his ideas.

"An academy of Readers at Zendi?" she asked. "How
will you persuade the empire to risk their precious Readers
outside their borders?"

"I don't think they would. Aradia, to make a treaty,
both sides must grant concessions. To gain peace, and the
aid of Readers, grant me the power to return the land that
includes the city of Zendi to the empire."

"Give back land honorably won?"

"You won it from Drakonius; thus you would not be
giving it 'back' to the empire but granting it as a concession
—with stipulations. The academy, and free access for
Adepts to work with Readers there."

Her violet eyes studied his face. "And you would be
Master of this Academy?"

"I . . . I suppose so, one day. I hadn't really thought
about that."

"Lenardo . . . precisely what was your mission on this
side of the border?"

"You know it. To find Galen and stop him from aiding
Drakonius."

"And that was all?"

"Yes. But after all I've seen here—"

"You are ready to stop merely doing what you are told."
She reached for the wolf's-head pendant he wore. "Do you
wish to continue to wear this?"

"Yes," he replied. "I will swear loyalty to you, Aradia—
freely, as I have fulfilled my agreement with you and won
my freedom."

"You have done far more than fulfill our agreement. But
if you swear loyalty to me, that is where your loyalty must
stay. If you do not succeed in making the treaty with the
empire, you must come back to me."

"I would want to," he replied. "If I cannot persuade the
senate or the emperor to listen to me . . . then you will

have one Reader, Aradia, and perhaps we shall find more among your people."

"The empire will think you a traitor."

"All but three people think so now. I am sure that, with your strength to back me, I can persuade the empire that making a treaty with you is to their benefit."

The wolfish grin showed her teeth. "With my strength to back you. Yes, Lenardo, you are beginning to understand how to work with nature—human nature. You shall have the power you require and the chance to learn to use it wisely. Now," she added more seriously, "there is a ceremony to be performed before Lilith leaves. Tomorrow afternoon, will you swear fealty to me before Lilith, Wulfston, and my officers?"

"Gladly, my lady."

The ceremony was held in the great hall, again cleared of tables, including the permanent one that had burned in the battle of Adepts. Aradia's treasure chest stood open, along with numerous other chests of gold and jewels, plunder brought back by the army. Other chests held gold and silver coins. Lenardo judged that there was as much value there as in the Aventine Empire's depleted treasury, unhesitatingly delivered by Aradia and Lilith's soldiers. Lenardo recalled Arkus saying that day in Zendi that Drakonius' soldiers were allowed to loot as they pleased—*and I suppose he didn't care if they killed each other over the loot, once the battle was over.*

Aradia, wearing the circle of twisted gold that had been Nerius' crown, began the long list of awards: to every soldier and watcher a measure of silver, to every wounded man two measures, to the family of every man killed a gold mark, and on to detailed grants to the communities that had sent men and supplies to her army.

Then each of the officers assembled there received one of the twisted gold bracelets, and Lenardo recalled that there was enough value in one to build and furnish a modest home. More than one mind among the younger officers began to fill with marriage plans, while others thought of horses or oxen, of new clothes for wives and

children, and standing out from the common melee someone's plan to build a mill to grind grain.

Charging the officers with taking their men safely home
and distributing their awards, Aradia turned to Lilith,
Wulfston, and Lenardo. "Although Master Lenardo long
since gave his personal pledge to me, and proved his value
and loyalty right well in the battle just past, he has not
made a public declaration of fealty. Master Reader?"

When Wulfston had rehearsed him in the ceremony,
Lenardo had been glad to find it needed no rewording to
avoid conflict with his Reader's Oath. He knelt before
Aradia and held the wolf-stone in both hands. "I, Lenardo,
Master Reader, take this sign in pledge to Aradia, daughter
of Nerius, and my liege lady. I promise to protect her life,
her people, and her goods, and to defend her life with my
own."

Aradia took his hands, saying, "I accept your pledge.
Arise, Master Lenardo, my sworn man. I promise to protect your life, your family, and your goods, and as with all
my people, to defend your life with my own." She kissed
him on both cheeks, quite formally, and he stepped back,
his part in the proceedings over.

Aradia then announced, "As you know, the battle just
past resulted in the deaths of Hron, Trang, Yolo, and
Drakonius, and the forfeit of their people, lands, and goods
to me. The lands of those Lords Adept will require hard
work and a strong hand to be made good for their people. I
cannot rule them all, nor should those who kept loyalty to
my father and me, risking all against Drakonius and his
henchmen, go unrewarded." She stepped to the wall, where
the three shields still hung, and took down the one with the
golden boar.

"Hron betrayed the alliance he had made with me. He
paid for that broken pledge with his life and the forfeit of
all that he owned. To Lilith, my ally who supported me,
and who kept her pledge and her honor, I award the lands
which formerly belonged to Hron."

She held the shield before her, and a smell of scorching
rose as the paint shriveled and blackened and the image of

the boar burned away. Then she handed the shield to Lilith, who said, "May the land and its people prosper under
my rule. Thank you, Aradia."

"The lands belonging to Trang and Yolo I retain for my
own," said Aradia. "The lands that Drakonius ruled, however, are larger than all these lands combined. Therefore, I
divide them, and give to my brother Wulfston, Lord Adept,
the lands from the western sea, eastward to the natural
border formed by the Western Hills."

As Wulfston moved forward to give his formal thanks,
Lenardo felt a warm triumph to note that Aradia had
neither claimed for herself nor given away the central portion of land from well north of Zendi to the Aventine
border at Adigia. So she had set aside land to cede to the
empire in negotiating peace. He felt inordinately pleased
that she had taken his advice, and more certain than ever
that peace could be achieved.

Until Aradia turned to the assembly once more, saying,
"Finally, the portion of land southward from the border of
Lilith's land, east from Wulfston's, and west from mine, I
give to Lenardo, Lord Reader, to hold or to distribute as he
sees fit."

Lenardo was dumbfounded. All eyes turned to him as he
stared in shock for a moment, then burst out, "Aradia, you
can't—"

"The land is mine, honorably won. I choose to give it to
you. Will you not thank your liege lady, my lord?"

The public assembly was no place to argue. Mustering
all the grace he could, he said, "I am unworthy of the
honor you do me, my lady, but I thank you."

That was the end of the ceremony. As soon as most of
the officers were out of the room, Lenardo hurried after
Aradia, who was heading for the staircase with Lilith and
Wulfston.

"Aradia—why did you do that?" he demanded. "I
thought you were going to hold that land to negotiate
with!"

She turned. "I would like peace with the empire, Lenardo, and you may be the one person who can achieve it.

Truly, I think the Aventine government's terror of Adept and Reader alike will prevent there ever being peace between us—but if there is a chance, I want to give it to you. My father was right: you must negotiate from strength, not weakness. There would be a degree of strength in negotiating as my emissary, but I think the only true chance you have—and that a slim one—is as a lord in your own right, representing an alliance of Lords Adept."

"But—"

"Go claim your lands, my lord. Make the people your own. Think of what I have said and what you know of human nature." She looked up at him, her violet eyes huge and deep. "If you must prove to yourself that I am right, to the detriment of us all, go now—present yourself to the Aventine emperor and give him the lands I have just given you: that is your right. He will take them, I guarantee it. And after that, he will listen to nothing you have to say; I guarantee that, too."

Lenardo stared at her, realizing how acutely she read the truth he dared not admit to himself. "Then what do you expect me to do?"

"Go teach your people to love you, as my people love me. You will have to overcome the fear Drakonius instilled in them, but if you work with human nature you will gain their undying loyalty as Drakonius never did. Then, Lenardo, we will work out a scheme to negotiate peace."

"Lenardo," said Wulfston, "we share a border. We should be allies. Will you swear here and now, each to come to the other's defense in time of need?"

"Defense? My personal service, of course, Wulfston, but I'm not an Adept, and I don't have an army."

"Neither have I," Wulfston said with a laugh, "but Aradia and Lilith will lend us troops until we train our own. If we make alliances with them, that is."

In moments, a four-way alliance was concluded, there at the bottom of the great staircase, Lenardo too bewildered to do more than follow the Adepts' lead. As the four began to climb the stairs, Wulfston hung back, saying to Lenardo, "My sister has plans for you."